# LAS VEGAS LUCK MAGIC

## B. B. GRIFFITH

Griffith Publishing

Cover art by James T. Egan at Bookfly Design

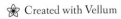 Created with Vellum

*For Christian, who makes his own luck.*

"Depend on the rabbit's foot if you will,
but remember it didn't work out for the rabbit."
-R. E. Shay

# CHAPTER ONE

I wake up in a hospital bed with the sensation that my life has been interrupted mid-sentence. Listening to the hissing and beeping of machines, I try to pull my brain together before I panic. My last memory is of a conversation cut short by a horrendous noise. Something about a party. No, not a party. A wedding. My wedding. Alli. My wife. She's my wife now. Where is my wife?

My sight is bleary, and my face feels puffy, as though I slept too hard. My right arm feels tacked on. I probe it with my left and find my whole upper body wrapped in gauze.

Something terrible has happened, then. My mind processes this in a floaty, disassociated way that tells me drugs are keeping pain at bay.

I say Alli's name, which comes out in a papery rasp, barely louder than the beeping machines in the room. Someone hurries over to me.

"Lee? Can you hear me?"

Mom. Fear I didn't know was building within me drains back out. If Mom is here, I can deal with this.

"Where is Alli?"

I know Mom hears me, but she doesn't answer. The fear bubbles back.

"There was an accident," she says. Her voice breaks.

My heart breaks too. That horrendous noise echoes in my head, a sharp slam like the world's biggest beer can being crushed in an instant.

Another voice, the dispassionate tone of a doctor. "Mrs. Baker, he needs to sleep. One thing at a time."

I feel a burn in the vein of my vampire arm. My mother grasps my other hand, and her touch is freezing. She leans down to my face, and I see she's still in her party dress. Some of the hundreds of hairpins jut from her updo. Tears have cut rivulets in her professional makeup job, little tributaries in the foundation of her face. Her eyes are brimming and bloodshot.

I wonder if I'm still in my tuxedo.

"I'm so sorry, Lee. This is all my fault."

I want to ask her to explain herself, but the burn in my vein kicks all thought from my head, and I float away on a dark cloud of dreamless sleep.

I SURFACE AGAIN, an inch at a time. The room is dark, the beeping muted. A machine whispers softly, printing a readout. I feel like I'm covered in ten blankets but freezing at the same time. I clear my throat and find my tongue fat and dry.

Mom is there with water. She puts the straw in my mouth. I sip until she takes it away. She's changed out of the dress.

She looks at me as though she wants to capture a moment. Her hand moves to my face to cup my cheek, but her fingers hover an inch away. She checks a sob and pulls away.

"I have to leave. I wish I could make you understand, but I don't understand, myself. All I know is what I see, and I see..." Her hands cover her mouth as she looks down at me.

I try to shake my head. *What are you talking about? Leave?* The words are fully formed in my head but turn to mush somewhere in my mouth and come out as a mumble.

"Please don't hate me." Again, she comes close to touching me but stops herself and pulls away.

I drop below the surface of consciousness again as she leaves the room, as if she is pulling the darkness over my eyes with each step farther away.


A TICKLING SENSATION WAKES ME, and I turn to see a nurse gently cleaning a row of staples that crosses my right shoulder like a zipper in my skin. The skin around it looks like green and yellow paint mixed by a child and wiped on in swaths. It itches like hell, but it's the first real sensation I've felt in that quadrant of my body since I ended up here, and the feather touch of the sponge is a weird mix of pleasure and pain.

"So sorry to wake you, but we need to check this dressing every four hours."

Daylight streams through slatted blinds. I wonder how long I've been asleep, how long I've been here.

"What day is it?" I ask, my voice hoarse and raspy but clear enough.

"It's Saturday," she says. "June ninth."

I suck in a little breath. My wedding was on the first. I've been here over a week. An entire week of my life deleted—pulled away from me with that horrible sound of crushing metal. I try to swallow the panic that comes with the memory. I remember the moments before, when Alli held my hand, her wedding ring throwing sparkles on the black leather of the town car as it pulled away from the chapel...

I twitch my head as if I could throw the memory bodily from my forehead, and the nurse lifts her hands, mistaking my mental agony for some pain she's caused.

She checks a dripping IV bag and notes the time. "Let me see what I can do about getting your next dose a bit sooner."

"My mother? She was here."

"She's been here the whole time." The nurse glances over at a small loveseat in the corner where some thin hospital sheets have been folded neatly into a square and set next to a small, puffy pillow. She frowns. "Must have stepped out just recently. You've had other visitors too. I have a guest book full. They all wanted to come in, but we can only admit direct family on your behalf."

"I've only got my mom."

That's not true. I guess I have Alli's family now. Although Kathy and Bob were a hard sell on the wedding to begin with. And without Alli in the picture...

That crunching sound again. It flips my stomach. Spit gathers in my mouth. A disgusting pocket of old air bubbles up my throat.

The nurse calmly grabs a bedside bucket and gently tilts my head toward it as whatever thin contents are inside of me come right up.

"That's okay," she says. "That's okay. You've been through an awful lot."

I lie back and rub my watery eyes with my good hand, breathe deeply, and take stock. Alli is just as dead. Mom is just as gone. But for some reason, the puking has made me feel a little better.

The sunlight is playing strange tricks in the room. I rub my eyes again and open them wide. No difference.

"Is it smoky in here?" I ask.

The nurse looks around and sniffs. "I don't smell anything."

"No, not a smell. Like... dusty."

The nurse smiles sadly at me. "This is a hospital room, sweetheart. It's cleaned twice a day, up and down." She pats my leg over the thin blankets. "You just rest."

I sit, staring at the strange sunlight, in this catatonic state where time seems to slip by me like a river around a rock. Some flowers are delivered. The front of the card reads Thinking of You in that thin, loopy cursive that seems to come stock with these things. I flip it open. It's signed by the wedding party. They would have had to go home by now. Back to their lives. My best man was a childhood friend I recently got in touch with online. The other two were guys I pulled into the party from the bar where I work to try to fill out my numbers. None of them were super invested.

I must have fallen asleep again because when I wake up, an old man in a dark gray suit is sitting calmly by the window, speaking with the nurse in low tones. I hear him whisper, "Just terrible... On the wedding day too." I clear my throat, and they both turn to me.

"Hi, Lee," he says. "I'm a grief counselor with the hospital. I just came to check in and see if there's anything I can do for you."

For some reason, the official title brings it all home to me. The loss settles on my chest like a weight, and I feel I'm being buried underneath these thin hospital blankets. The nurse comes to my side and takes up the bucket again, but I have nothing left. She holds my hand until I dig a big breath up from within myself then another. And another.

"So she's really dead, then," I say.

"She died instantly," he says. Softly. Evenly. "She felt no pain."

I remember. One moment, she was smiling at me, reaching over to place her ring over mine. The sunlight was catching her hair, brushing her neck with liquid gold. The next moment, the car was crushed. Her entire side caved in an instant. She wasn't taken from me so much as snuffed out, her hand gone from mine as though it never was.

That's all I remember. That's all I'll never forget. I already feel the memory heating up, burning itself into the back of my brain like a watermark that will never leave my sight.

When I wave away some of the dust floating around, the counselor takes it as a dismissal, nodding sadly. "When you're ready, then," he says as he leaves.

So many sad nods—doctors, nurses, guys in suits. All nodding sadly to one another. Seems like they're having a much easier time accepting things than I am.

"What's with all the dust?" I ask.

The nurse looks at me, more concerned this time. "No dust in here, Lee."

I point at an area in a corner, right near the window where she's standing. A golden fog is gathering there, swirling and moving like glitter caught in some unfelt breeze.

"Right there," I say. "You don't see that?"

She looks down and around. "See what, sweetheart?"

I squint. Close my eyes. Blink a few times. Open them

wide. Still there. As though it's sifting through the cracks in the window.

The nurse looks at me curiously then pouts slightly. She notes something on the computer—a lot of typing.

She walks back over to me. "I want you to tell me if you see more of this dust, okay, Lee? I think it might just be a symptom of the concussion."

"Okay."

I'm not sure why I don't tell her about the golden dust coming in under the door like low-lying fog. And dripping from the ceiling lights like floating sand. Maybe talking about seeing things like this after a car wreck isn't such a good thing. Maybe this gets you taken from one hospital to another, where they strap you to your bed.

About five episodes of garbage daytime television later, the nurse comes back in with a doctor I vaguely recognize. The doc tells me about how my shoulder is good to get sutured. They're gonna give me a little something for the pain and remove the staples.

I nod, trying to ignore the dust flowing around their feet as they prepare a little station near my shoulder. The nurse pumps something into my IV, and I conk out.

I wake again to find a fresh bandage and sling on my arm and food nearby—cold grilled cheese and room-temperature Jell-O. I eat it anyway, and it stays down. The sun is setting. I don't know how I can sleep as much as I have and still be tired.

I blink, and it's nighttime again. But the room isn't dark. The dust floats all about like sand blowing across a lonely highway. Bits of it are kicked into the air here and there in swirls and cyclones. A low light emanates from the ground, where the dust is playing around like veins of slow-moving lava glowing at night. One tendril of it is snaking its way about my bedcovers. When I reach out, it scatters with the passage of my hand. My fingers feel briefly warm then cool.

I lie back again. Breathe. Breathe. I don't fall asleep quickly this time. Maybe they dialed the meds back, or my body is thinking it's about time to start doing things again. Either way, I nod off only when the dusty glow is dampened by the rising rays of the sun.

When I wake up, another man is standing in the room. He wears a crisp suit of dark blue and the flat gaze of a bureaucrat, and his lapel pin is the hospital logo. He speaks unprompted and without introduction.

"Mr. Baker, how are you feeling?" he asks.

"That's kind of a loaded question."

"Physically, I mean," he adds with a hint of a sad nod.

"Okay, I guess. Better."

"Good to hear." Still nodding. "That's really good to hear because we're going to be discharging you today."

I look over at my arm still wrapped in its sling, trying pointedly to ignore the dust that seems to be reaching out to me like creeping ivy.

"Are you sure? I'm still kind of banged up."

"That's the recommendation of the hospital, Mr. Baker."

"Can you bring the grief counselor back in here?" I ask. "I liked him better."

"You'll have to take that up with your insurance," he says. "Sign here, please."

I see what's happening here. I've run out of money. Or Medicare thinks I did. Or thinks I can't pay what's coming. I bet I've been here damn near two weeks. That ain't cheap in New York—or anywhere. I don't know the specifics of all these things, but I'm pretty sure whatever government plan is out there, Mom and I are on the bargain side.

"You think I'm broke," I say flatly.

The suit returns my gaze in a way that is somehow neither threatening nor friendly. It just is. He's a born administrator. He probably hit his mother with that look after the doctor slapped his ass at his birth.

I take up the pen and scribble a signature and the date.

"Well, guess what, Mr. Suit? You're right."

## CHAPTER TWO

I call Mom as soon as I put my pants on and fish my phone out of my pocket. After five rings, her voice mail fools me, and I start talking over it as though I haven't heard it a hundred times before: "This is Claire!" Half a beat. "I'm not in at the moment, but I'll get right back to you. Thanks!"

"Mom, where are you? I need you here. You said some stuff about leaving, a bunch of other stuff, but I was out of it. Call me back. I'm heading home right now."

I fish out my wallet with my good arm. After saying a little prayer, I open the billfold. Five bucks. Well, it's something. A bus fare home, at least.

The dust moves around me as I walk down the halls of the hospital. Little piles here and there. I'm looking down, left to right like a nosing hound dog, and I nearly run into an orderly pushing a bedridden patient.

"Watch yourself," he says, not unkindly.

"Does it look gold in here to you?" I ask, gesturing at the floor.

Dust is also floating over the woman in the bed. She watches me warily.

"Gold?" he asks. "I wish." He moves on without another word.

The woman turns to look at me carefully, eyes narrowed. Then she turns away.

More dust is outside, on the sidewalks, on the streets. Little veins run here and there down the buildings. Rivulets play on and around the people walking about. A pool of the stuff moves around two men smoking just off the entrance, speaking in low tones to each other.

Nobody seems to notice a damn thing but me.

The bus pulls up. The door opens, and a little puff of dust follows me in. I feel it on the back of my neck like faint mist. The dust hits the driver, too, but he only stares dumbly at me, hand out.

I hand him the five, and he gives me some change. I move in and sit down by the window, wincing when I bump my arm settling in. Outside, the gold dust puffs this way and that. Sometimes, it kicks up with the passing of certain cars and people. Other times, it seems to pay no mind at all, as if the world around passes right through it.

I hit redial on my phone and close my eyes. This is all a lot to take right now.

"Hi, it's Claire!"

"Mom, I really need to talk to you."

"Hi, it's Claire!"

"Hi, it's Claire!"

By the time I get to my stop, I've convinced myself my brain is bleeding to death. I signed my life away when I allowed that goober to discharge me. Any second, all this gold dust is gonna overwhelm my vision, turning it into a tunnel of light. I'll follow it down, down, down... See you later, alligator.

But I don't die on the bus. And I don't die on the sidewalk in front of our half of the duplex, either. Mom and I have lived in this rent-controlled apartment for as long as I can remember, just the two of us. If she's not here, it'll be empty. My dad was never in the picture. I've never known him. Mom doesn't remember him either—a time in her life she calls a "dark chapter"—and I've never pressed.

I don't die when I open the door or when I step inside, although a good amount of gold dust follows me in, rolling over my legs in a little wave and spreading out on the floor of the living room.

The hallucination is remarkably vivid. Every square foot of dust seems to have its own agenda. The closer I look at the stuff, the more detailed it becomes, a little like trying to find the black space between stars, only to find more stars.

My home is frozen in time. Remnants of the wedding are everywhere. The gold dust plays over unopened boxes of towel sets, glassware, and kitchen utensils I doubt I'll ever use. Two empty bottles of cheap champagne stand around a vanity near the sink, from when Alli's wedding party used the kitchen for makeup. I almost can't look at them, yet I'm fascinated. The world simply can't go on around these things with Alli gone, yet it does.

The dust seems drawn to these vignettes of a life now gone, swirling around the champagne bottles like a ghostly hand and flitting over a pile of hairpins. More recent lines of life draw the dust as well: the front closet door thrown open, with bags strewn about. The everything drawer, where we stashed a few bucks every now and then for our rainy-day fund, pulled open, riffled through. Mom's trusty notepad on the counter, the top sheets torn off. A few odd bits of clothing trailing from her room in the back. The dust flows over these clues as well.

I follow the trail back to Mom's bedroom. Her jewelry box is open, and I see some key pieces missing, things she would know she could get money for. She doesn't have a lot of clothes, but much of what she has is gone from the shelves in her closet—same with the picture of her and me standing outside on a particularly beautiful fall day a few years ago.

The bed is made but dimpled where she must have sat, packing. The little roller trail of the suitcase has marked the carpet. I sit where she sat. The covers puff around me, and a dusting of gold puffs as well. I'm suddenly very tired. My room is just downstairs, but it seems a mile away.

I lie down on Mom's bed, surrounded by a presence of her that I feel growing fainter with each heartbeat. I bet she came home that day she said goodbye, packed up in a hurry, and walked right out the door. A stale, dusty smell is replacing the warm, lived-in scent of the house. But what little of that scent is left is still a comfort.

I tell myself that maybe tomorrow, somehow, Alli and Mom will be here, flitting around the kitchen, banging the screen door to the back porch while coming and going.

It's not much, but it's enough to get me to sleep.

I WAKE up in the early morning to find the gold dust dancing in and out of the first rays of sunlight flitting through the blinds. A quick glance around the room tells me there's no more gold dust than yesterday, which is a good sign for whatever head trauma brought all this on, but there's certainly not less. And it seems no more faded. If anything, the gold has an inner glow in the muted light of morning that makes it more startling.

I sense no other signs of life in the house, though. No flitting around the kitchen. No scraping bowls of cereal. And of course, nothing of Alli at all. Alli already seems more distant to me than my mother. Both women are gone, but one has been obliterated.

The other is still out there somewhere.

I pick up my phone, thinking I'm gonna give Mom's number another shot, and I find I've missed a text from her. At 12:45 a.m., my mother wrote: *McCarran Airport. Stow-and-Go. 777.*

I frown even as my heart hammers. I was hoping for something a bit more enlightening, maybe an *I'll be back soon. I love you.* And a few smiles and hearts like when she usually texts. But that's all I get: three words and one number.

I do some quick phone research. McCarran Airport is in Las Vegas. Stow-and-Go is a storage company that offers long-term lockers at McCarran and other airports in the west.

I have no idea what 777 means. It could be a flight number. It could be a lucky number. It's sure as hell a lucky number to me—lucky because it's something, at least. A hint of where she may have gone.

I call her, but this time her phone jumps immediately to voice mail, as though it's turned off.

"Hi! It's Claire..."

I mutter a curse and try texting: *Mom are u okay? Call me!*

I wait for an infuriatingly long span of seconds after sending it, willing myself to see the three little dots that tell me she's typing. But I get no dots.

After a full minute, I toss the phone onto the bed, and it passes through a thin mist of gold that's accumulated on the bedspread like fog on a grave. I rub my face and eyes in frustration. I've got a full-blown beard going on now. I need to trim that back. I catch myself in the wall mirror as I sit up and start at the subtle silver that streaks my wiry black hair at the temples. That's new. I look a bit like a starving badger.

Next, I do what I always used to do to get myself out of bed after a long shift at the bar. I list out steps.

Take a shower.

Make myself presentable.

Eat whatever didn't go bad in the kitchen.

Empty my bank account.

Buy a ticket to Las Vegas.

Find Mom.

That last one does it. I swing my legs over the ground and ease my arm along to follow.

I stand up and move through the low-lying gold.

## CHAPTER THREE

I land in Vegas at high noon. Heat waves start radiating off the wings as soon as the tires hit the ground. The arm sling seemed more a hindrance than a help on the way out, so I ditched it, but after five hours on the airplane, my shoulder is sore as hell. The beard I shaved off feels like it's grown back. I spent my last five bucks on a tiny bottle of whisky that did nothing to calm my nerves during the flight.

I'm pretty sure the poor old lady that had to sit next to me thinks I'm running from the law. As soon as the seat belt sign is off, she's up and out, scurrying to get as far down the aisle and away from me as she can before the rest of the passengers clog things up. I can't blame her. I've been hunched in the corner, staring out the window ever since we left New York. I jumped every time the intercom dinged or the stewardess spoke. I look like... Well, I look like a guy who's seeing things.

People start deplaning. I'm not sure what I'm gonna do once I get off this airplane, so I'm sort of frozen to the seat—analysis paralysis. A bachelor party passes by my row—these are people my age, but they seem a world apart: carefree, laughing and joking, excited to start an epic weekend that they'll barely remember and never forget. Everyone passes me by. The dust plays off each of them until I'm alone, still buckled in, arms crossed, shoulder slumped awkwardly. I can't bring myself to get up and moving. Eventually, a stewardess does it for me.

"Sir, this is our final destination," she says. Her eyes look almost as tired as mine feel. She takes one look at me and adds, "Is there something we can help you with? Hotel? A connection?"

The dust moves slowly around her feet. Little tendrils still snake down the aisle, but most of it has gone, following the people. It seems attracted to movement, interaction, life.

"No, thanks." I clear my throat. Those are the first words I've spoken in hours. "This is my stop."

I get up and make my way down the aisle, taking nothing from under the seat in front of me and ignoring the overhead compartments.

"Good luck in Sin City!" she adds.

I nod and try to muster a smile. If only she knew. I think I could make a pretty good case of being one of the unluckiest people in greater Nevada.

My mom went to Vegas once for a friend's fortieth birthday. She somehow made it work with two hundred bucks for two nights. She said your brain starts changing as soon as you step off the plane. I never got what she was saying then, but I do now. Even walking into the airport gives me a bit of a jolt, like somebody wafting smelling salts under my nose. I square my bum shoulder and don't even wince. Much.

The blinking neon bulbs greet me in the terminal and don't stop winking, each one blending with the next in a glittering line, beckoning like a finger.

I try to picture her walking out like me. I try to sense her, to see things as she did. But the dust is too distracting. My eyes flit along one vein of gold and jump to another and another. And as for what she was thinking... Hell, I can't even touch that. Whatever made her run is something I can't fathom. We each held to our own at home, but we were always open. Yet I missed something—something big. She wouldn't run out like she did, when she did, unless she had a bad secret.

Maybe I don't know my mom the way I think I do. Maybe I don't know her at all.

The harsh reality of that thought sears me like the baking heat of the desert air as I step outside. I breathe it in, letting it fill my lungs.

As I breathe, my heart slows, and a faint ringing starts in my ears. My stomach does a little flip, like when you look up at the last second and stop yourself from crossing the street just as a car barrels through. Faint tendrils of golden smoke stir and settle low to the ground. Strings of it snake everywhere, like glittering snow dusted on a frozen highway, some of it swirling as people walk by, most of it dancing to the beat of some unheard drum.

Right now, the dust shimmers with particular strength along the sidewalk, past the rental-car booths, just beyond the ride-share pickup, to pool around the entrance of a grubby little storefront with a faded neon sign that reads Stow-and-Go. I can't figure out whether the stuff is guiding me or maybe egging me on. I don't think it likes me. I seem to agitate it with my passing, setting it boiling briefly with each step. But if it's not gonna kill me, maybe it can help me.

I don't even need to look at the numbers on the rows of lockers when I walk inside. One of them shimmers like a lone light in the window—locker 777. I walk right up to it and give it a little tug. Locked, naturally. Not sure what I expected.

I step back, thinking. I close my eyes and picture Mom here. I breathe and feel the faint pressure of the dust around me, a sensation that's pleasantly numbing. I open my eyes and try our address in Brooklyn, 1115. No go. I try her birthday, 0512. Nope.

The dust dances around the numbers. It tickles up my fingers and trails up my arms. I find myself smiling stupidly.

I try my birthday, 0910.

The light beeps and turns green, and I hear the mechanical lock roll back. The locker scoots open a half inch, and gold dust leaks from the crack, spilling all over me. I shake my hand free of the stuff like gossamer spiderwebs.

I hold my breath and open the locker. Inside, the dust swirls and billows like smoke in a bottle. At first, I have a hard time seeing anything. Then I realize there's not much to see.

A single casino chip lies flat at the bottom of the locker, a chip worth one dollar to a place called the Diamond.

I start laughing, unable to help it. The little snicker turns into a silent shaking. *Here it is, folks! The pot of gold at the end of the rainbow! All my questions answered!*

I calm myself when I notice that a greasy-looking teenage kid pulling a beat-up backpack from a locker down the row is staring at me.

"Hey, let me ask you something," I say, still feeling a bit loopy. "D'you see all this dust?"

He rolls his eyes in spectacular teen fashion. "We live in a desert, man. There's dust everywhere."

Boy, is there ever. I pluck the chip from the locker and turn it over in my hand. The dust seems to bubble up a bit around the lettering, giving it a strange, unnatural glitter. Or maybe I'm just seeing things.

I shake my head. Of course I'm seeing things. That's the whole problem.

~

I WAIT for a shuttle in the oppressive heat. Beads of sweat sprout on my brow almost faster than I can wipe them away with the slick back of my hand. I could use about a gallon of water. And a few shots of whisky. And a cheeseburger. Maybe I could swap some of this golden dust for a cheeseburger. I reach out to try to grab a handful, but it passes through my fingers with barely a jolt.

A car pulls up, and it occurs to me that I may have inadvertently signaled for a ride when I sure as hell can't afford one, especially not this one. This is a jet-black Mercedes with tinted windows. This is the kind of car I might be lucky enough to gas up one day, not drive.

The doors of the airport open across the street, and a man and woman step out, quick time, toward the car.

"That's us," says the man. "Right here."

He's dressed in bright-white loafers and dark-blue slacks. He wears a linen jacket over a crisp white polo. He's tan, his teeth are as bright as diamonds, and the dust roils around a gold watch hanging loosely off his wrist.

I stumble back into the bus-stop overhang. The sheer force of this guy plowing across the street seems to send waves ahead of him. Plus, that watch... I don't like the look of that watch at all. The dust around it is dirty, like coffee that's boiled over until it turns to burbling sludge.

"They used to bring these goddamn things right to the

jet," he tells the girl next to him. "The private service here has gone downhill."

She shakes her head softly. "It was a one-minute walk. You lived."

"This homeless man almost poached our ride, for God's sake," he says, gesturing at me as if I'm not right here, able to hear his every word. "I mean... What's the world coming to?"

"You'll be fine, Huxley," she says, looking up at me shyly, shaking her head as if embarrassed. She has a sort of effortless beauty that makes the bronzed and pressed look of this Huxley fellow seem foppish and overdone. She shrugs at me as if we have some private joke between us: *"He's ridiculous, I know. I'm sorry."*

Perhaps she'd have said something if Huxley hadn't shot me a look that sent me back another step. I've looked at rats in alleys with more compassion than this man looks at me.

He helps the woman into the car a little too quickly, and she balances herself with one hand briefly on the roof. A square diamond engagement ring the size of a front tooth flashes briefly.

He shoots me another cold look that I deflect by looking elsewhere, I'm a little ashamed to say.

I'm not sorry to see Huxley leave. However, I play the woman's slight shrugging smile over a few times in my head until the shuttle bus comes.

The windows of the bus are dripping with condensation from the blasting AC. The Strip shimmers like a mirage as we turn onto Las Vegas Boulevard. The dust is everywhere—on the sidewalks and streets, on the cars and people. It sifts from the neon signs and puffs in and out the doors of the casinos, dancing up and down the waves of heat like a spoon on a washboard.

The sun cuts at my eyes when I get off the bus. I add sunglasses to the long list of things I should buy but can't afford. My newfound single-chip fortune hasn't exactly put me on easy street. I've heard Vegas is a tough town for broke people, and I'm not much into panhandling, either. I'm going to have to figure out some way to get food, too, but all those concerns are secondary. First order of business: The Diamond. Maybe Mom is there. Maybe all these problems go away.

The Diamond is built like an actual cut diamond—its flat crown, twenty or so stories up, tapers down, down, down and gives the impression that the point is dug another hundred feet or so into the ground. Two towers of hotel rooms support it on either side, and a VIP-looking rotunda sits way high up on the crown. Brightly lit elevators inside the main plaza shoot up and drop down, stopping here and there. Subtly mirrored glass on the outside gives the impression that the entire structure sparkles with some bright inner fire that can surely be seen from outer space.

A dune's worth of dust sifts down the facets of the main plaza with the slow certainty of sand through a massive hourglass. The dust seems to like this place a lot. I get a feeling that it's expecting me.

As I walk along the sidewalk toward the front entrance, I pass a string of Hispanic guys wearing utility vests, slapping their hands with cards and fliers to get the attention of the people passing by. One of them—a young guy with sharp blue eyes, close-cropped hair, and one gold tooth—thrusts a baseball card into my hand, advertising airbrushed models with black stars edited over their naughty bits. They're straddling a phone number.

"I'm not interested," I say, trying to hand it back.

"Good luck in there, *ese*," he says and winks at me. He leaves me hanging and starts slapping again.

After a second, I pocket the card and walk on. I'm thinking I should just drop it like all the others. I have no intention of calling the number—even if I had money, I wouldn't—but for some reason, I feel good about having something in my pocket other than a featherweight wallet, a dollar chip, and a busted cell phone that's about to get cut off.

A footman opens the front door, his eyes lingering on me as I step inside, but I quickly forget him as I take everything in. The smell is a mix of wildflowers and new money. A crystal fountain in the center in the shape of a free-standing umbrella gently splashes falling water into a marble basin. *The Diamond* is written in large glittering cursive on the floor at the foot of the fountain. The black marble floor beneath my feet glitters like a starry night spreading in all directions. A plaque on the wall by the doors calls it the 7,777 Karat Foyer. I believe it.

Everything else glitters too. Four cut-crystal chandeliers hang from above on hundred-yard chains of glass. The many front desks are mirrored. The walls behind them aren't walls at all but flat sheets of evenly poured water, lit from behind to cast a shimmering effect on the steady stream of folks coming in behind me.

Add a slowly roiling layer of golden dust to all this, and you've got a sensory explosion.

I don't know how Mom can be here. This isn't like her. It's stunning, but it isn't like her. I brush off my front and try to wipe the residue of exhaustion from my face. I scrape bits of scuzz from my scruff and retie one well-worn sneaker. I've never felt so out of place in my life.

Most of the employees are busy checking people in, but

the concierge desk is empty and staffed by four or five eager beavers. They look increasingly disappointed as I approach. One eventually steps forward, wearing a tight black suit with a round fez perched jauntily askew atop his head. Dust dances about the desk but doesn't really seem to want much to do with him.

"Can I help you, sir?"

"Can I ask after a guest?" I ask.

"If they're staying on premises, I can ring the room phone if that's what you're asking."

What I'm asking is *"Where's my mommy?"* but that won't do to say out loud. "Sure," I say. "Her name is Claire Baker. I'm her son."

The concierge does a strange thing. His fake smile lingers for about two seconds too long, as if whatever program he's running hits a glitch and lags. When he snaps to, he taps rapidly on the keyboard at his waist and purses his lips.

"Nobody by that name, sir."

"Are you sure?"

"Quite sure."

I wasn't expecting a dead end so soon, so I start hurling Hail Marys. "Can you give 'Baker' a search? It's a pretty unique name."

After a few more taps, he gives a sad shake of the head, oddly reminiscent of the administrative suit that kicked me out of the hospital.

I slump. Then I feel around in my pocket for the chip and pluck it out to give it a glance as if the name might have changed. The concierge watches me carefully until I protectively tuck it away again.

"How about 'Claire'?" I ask. "Maybe she just put her first name."

"No Claires at this moment either," he says without looking at the screen.

"She's missing. I think she might be in trouble. Have you seen a woman about my height in her fifties, short cropped black hair, thin, sort of pixyish, dark-green eyes?"

"We see a lot of people every day here," he says, shrugging. "I mean, maybe?"

"Eyes like mine," I say, pointing at my face and fully realizing what a fool I must look like.

"Have you gone to the police?" he asks pointedly.

I open my mouth to speak then close it. "Well, she wasn't *taken*. She left. But she's not thinking right."

"I'm sorry, sir. That's about all we can do."

"All right, then," I say. I look around helplessly, hands on hips. "Do you have any job openings here, by chance?"

The grating smile returns. I already know the answer.

"Not at this time, no."

"Not even a bellhop?"

"Our front-door ambassador positions are quite competitive."

"A dishwasher, then."

He shakes his head.

I point at the system of interconnected mirrors that give the Diamond its inner fire. "Who polishes all those mirrors? Maybe they could use some help."

"We take care of any smudges that do arise with flying drones."

I lean back against the concierge desk and scan the soaring rafters. "Drones? Really?"

The concierge looks with aversion at where my hand has left a mark near his console. "Really."

I let out a breath. "Well... thanks for nothing."

"My pleasure," he says, flashing that hollow smile again,

faker than the Rolex knockoffs they're hawking down the block.

I can feel his eyes on me as I walk away, but I'm not quite ready to leave just yet, so I decide to take a walk around the casino floor. As soon as I turn that direction, I can't help but notice one of the "ambassadors" peeling away from his post at the door to follow. I turn and smile at him. He doesn't smile back. I put my hands in my pockets and keep walking. He follows but at a distance. My guess is that as long as I don't touch anything or talk to anybody, he'll leave me alone—for a little while, anyway.

The casino floor just keeps going. Rows and rows of slot machines line the walls on either side of winding pathways that twist and turn. I pass table games of every variety, raucous games of craps, the slotted ticking of roulette wheel after roulette wheel. I can hear the whirring shuffle of thousands upon thousands of cards, the dry slap of them hitting the tables, the buzz of the people, their cheers and jeers. Soon, I'm hopelessly turned around, lost within a glittering jungle where time seems to have stopped, which is exactly what these casinos want—a willingly captive audience.

Dust coats everything. It swirls around on the floor and puffs with the movement of the dealers' hands on the bright-white felt of the tables. It drips from stacks of chips and billows like gossamer cobwebs from the handles of the slot machines. Some tables and some machines have more than others. So do some people. One woman dripping in dust tosses the dice down a craps table and receives the loudest cheer in the room. Another man coated in dust puts all his chips on the number seven for a roulette spin. The ball races around the outer slot of the wheel then bounces off the wood. It skitters over the numbers, dropping in and popping out of slots, pauses for a moment on the seven long enough for the whole table to lean in, nobody breathing... then it pops out and settles in the zero: the table loses.

The man drops his head as everyone sighs. "I just don't got it tonight," he says.

I move on. This is the oddest brain bleed I've ever had. First, it leads me to the right locker for Mom's chip. Now, it almost seems to be pointing me in the direction of where the action is, good or bad.

This must be exactly what truly insane vagrants think— the poor guys I used to see rambling at pigeons when I'd take the trash out late at night, at the bar back in Brooklyn.

I guess this is my life now. I'm a pigeon rambler.

I'm distracted from my slow descent into insanity by an elevator at the far back of the casino. The clear tube whisks people up into the top floors of the Diamond, maybe even all the way up to that crown jewel I saw plopped on top. So much dust is moving in and around this thing that it looks like those clear wands I used to play with as a kid, where an air bubble would stir up a bunch of glitter and confetti when it was tilted this way and that.

Something is up there, something big. In front of it, an attendant stands with his hands clasped behind his back, face impassive, tiny little fez cap perfectly askew on his head. I'm not sure how I'll get past him, but I'm gonna try. I've literally got nothing to lose. I take a step toward the back and feel a heavy hand on my shoulder. I'm spun around and come face-to-face with Mr. Ambassador.

He shakes his head at me. "Time to go."

With a subtle touch on my arm, he leads me back, winding through the casino and foyer. I don't protest. He's just doing his job. I've led out a few crazies myself in my time—a bit weird, to be on the other end of it.

He leaves me out front, turns around, and goes inside

without a word. His hand touches his earpiece, already on the next call. I stand with my hands in my pockets, one around the chip and one around the card, staring up at the cut glass of the Diamond as it reflects the waning rays of the day.

It's quite pretty. A truly golden hour. Shame almost everybody's inside, missing this. Then again, it's probably a hundred degrees. Also, every place on this block is designed to keep you in, not out.

Unless you're me, of course.

"Tough luck, *cabron*?"

The voice comes from the sidewalk behind me and to the left, where the gold-toothed Mexican man is still slapping his cards and offering them to passersby. At first, I think he's talking to one of the other men in his group. Then he looks over at me.

"You could say that," I reply.

The man nods, his sharp blue gaze alternating from my face back down to the hands of each person that passes. He wears a battered construction helmet with a faded rag tucked in the back and draped over his neck. He's dressed in well-worn jeans and a clean white T-shirt, and he doesn't seem to be sweating at all, incredibly. He slaps and offers his cards with a rhythm. All of them do. It makes a sort of papery musical sound in concert.

"They won't even let me wash the windows," I say.

"That place?" He shakes his head quickly. "Nah. You don't want to work at that place."

"Any open spots on the corner, handing out the nudie cards?" I ask.

He smiles, and the gold glints in his mouth. Dust refracts the light all around him. The dust likes him.

"You can't have this job, *hombre*," he says. "This job hires only real special people."

As he speaks, a beat-up old truck turns the corner and slows in front of the men. A rough-looking Mexican man gets out and pops open the rusty bed. Another group of guys and gals in vests jump out. They each grab banded bunches of cards on their way and put them in the front pockets of their construction vests.

"Oh yeah? And what makes you so special?" I ask Gold Tooth.

He looks at me, and for a moment, his gaze is hard. His blue eyes squint as they scan me from top to bottom. The dust that swirls quietly around him suddenly bubbles and spits, and I make a conscious effort not to look directly at it.

"You got a driver's license in your wallet, *cabron*?" he asks me.

"Sure."

"See, I'm special because I don't got nothing like that. Or any other papers. If you know what I'm sayin'. None of us do."

*Ah. So that kind of special.* I nod. "I get it."

He spreads his hands and flips them over like a blackjack dealer tapping out of a shift. "And I'm all done with work for today." He pulls himself into the passenger's side of the idling truck and slams the creaky door behind him. He turns to look at me again, elbow out the open window.

"If I was you, I'd try my luck at the Golden Swan," he says. "They're looking for good people."

"Oh yeah? Where's that?"

He points way down the street to a big property in the distance—a glittering castle with spotlights swirling from every rampart and parapet. The Diamond dwarfs it in terms of a light show, but it's still impressive in its own right, even as far away as it is.

"You see that pretty place?" he asks. He moves his finger a tick to the right. "It's the shithole next door."

I strain my eyes. Something drab and old is jammed between the castle and an outdoor strip mall beyond, but I can't quite make it out.

"Don't worry—it's there," he says. "When you get there, say Berto sent you. Might help. Might also get you thrown out on your ass." He shrugs as if to say, *"Such is life."* I'm about to ask him whom to ask, but he taps the car door twice, and the truck pulls out in a cloud of dirty oil exhaust. When the air clears, the other card slappers have already moved on down the street, dispersing to other corners, and I'm left alone.

The blocks in Vegas are deceptively long. I walk for five minutes, but the glitzy castle doesn't seem much closer, and the Diamond still looms behind me. The sun is setting, and the lights of the strip fire up all around me. The dust still shines in the low light, tossed gently about like glowing ash in some unseen wind. I still catch myself rubbing my eyes as though I might be able to clear them. I feel like I'm walking through the hot zone of a forest fire while all the other animals play on, unaware.

Fifteen minutes after I start away from the Diamond, I reach the castle. It's called the Avalon. They went all in on the King Arthur theme, with a moat and drawbridge and everything. Handsome knights in glinting metal armor that you could probably fry an egg on beckon passersby. Buxom ladies call down from the turrets above. There's even a Sword in the Stone out front that the kids are going nuts over. Every now and again, one of them manages to make it rumble and hiss smoke, and all of them scream with delight.

A massive metal dragon with iridescent green scales shoots great gouts of flame from its perch atop the drawbridge. I can feel the heat from each blast.

I keep walking.

And walking.

Ten minutes later, I get to the Golden Swan. My jeans are chafing me something awful. The short sleeve of my T-shirt is soaked with brow sweat.

Compared to the Diamond, the Golden Swan looks like it fell asleep in the 1970s and has just woken up to an entirely different sort of Vegas party. The sign above my head shows a faded yellow cartoon swan looking a bit drunk, clutching wads of cash in both wings. It blinks on and off in measured time with all the brightness of a desk lamp on the fritz. The swinging-double-door entrance is flanked on either side by huge golden eggs in big planter pots. The building looks a bit like a bong: squat at the base and thin up top, where a handful of neon-tinged windows indicate hotel rooms. The entire place is maybe half the size of the Diamond's lobby.

I sit and watch the front doors for five full minutes, and in all that time, I count no more than ten people going in. Three of them come right back out, laughing as they head toward the castle.

The Avalon obviously gets the lion's share of the crowd around here, but the Golden Swan gets as much dust as the Avalon—which is to say, not much. A little stream of shimmering gold trickles into this hole in the wall, but I'd probably pass it by if I wasn't looking for it. Nothing like the amount drenching the Diamond.

I don't bother tucking in my rumpled shirt. As I push inside through the swinging double doors, I decide I'm going to take a different approach: let the dust do the work.

The entrance of the Golden Swan has a faded opulence that reminds me a bit of the set of an old game show. It's more open than I imagined. A sequined swirl accent grabs my eye from the doorway and takes my gaze along the wall, down the length of the foyer, swirling and looping. The same drunken cursive pattern is sketched into the marble flooring, which is a soft brown, faded and feathered here and there with cracks. Brass light fixtures hang from above, adorned with little tassels that flutter with the hot wind that follows me in.

I see only one check-in desk, and it's doing double duty as a concierge desk. A fat man with cinnamon-colored hair and a walrus mustache stands behind it. He wears a tired-looking suit with a comically long tie, and he is resting his clasped hands on top of his belly, placidly listening to an old woman insisting he check the lost and found again for something. Dust dances about the desk but mostly leaves him alone. Can't say the same for the old lady.

To my right, a neon sign says Shop at the Swan in that same drunken cursive. I remember that as I was getting kicked out of the Diamond, we passed a shopping area with ten or so designer boutiques and jewelry stores, and I have to laugh. Here I see three. The first two are a sundry shop for last-minute toothbrush purchases and the like and a souvenir shop with shelves of drunken-looking swan figurines, hats, and shirts. Not a lot of gold dust in there, but I do see a fair amount of real dust.

The third shop is tucked in a corner behind a bead curtain. The heady smell of incense hits me like a mouthful of bad cologne as I walk by. What little dust is in this joint seems to want to come in, so I push through the beads into a small, dark room covered floor to ceiling in swirling tapestries of purple and red. A single table is illuminated in the center of the room, not much bigger than a nightstand and draped in black velvet. Beaded pillows are piled in the corners. Chimes and baubles hang from strings throughout. I accidentally knock into one, and it sends a sound around the room like dice rattling in a can.

Someone calls from behind a wide tapestry to my right, "Take off yo shoes, honey. I'll be there in a second!"

This place is either a fortune teller's shop or a shady massage parlor—I'm not a hundred percent sure which. Either way, I'm out.

"Oh, no, thank you. I'm just looking," I say.

"No, you ain't," comes the reply. "Now take yo shoes off and sit yo ass down."

I pause a second more, blinking in the cloying incense. After I kick off my shoes and step up to the table, I sit down like a chastised schoolboy and wait.

The music from the lobby is muted. Even the ringing of the slots doesn't seem to reach here. The quiet is strange. Deep. Then I hear a low whirring, like an electric toothbrush.

Something bulges at the large tapestry in the back, like a monster poking a finger, testing the barrier between our worlds. The whirring stops, and I hear a muttered curse. With a series of backup beeps, the shape recedes, then the whirring starts again, and the tapestry opens in the center to reveal a huge woman on a motor scooter. She whirs herself up to the opposite side of the table and stops with a flourish, flipping a long purple weave with a flick of her hand. Her face is the size of a pumpkin, her skin is a rich black, and her lips are full and bloodred. Her eyelashes are long and jeweled at the tips. She turns sidesaddle on the scooter and clasps her hands elegantly on the velvet between us. Her long, purple nails click softly against one another.

A massage is looking less and less likely.

This woman stirs up dust like I've never seen before. She brought in a fair cloud of the stuff with her from behind the curtain. It bubbles and burbles, and the turbulence is coming my way, spreading out and misting up like cold water sloshed onto a hot tin roof.

Suddenly, I don't want to be here anymore. When the dust rumbles, things happen. Maybe good but maybe bad. And I'm thinking maybe I ought to just let my brain bleed in peace—find some bench in a park to lie down on and never wake up again. I start to stand.

She throws up her hands. "I was eating my dinner, I come all the way out here, and now you just gonna leave?"

"I don't have any money—"

"Don't take a psychic to figure that out, honey."

The dust crawls up the velvet table like smoke falling in reverse. I try to calm myself. Maybe it reacts to my anxiety level. I take a few deep breaths, but it keeps building, getting thicker and thicker out of nowhere, like glowing water seeping from the ground.

"I really should go," I say.

The woman seems intrigued, wholly unaware of the dust creeping up the long folds of her patchwork dress. It encircles her massive waist as I take deep breaths, willing the cloud to calm itself, but it doesn't seem to care what I want. The dust is nearly to her neck now, and she reaches up as if to scratch at it. Instead, she fingers one of her many necklaces, a beaded leather thong with a polished river stone hanging low at the center. Her fingernails find the stone, and she taps it three times, flipping it on a little spinning axle to expose a crudely carved pictograph of an eye, wide open.

The dust pauses… or at least appears to pause. I blink and look harder.

The woman spreads her substantial arms wide. "Let Zja-Zja—the Eye of Sin City, the Oracle of the Desert—give you a taste, then let's worry about payment later. That's how we work. Fortune tellers and drug dealers. Same thing."

She pulls a thin, tattered scarf from one of her many folds and flicks it open to lay it flat upon the table.

The dust puffs off the velvet and falls calmly to the floor —a strange real-life interaction. The dust retreats from us and moves to the edges of the room, eddying in pools against the walls… as if waiting. I catch myself staring at its sudden change of heart for too long and snap back to Zja-Zja. She's watching me with a twinkle in her eye.

"Something got you scared," she says as she pulls a folded knife from her sleeve. She grasps it by its worn bone handle and flicks it open. "Let's see if we can't find out what."

For a second, I think I'm about to be robbed by a woman on a motor scooter. And Zja-Zja won't be too happy with what she finds unless she wants to call a hooker. But then she positions the knife sideways, flat along the edge of the handkerchief, the blade facing inward.

"My great-grandmother made this kerchief. I like to call it my first tapestry. I don't bring it out for just any reading, but something about you got me going." She winks.

I smile weakly. "And the knife?" I ask. "That hers too?"

"Hell no. Gammy was more a gun woman. Eddie took this knife from some drunk hick that tried to pull it out at a blackjack table after a bad beat. I snatched it from the lost and found 'cause I like the bone."

"Eddie?"

"He's the walrus-lookin' man at the front desk. Runs the place. But don't you concern yourself with what's out there," she says. "All that matters now is what's right here."

She pats her sleeves and digs around in pockets I can't see. "Hmmm." Then she looks down her shirt. "Aha. There you are."

She pulls a black velvet sack from somewhere in her ample bosom, loosens the drawstrings, and pulls a deck of cards from within.

"Damn things have a mind of their own sometimes," she says and starts to shuffle.

"I take it we're not playing blackjack."

Zja-Zja shakes her huge head slowly. "These are tarot cards. I'm the best tarot reader this side of the Rocky Mountains. You stand to gain a lot more than money at my table."

The dust creeps back in but slowly, as if curious. I watch it out of the corner of my eye.

"Or lose a lot more," I add.

Zja-Zja shrugs, but her gaze never wavers. She spreads the cards face down in a messy pile over the kerchief and starts stirring the pot. The dust follows like a hypnotized cobra, darting out here and there as if to touch certain ones. I can't help but lean away. My chair creaks softly. The silence stretches as she gathers up the cards and begins to shuffle them in her big hands, her eyes closed. She's humming some sort of tune. At first, I think it's an old lullaby or spiritual, then I realize it's the theme to *The Price is Right*.

She suddenly stops and opens her eyes. "That'll do," she says. "The shuffle is all about feel."

She sets the cards neatly in front of herself upon the table. She edges them with a few taps from the flat of the knife blade to even them out.

"My Gammy's hankie, the bone knife, these are what we all-seeing folks call *significators*. Objects of importance. Things that mean something to me or that I've grown fond of without knowing why. They focus the power of the cards." She taps lightly on the top of the deck. "Now, I need a significator from you."

"I told you, I don't have anything—"

"Everybody's got something. Bracelet? Key chain?"

I shake my head.

"How about a picture? You got a lover's picture in your wallet?"

"No lover. No picture," I say as I reach into my pocket. "All I got to my name is this."

I set the hooker's call card and my one-dollar chip on the velvet. We both look at them in silence for a minute. Disconcertingly, the dust crawls my way like a snake that has noticed food dropped in its cage.

"A titty card and a one-buck chip? Damn, boy, you really are broke. What about that wedding ring?"

The creeping dust freezes. I look down at my ring, bright gold and brand-new, smooth as the day it was forged.

"I don't like to take it off," I say. "Try the card and chip. I think they'll work for you."

She watches me carefully then shakes her head and picks up the card and chip. She sets them gently on the corners of the kerchief opposite the knife. Then she leans back and clears her throat, looking sidelong at the table. I'm not sure what she's seeing, but eventually she shrugs.

"They fit. I think you may be right."

The dust thinks so too. It spreads over the kerchief like shimmering oil in a pan. I feel a need to pop my ears, like the pressure in the place has dropped. Zja-Zja pulls the first card, and I feel like I'm strapped in for whatever comes. She touches the card's face gently to the stone eye on her necklace and pauses.

"The three-card spread is a simple and powerful draw. It reads the past, present, and future. This is your past."

She sets the card on the kerchief, and the dust pours over it—a picture of a foppish jester with his chin up, unaware that his next step will take him over a cliff's edge.

"The Fool," says Zja-Zja.

I think of missed opportunities. Slinging drinks at a Brooklyn dive for nearly five years with no urgency at all. Fooling myself that Alli and I would be able to live young and carefree forever. Day in and day out, completely unaware of whatever my mother was going through—whatever drove her away—until it was too late. And everything came to a crashing halt.

"I could have told you that," I say.

"In tarot, a Fool is different from an idiot," she says before cocking an eye. "Although I ain't sayin' you can't be both."

She taps the edge of the card lightly to align it with the side of the kerchief.

"The Fool tells me you were unaware of what life can throw at you. But that's in the past now. You're no longer unaware."

The dust spins gently around the card, making room for the next draw. Zja-Zja slides it off the top of the deck and taps its face against her stone.

"The present," she says, then she sets it down.

It's a man in a robe and cowl, staring straight at me. In his right hand, he holds high a burning candle. His left hand points at the ground and glows with a white aura.

"The Magician," says Zja-Zja, and she narrows her eyes to look up at me.

I snort. "I'm no wizard."

"The modern magician doesn't cast spells, honey," she says, setting the card down front and center. "He comes in two types. Either he's got true untapped capabilities others don't have... or he's a nickel-and-diming huckster, hiding balls under cups and thinking himself something special."

As if in answer, the dust flows softly over the card toward me.

"Which one are you, I wonder?"

The dust shows me the jutting corner of a third card. It's not up top but buried deep in the pile. Yet somehow, I just know she's gonna pull it. Zja-Zja's hands dance over the stack until she picks that very same card. I wonder again if maybe the way I'm dying might have a bit of magic to it.

"Your future," she says.

As she sets the card down, it glides an inch toward me on a pocket of air. Zja-Zja grumbles. The sound is low and half hidden deep in her mighty bosom. She coughs to try to cover it, but I catch on.

The card is called the Tower. It depicts a tall, angular stone structure on fire and half blown to pieces by a jagged lightning strike. Two figures, a man and woman, are falling headfirst from the burning top, their faces frozen in torment.

"That doesn't look good," I say.

"In some readings, the Tower can mean freedom, higher learning..." she says before trailing off into a frown.

"But not this reading."

"No, honey. Not this reading. Sometimes, a cigar is just a cigar. The Tower most often means danger. Crisis. Destruction. And that's the reading I feel here."

She looks carefully across all three cards of the draw once more, as if she might be able to see them differently on a second pass. She shakes her head. The dust all but confirms it as well as it spins in a slow, mesmerizing circle atop the Tower.

"I wish I had better news," she says, sincerity in her voice. Then she changes tracks entirely and says, "And now, the matter of my payment," the pop back in her voice.

"Like I said, I don't have any money. The chip and the card are all I've got—"

"And I feel you best be hanging on to those," she says, gathering up her cards. "But I gotta get paid nonetheless, baby, which means you gotta get a job. Which means you gotta talk to Eddie up front and tell him Zja-Zja the Eye sent you."

I lean back, puzzled at this change of fortune. "You mean Eddie, the walrus-looking guy?"

"Well, I wouldn't lead with that. But yeah. Eddie, out front. Now get." She shoos at me. "I need to lock up, get home, and get my beauty sleep."

I stand, unsure of what to say, how to thank her, or if I even should. She's packing up, but I can tell she's making a concerted effort not to look at me, as though she knows something she's not telling me, something more from the reading, maybe. I never held by any of this junk until right at this very moment, but we both seem to be seeing things others can't.

I end up muttering an awkward thanks that I'm not sure she even hears as she rolls herself back behind her huge curtain and disappears.

I push back through the beaded curtain, and it melts closed behind me with a soft swish. The neon eye above is dark already, and the lights in the room go out one by one.

In the foyer, Eddie is still talking with the same shrill old lady. I feel like she's been complaining for hours, but my guess is that I was probably with Zja-Zja for no more than ten minutes. I can't be sure, though. The Golden Swan has no clocks that I can see.

I walk to the desk and can't help but pick up on the conversation.

"Your housekeeping staff stole it, then," says the old lady emphatically, rubbing at an empty spot on her bony wrist. "I keep it in the same pocket of my luggage whenever I'm not wearing it, and when I went to dress for supper, it was gone."

Eddie's hands still rest atop his flowing tie, on his rounded gut, but they're starting to scratch at each other in a way that suggests Eddie is growing weary of his accommodating smile.

"All I can tell you is that we've looked high and low for your bracelet, ma'am. I'll have everyone on staff keep an eye out for it—"

"It's very dear to me. It's lucky, you see. A charm bracelet my mother wore."

As she speaks, the dust that moves around her flashes like dominos falling down in a line. A single pulse flows through the gold that snakes around the check-in desk, through the foyer, and onto the casino floor. I glance at Eddie and the old woman, still not sure of what can be seen or not. She's launched into a full-blown history of the bracelet, ticking off each charm one by one. He's nervously eyeing the guests that have recently arrived behind her as if they might bolt at any minute. They look unimpressed already.

I walk through the foyer and past the front desk, following the dominos into the casino.

The casino has five tables: one craps table, one roulette table, and three blackjack tables—the bare minimum. I count maybe twenty people in here, and I'm easily the youngest. The place has more of the feel of a bootleg operation in the basement of some dated mansion than something you'd find on the Strip, but I do see a thin film of gold dust. The ground mists with it, and it sifts softly from the table games. The dealers have a little bit on their hands and shoulders and hair. Many of the gamblers do too.

My dust dominos wind around the tables and toward the slot machines along the far wall. They lead me to a cluster of classic slot machines—huge crank-handle things with one row of spinning reels. They've got bars and sevens and occasionally a drunk-looking golden-swan character thrown in the mix. The dust sits heavily on one in particular, specifically in the gap between it and the next machine.

I reach into the thin gap with my index finger and pluck out a silver charm bracelet.

Lucky me.

I walk right up to the front desk, where Eddie continues to patiently listen to the old woman's story of the bracelet. Fortunately, a young man who smells fresh from a cigarette break is now checking in the couple waiting behind her. I thought they were gonna bolt for sure.

The old lady's back is to me. Eddie notices me for the first time and raises a brief, accommodating finger to tell me he'll be with me as soon as he can. I hold up the charm bracelet and pop my eyebrows questioningly.

Eddie furrows his brow for a moment then interjects, "Ma'am, is this the bracelet, by chance?"

She turns around and sees the bracelet before she sees me. Her watery eyes light up, and she looks from the bracelet to me, seeming to study me more than it, actually.

For a second, I think maybe she knows that this bracelet

looks different to me. Zja-Zja's third-eye necklace was more than just an engraved river stone. The bracelet matters to the woman like the necklace and the knife and the kerchief matter to Zja-Zja. Like the dollar chip matters to me. Somehow, the dust recognizes these things. The dust is affected by them.

Or maybe she thinks I stole the damn thing.

"You found it!" she says, and her fingers shake slightly as she takes it from my hand.

I let out a breath. The last thing I needed was some old lady calling me a thief before I ask for a job.

"Where was it?" she asks.

"Were you sitting at those machines? It fell in a crack between two of them."

The woman looks suspiciously at me for a moment. Eddie preempts an unasked question on her lips when he says, "Cameras everywhere, ma'am. We were able to run back some of the footage while we spoke," he says. "Find where you'd been sitting."

She nods, brow still furrowed, but thanks me several more times as Eddie offers to help affix the bracelet once more.

I'm still processing Eddie's little white lie. Nobody ran any film. And "cameras everywhere" seems a slight exaggeration.

"Next time, try the machine to the left," I say, not thinking.

Eddie snaps his gaze to me, and the old woman looks up.

"Why's that?" she asks.

Eddie's eyes narrow, and he looks from me back to where the Eye's parlor is darkened and quiet, then back to me.

"I, um..." I clear my throat and pick at my fingernails. "I got a hunch it might be ready to hit."

"Oh," she says, nodding politely. "Well, perhaps another time. I've had enough for today."

"Of course, ma'am," Eddie says, gesturing her toward the elevator bay. "Some rest, then."

"Yes," she says, muttering thanks as she slowly walks away, one hand toying with the charms.

After we watch her go for a moment, Eddie turns slowly to me. "Let me guess. Zja-Zja sent you my way."

I nod. "She said you might be able to get me a job here."

"Why don't you just waltz over to that machine and make a month's worth of wages in a single pull."

I shrug. "Maybe because I'd need that bracelet. Or to be that old lady. Or maybe because I'm half convinced I'm full of shit."

Eddie seems to ponder that for a moment, his hand running down the length of his tie.

"Interesting," Eddie says.

The fact that he hasn't laughed me out of the Golden Swan tells me something important and slightly terrifying.

Maybe this brain bleed isn't as much of a brain bleed as I think it is.

"I can clean, valet cars, fetch bags, answer phones—"

"Help old ladies clean me out," he finishes.

"If I see anything like that again, I'll keep it to myself."

"See that you do. Can you tend bar?"

I nod. "I was a bartender in Brooklyn before coming here. I know my way around booze."

"Can you tend bar without drinking everything?" he asks point-blank.

I nod again. "I clean up well." Then I look down at myself. "I just haven't cleaned up in a while."

"The pay isn't great. But then again, something tells me you're not here just to get paid."

I nod again but offer nothing more. I finger the chip in my pocket.

"Why *are* you here, Mister...?"

"Baker. Lee Baker."

Eddie pauses after hearing my name, just long enough to make me wonder if he's heard it before. "Why are you here, Mr. Baker?" he asks again.

"Well, a drone beat me out for a spot at the Diamond, so I decided to try my luck here."

Eddie lets out a single snuff of a laugh, which I guess is a win. "You start tomorrow. Our bar is called the Swan Song. It opens at ten a.m."

"Thank you," I say, and I mean it. I decide to press my luck. This is Vegas, after all. "Is there any chance I could maybe crash here tonight? You could maybe put a room on my tab or something?"

"Tab? This is a casino, not a charity house," Eddie says. "Ten a.m. tomorrow."

So much for luck. I'll figure out somewhere else to crash, I guess.

Eddie pauses and turns back to me. "Oh, and speaking of luck, I don't know if that trick you pulled with the bracelet was real or not, but either way, you don't gamble here. No slots, no tables—don't even throw a business card in a bowl for a free steak. Understand?"

I think of the only business card I've got and smile. "I understand."

"Good."

Eddie walks back behind the desk, settles his tie, and looks longingly out the front doors for the next guests. I follow his gaze. The sun has fully set, and the crowds are picking up. Streams of them pass by the Golden Swan on their way to the Avalon and beyond, toward the heart of the Strip. This is when Vegas shines, but I'm suddenly exhausted, as if my body was keeping me going just long enough to know I'd have a paycheck coming.

I recall my walk over here. Maybe I passed a quiet alcove or a bench where I could sleep without getting hassled. I've heard the desert gets a little chilly in the witching hours, but otherwise, I'd be plenty warm outdoors. I ain't afraid of a little chill.

Between the Avalon and the Swan is a windy little walkway with a few benches plunked down facing the castle and moat. I think perhaps the architects that built this place were expecting more people to walk here, but they were mistaken, and I'm thankful. I find one that sits up against a little metal overhang like a cupped hand. I take a seat and test it out, rolling my neck and mentally preparing for the crick it'll get.

A few people walk by on the main drag, but nobody turns off the Strip. One couple sits on the concrete down the walk, laughing and sipping something. One guy is smoking a cigarette farther back, toward the rear of the Avalon property, but he doesn't seem to notice me.

*Looks like home for tonight.* I lean back, rest my head on my arm, and close my eyes. I'm not actually that uncomfortable, which I suppose is more a testament to exhaustion than to the slatted wood of this bench.

I start to drift.

A shadow passes over the lids of my eyes, darkening what is already dark. I snap out of my groggy drift to find the guy who was smoking down the way now standing an arm's length away from me, staring at me with unblinking, fishlike eyes.

My heart goes from sleep mode to race car driver in the blink of an eye. I throw myself to sitting with my hands up, brushing my face awake again as if a spider has plopped from the sky onto my resting head.

"What do you want?" I yell loudly.

He stares at me with a strange, manic stillness. His cigarette seems forgotten, but its glowing red cherry is clearly burning the space between his fingers. He looks rough—homeless, maybe. His skin has an unhealthy tan, and his lips are chapped.

"The ring," he says.

Thirsty for my wedding ring, he's not even looking at my face at all—only my left hand.

"Get out of here," I say, looking around frantically.

The couple I saw before is gone. Nobody is walking by on the Strip either. Tough luck. The smoker shakes his head slowly as if my voice is white noise he doesn't understand. He steps forward. I get up.

"I'm warning you, man," I say. "Back off."

As soon as I stop talking, he reaches for my hand. His arm strikes like a snake and grabs me before I know what's happening. I pull away, but his grip is like a vise. *If you can't back out, move in.* I step in and knee him in the balls, an old Brooklyn bar fight trick.

He grunts in pain and redoubles his grip. I realize with slowly dawning horror that he's trying to bring my hand to his mouth. He opens a barely-there set of stained teeth. His tongue looks like a salted slug.

This crazy asshole thinks he can bite my finger off.

I ball up my right fist, pull my left hand down, and use his crazy grip strength as a fulcrum to slam my knuckles into his temple.

I try to keep my busted shoulder as tight as I can, but

when my fist hits home, I feel a stitch pop. My whole shoulder shakes like a Jell-O mold. I yell in pain as he drops wordlessly to the hot concrete.

Swearing at the crazy man, I pull my arm in close then try to soothe it, as if words might help.

Words don't help. But the dust seems to. Gold mist creeps up and over the bum, dancing along my ring finger before crossing my shoulder and settling over my busted right arm.

"Please don't be a mess," I mutter. "Please don't be a mess. Please don't be a mess."

I dare to peek under my sleeve.

One stitch is busted, with a little spotty bleeding. Nothing too terrible. I let out a breath. Lucky me, after all.

I look down at the bum. He's totally out. But maybe he should've thought of that before he tried to eat my finger. He's on his own.

I take off at a brisk clip back toward the Strip and humanity, shivering all the way, despite the heat.

AN HOUR LATER, the adrenaline has mostly run its course through my system, and I'm not visibly shaking. Now, I'm twice as exhausted and still without a place to sleep. No way on this earth am I gonna sleep outside tonight after that little encounter. But the only place I know that hasn't spat me out so far is the Golden Swan.

I've been sitting with my back to a concrete retaining wall across the street from the place for twenty minutes, wondering how I can beg a room for the night.

Nothing for it but to ask. I stand and walk across the street and between the golden eggs. At least no bullshit ambassador is here to give me the boot before I can even try.

Inside is blissfully cool. A quick glance tells me Eddie is nowhere to be seen. The bored-looking guy who was on a smoke break is manning the front desk. He's deep into his cell phone. I don't feel good about asking him. *Doubt he has any sway.* The dust doesn't seem to care about him either. But he's all I got.

As I walk across the atrium, I notice a flash of dancing gold by the draped and shuttered door of The Parlor of the Eye. The bead curtain looks like it's glowing.

A closer look reveals dust spilling from the thin crease between the door behind the curtain and the frame to the right of its handle.

As I walk over, nobody even spares me a glance. I push apart the beads and am showered in dust. I grab the handle to peer down and get a better look, and the door slides open easily. A tarot card falls to the ground facedown. It was keeping the latch from locking.

Inside, the parlor is dark and quiet. The couch against the wall is piled with soft pillows. The velvet reading table has been pushed alongside the couch, and a tall glass of ice water gleams atop, along with a packet of cookies.

"Zja-Zja," I mutter, smiling. "Maybe you really are all-seeing."

The tarot card shines on the ground with an eerie gold ghost light that can't cast itself against anything, like the insulated shimmering of a star. I pick it up and flip it over. The Magician stares back at me with his flat gaze, one hand still held high.

The hairs on my neck prickle. I turn around, wary of being seen, and not just because I don't want Zja-Zja to get in trouble for letting me crash here tonight.

Just outside the doors of the Golden Swan, a man stands in the middle of the sidewalk like a rock in the flow of people walking the strip. When I see him, our eyes lock, and he makes no effort to hide the fact that he's watching me.

I recognize him—not the bum, as I'd first feared. He's the stone-faced casino attendant from the Diamond, the one who escorted me out with a press of his finger. He must have followed me here, fez in hand. Seems like a lot of trouble to go through, just to keep tabs on a drifter looking for a job. Or maybe somebody in that glass palace recognized the way I followed the dust through their massive casino and didn't like the way I looked at that elevator.

The bouncer's eyes linger on me unabashedly before he simply turns and walks away.

I step inside The Parlor of the Eye and close the door behind me, double-checking the lock. I'm not sure what kind of message the Diamond wanted to send, but I don't want to take any chances.

I set the tarot card gently upon the velvet table then chow down all the cookies in a few bites and slam the whole glass of water.

My last thought as I drift off to sleep is that I have been grossly misinformed about Las Vegas.

# CHAPTER FOUR

I wake to the muted sound of ringing slot machines. I pull out my phone and check the time: eight a.m., with two percent battery. In a sudden moment of sick desperation, I try Mom's number again.

I get no voice mail this time.

"We're sorry. The number you have called is no longer in service."

I have just enough time to double-check that the number is right before my phone dies. I guess that's that, then. If I'm gonna find her, I'm gonna have to find her on my own.

I sit up, plant my feet on the floor, and rub the sleep from my face. My hands come away shining. *Gross.* I can't go in on the first day on the job looking like I haven't showered in three days, even if that's the truth. And I have to do something about my greasy hair. Nobody's gonna want to buy a drink from a guy who looks like he's got a bird's nest on his head.

Behind the huge purple curtain, Zja-Zja has a little makeshift dressing room with a standing sink. I turn on the hot water and stick my head underneath, pump a bunch of soap into my hands and lather up as best I can, then wash it all away. After that, I scrub my face until it's pink. I borrow the hand towel and dry off then fold and replace it. Zja-Zja has enough makeup and hair accessories here to make a drag queen jealous, but I don't know what's what, so I just push my hair back from my face, Wolverine style, and hope it dries well. I can't do much about the neck beard, but I do grab a canister of ladies' deodorant and give myself a few spritzes. I'd much rather smell like a flower than the homeless bum I am.

I walk back out to the couch, fluff up and arrange all the pillows, and pluck a few stray cookie crumbs from the velvet table. I stand back and take a big breath, testing my shoulder carefully. It's not great, but it's not throbbing and doesn't feel hot. As a matter of fact, I feel more human than I have in weeks.

I eye the front door, still curtained. I don't want to take a chance of running into Eddie. He seemed decent enough, but I doubt he'd be too pleased with Zja-Zja for letting me crash here. Instead, I turn and walk through the back, past the dressing room, and down a thin little hall marked up along the baseboards by passing food carts and maybe the Eye's rolling wheels too. A door at the end of the hall pushes open easily, and I find myself on the back docks.

At eight in the morning, Las Vegas has an expectant quiet to it. Whatever was done last night feels forgotten in the morning sun, and whatever the night has in store feels like it's patiently waiting.

Two men are unloading boxes of food from a delivery truck into an open bay. One looks over at me and nods. The other whistles a tune to himself and moves the boxes down the line. The desk clerk from last night is smoking a cigarette against the wall beyond the truck, lost in his own thoughts after a long shift. I walk down the delivery alley, stepping over questionable puddles of water here and there and turn the corner onto the side street between the Golden Swan and the Avalon. The castle glints in the morning sun like a slightly faded knockoff version of the Disney Cinderella castle. The bench where the bum tried to eat me is here. In the morning sunlight, that awful encounter feels like something that happened to another person.

One thing that hasn't changed is the dust. It's not so visible in the bright light but still there, glinting like untouched snow. It moves more slowly, simmering instead of playing about. A tendril of the stuff brushes against my leg briefly then moves on, like a cat about its business. Whatever rapport I seemed to have had with the stuff last night with the bracelet seems entirely gone.

The people out and about this early and this far down the Strip are mostly either joggers out on a defiant morning run or poor souls that are hungover and slightly lost, trying to get their bearings. I hear a faint and familiar sound, like a playing card in the spoke of a slowly turning wheel. Across the street, two men in grungy reflective vests stand in the shadows just past the crosswalk, handing out cards to the men passing by. Not many takers at this hour, but I gotta respect the hustle, such as it is.

One of the men looks up at me, and I catch a flash of a golden front tooth as he grins.

I think about crossing over to talk to him, but Berto is already walking away. He looks back once, and I think he might see me, but he puts his hands in his pockets, clomping away in his boots and joking with the guy to his right.

For an illegal immigrant peddling call services on corners, Berto certainly seems comfortable in this city. I'm

fairly sure there's more to him than meets the eye, but he
was the one who pointed me toward the Swan. If he wants
to keep an eye on me, I'm all for it. I could use the frickin'
help.

I pass between the golden eggs and walk into the Swan
at nine thirty as though I didn't just wake up in the shop to
my right twenty minutes ago. *Fake it till you make it.*

The foyer is quiet. Two new attendants stand behind
the front desk. One yawns hugely. The other watches me
with interest until I pass by. They're dressed in high black
slacks and faded flower-print topcoats with a bit of an island
flair, which I gather is something of the outfit around here.
A few guests are helping themselves to a modest continental
spread by the shops, hissing coffee into their cups and
rubbing their eyes. The Parlor of the Eye remains curtained,
but a light is on inside. I find myself grateful for missing an
awkward reunion with Zja-Zja this morning. Her gift of a
free night when I desperately needed it was best given and
received in secret.

The casino floor doesn't have much action. One blackjack table has two players at it, and another is staffed by a
dealer who leans heavily on the scuffed red felt, an uncut
deck of cards in front of him. The craps table is staffed as
well, but nobody seems to want any part of an empty craps
table, so the dealers are talking among themselves. I can
hear a few slots running, including the one the dust told me
about. Sure enough, the old lady from last night is sitting
there. She's sipping a glass of orange juice and looks to be
settling in for the long haul. Her player's card is plugged in
and attached to her lapel with a bedazzled pin. I wish her
luck.

The bar is a half circle of dark wood set against the back
wall in the middle of the casino. I count eight seats, each

with a dug-in screen for video poker. The polished lacquer of the wood is faded in spots from years of resting elbows. The booze stands at attention on three rows set against an ornate mirrored backsplash. Two racks of glasses hang suspended from the ceiling to either side, making a nice frame. A brass bar runs along the outside of the bar top and curls up at either end into a surprisingly delicate statue of a swan about the size of my hand. A sign etched into the glass back above the glittering bottles reads The Swan Song.

Eddie is the only person there. He's standing behind the bar, holding the hook of a hanger and a freshly pressed uniform in a plastic dry-clean bag. As soon as I step up to the bar, he hands it over to me. It's a Hawaiian shirt, pink flowers on black, well-worn but clean—no jaunty cap, thank God.

"Take a knee and throw the shirt on. The pants are still at the cleaners. I'll get them to you tomorrow. We launder uniforms every third day now, on account of the budget, so try to keep yourself clean."

After stepping behind the bar and ducking, I peel my old black T-shirt over my head and stuff it into a little cubby behind the trash can. I should just throw it into the trash can, but I don't have many shirts and even fewer pants. I realize now that I should have brought more out here. I wasn't thinking about the long haul. I thought I'd find Mom and turn around. As I button up, I realize just how wrong that thinking was.

Eddie looks at me and nods almost imperceptibly. I guess the shirt fits.

"You look like a man that knows his way around a drink, but I gotta be sure, so pop quiz. I want you to make me the three most ordered drinks at the Swan Song. Number three, a whisky and Coke."

I take a quick look around, find a tumbler below, pull it out, and flip it over. I fill it to the rim with ice from a scoop and trough below then turn around and reach for the Jack Daniel's behind me.

Eddie stops me right there. "Whoa, whoa, I said whisky and Coke, not Jack and Coke. Give customers the good stuff if they ask for it. Otherwise, go with the well." He points at the sleeve of off-brand booze in plastic bottles in front of me. I finger through them, find a brand of whisky I've never heard of, and pour what I guess to be a jigger full into the glass. I expect Eddie to chime in, but he just nods. I top it with Coke.

*Easy enough.*

"Number two," he says. "The skinny cosmo."

I pluck a martini glass from the hanging rack underneath the back shelves, flip it, and fill it with ice to chill. I grab a gleaming silver shaker from the hardware set to the side and fill it with ice as well. I turn toward the bottles behind me before catching myself. I look at Eddie, who's watching me with a schoolteacher's gaze. I turn back to the cheap stuff.

"There you go," Eddie says, nodding.

The vodka also comes in a plastic bottle and has a vaguely Russian-sounding name. I pour a little less than a jigger full into the shaker and top it with two quick pours from a glass bottle with tape marked Pomegranate. Shake, shake, shake. Clear the ice from the martini glass and pour. I cut a sliver of lemon in a little curlicue and set it down as delicately as I can manage.

Eddie takes a sip and nods then sets it back down.

"Last one," he says.

I wiggle my fingers like a sharpshooter before the draw.

"Hot tea."

I pause. "Hot tea?"

Eddie sighs softly. "We get a lot of orders for tea from our older customers," he says, nodding back in the direction of Agnes, at the slots, which are steadily dinging with another decent payout. Eddie clears his throat and looks straight at me. "We pride ourselves on our tea."

"Right. Hot tea," I say, looking around, lost. Eddie points behind me at a glass-topped wooden box underneath the hanging martini glasses.

"We've got black tea, white tea, green tea, Earl Grey, lemongrass, peppermint, chamomile, chai, and yerba mate," he says, ticking each off on a finger. "Hot water from the side spout of the coffee machine. Cup and saucer sets in the far cabinet. It's good tea. You're gonna get a lot of requests for tea."

I pour some hot water into a single-serving white ceramic pot. I grab a satchel of green tea from the box, drop the string down, then set it on the saucer and look at Eddie.

He shakes his head. "The bag opens at the top. It's basically loose leaf. Two minutes and fifteen seconds to steep. Not a second more or less. You understand me?"

I nod. Eddie watches me as I fill the order and let it steep for two minutes and fifteen seconds by the coffee timer. I pull the bag out and pour. Eddie takes a sip and nods. He takes another before looking at his watch. He settles his tie over his belly.

"I have to keep up the rounds. Do you think you can handle this?" he asks.

"I think I got it, yeah."

"Good. Shift is up at six. You get thirty minutes for lunch and three ten-minute shift breaks. Call me when you want to take any of them. We don't have another bartender. Or any barbacks, for that matter."

"Just me," I say.

"Just you." He nods. "You'll be serving and clearing."

"Got it."

"And one more thing. You might get more tips without the wedding ring," he says. "Especially from ones like Agnes over there. We get a lot of Agneses."

I turn the thin gold band over on my finger. "I think I'll risk the tips," I say quietly. "For now."

Eddie nods and doesn't ask any other questions, which I appreciate. "Good luck," he says and walks off.

I spread my arms and lay my hands flat on the bar. I'm surprised to find myself wearing a small smile. Ever since I left the hospital, the world has seemed like a relentlessly moving train, and I'm trying my best to hop cars. For the first time in a while, I feel like I've found a place that fits me. I can see the whole of it, end to end, goose to goose. No surprises. The bottles behind me seem to prop me up. The soft running of the wash and the quiet rattle of the beer fridge are like white noise. The Swan Song feels weighty, like it's been around a long time, seen a lot of things, and served a lot of drinks.

My first customer steps up and asks for a Bloody Mary. No problem. I get to work.

When I first stepped up to the bar and took the uniform from Eddie, the Swan Song had no golden shimmer to it at all. Now, it's as if I've arrived at the beginning of a golden gloaming. Dust seems to rise from the old wood like mist right before my eyes.

EDDIE WASN'T KIDDING about the tea. The next four drinks I serve consist entirely of steaming hot water and bags of loose-leaf chamomile, then a few orders for beers and a double Bloody Mary come in. The cocktail waitresses working the floor introduce themselves in stride. All three are Asian women, possibly from Thailand, although I can't be sure, and all three have affected matronly American names that make me think they're perhaps older than they look: Barbara, Nancy, and Susan. They wear uniforms of similar faded island-glam style, cut a good deal lower at the chest than mine. I fix each drink as they rattle it off, setting each glass atop a cocktail napkin that features the drunken, winking swan. If they're surprised to find a new bartender, they don't let on. I get the feeling they think I might not last long.

It feels good to work. Focusing on the task at hand, simple though it is, has a strange effect on me. I feel like the half of my brain that's keyed up in sleuth and survival mode is finally able to rest. My shoulders relax. I can roll my neck without wincing. The hours slip by, and I forget to take a break—don't really want to, to be honest. When Eddie comes by and asks me if I want to put in a lunch order, I'm caught off guard. For the first time in months, I've spent a solid hour without constantly thinking about my mother and my dead wife.

And I feel guilty for it.

"The way you've been eyeing the cocktail olives, I'm guessing you didn't pack lunch," Eddie says after a moment of me staring at nothing.

"No, I... I don't have anything today."

"You gotta eat, Lee."

"I'll be all right."

Eddie looks at me a moment and shakes his head. "I'll have the kitchen make you a burger. Employees get half-off lunch entrees," he says.

That's still half again more than I have. I'm about to protest, but Eddie murmurs something about putting future tips toward it if I have to and walks away before I can say anything. And I'm not in the mood to protest much anyway. It's been a while since I've had any protein to speak of, and my stomach feels like it bent over backward just at the word *burger*. I take another sip of water to calm it down as much as I can, and that's when I notice the dust on the bar shift as a single sheet, like a change of wind pressing a golden field of wheat first one way, then another.

I stop sipping. The hair on my forearms stands straight up. I raise my head and scan the casino floor. The tables have picked up a little bit since I started my shift. Barbara, Nancy, and Susan are circling. A few people mill about, watching others play, but nothing looks out of the ordinary to me.

Then I see him.

A man is leaning with his back against one of the columns separating the front foyer from the casino. The Swan Song is slightly raised, compared to the rest of the casino, so I can see him clearly. He's older, early fifties, maybe. He's got a close-cropped haircut, almost buzzed, but it's gray. He's tall. Even from across the casino, I can see he's at least six feet five, maybe taller. He wears a light-green track jacket despite the heat, and his hands are stuffed in the pockets. Standing flat-footed, he's resting his head back against one of the support columns and looking directly at me.

As soon as our eyes meet, he smiles coldly, like I proved him right just by looking at him. He pushes himself standing like a big greyhound and walks toward me in long, even strides. I straighten and plant my hands firmly on the bar, suddenly glad I have three feet of solid wood between me and the rest of the casino.

He's even taller than I thought, easily a foot taller than I am. Thin but not skinny. His gray buzz cut is thinning at the temples and peaks high back over a creased brow and sharp brown eyes.

"I'd heard this old place got a new bartender," he says, his voice low and conspiratorial. "Couldn't believe it. Had to check it out for myself."

*Odd thing to say. As if bartenders in Vegas weren't a dime a dozen.* Yet this man actually steps back and appraises me, and I feel strangely exposed. I wish even one other person was in the bar proper to strike up a conversation with, but I'm all out of customers at the moment. It's just me and him.

"Well," I say, spreading my arms. "Here I am. In the flesh. Can I get you a drink or something?"

He doesn't respond, and that's when I notice he's not really looking at me any longer. He's looking at the bar. I follow his eyes and see that they're focused on the flat wood in front of me, where the dust has begun to swirl in strange patterns I've never seen before. Fractals and geometric shapes spread out across a section of the wood about the size of a place mat, like water vibrating atop a speaker.

For a second, I'm too mesmerized by the dancing dust to catch on to the bigger point. The guy is watching it too. *He sees it too.* And unless he got in a car wreck or something similar, the dust isn't just in my mind.

When I piece that together, I find myself gripping the bar for support. He smiles that cold smile again, and suddenly the dust is on the march, jittering its way along the bar top like a twitchy caterpillar, an inch at a time, headed toward the brass swan to my right.

"Funny thing about this bar..." he says, carefully watching the dust move, his hands in his pockets. "Used to be a pretty live place. All sorts of interesting things happened here. Once upon a time."

The twitchy caterpillar puffs apart and reforms as a golden dust devil the size of a tumbler. It swirls around the swan's head then makes a Slinky-like jump to the bottles behind, entwining a few like swirling vines.

I turn back to the man, whose right hand looks like it's messing with something inside his jacket pocket.

"Now this place is just old history. That mirrored sign? I happen to know that it's over sixty years old, put in the day this place opened. Imagine all the things it's seen."

The dust crawls past the line of bottles and spreads out over the mirror, still jittering as if pulled along on an unseen string, dancing to a silent beat. It spreads wide until a thin film of gold covers the drunken cursive of The Swan Song. The whole name shimmers like the skin of a bubble about to pop.

"What are you doing?" I ask. My voice comes out confused and a little scared, like I stumbled across a grown man burning ants with a magnifying glass. "Stop that."

"I can see this place already means something to you," he says, taking a swipe at the dust already pooled on the bar top. "The luck never lies. I'm just signing my name is all. Like carving initials in a tree. I feel like I deserve it. We'll call it a tax for time paid."

He tenses his hand in his pocket and focuses on the mirror. The dust shimmers wildly then pops. The crack of the glass can be heard throughout the casino. A jagged scar feathers right between Swan and Song.

The man doesn't flinch or wince. He doesn't smile either. He closes his eyes and raises his pointed chin as all the dust that has pooled quietly on the bar flows to him in a stream. He breathes deeply, and it seems to infuse him, pouring into his nostrils until it's gone. The bar looks colder and older without it. I feel colder, too, drained.

He radiates. His skin glows, and his eyes glitter.

He finally takes a seat. "You know, I think I'll have that drink now," he says.

"I'm not serving you anything," I say, my voice scratchy. I feel parched.

"I think you will. Unless you want that mirror to just be the start of things. A tea, please. Chamomile."

I look around for Eddie, but he's nowhere to be seen. The man waits at the edge of patience, eyeing me with those too-bright eyes. I move over to the cupboard, grab a steeping kettle, and take it to the hot-water spout. It fills halfway until it cracks. I freeze, watching the crack grow, rooted to the spot until the whole thing shatters in my grip. Boiling water pours over my hands, and I instinctively fling the shards away. Bad move. Dull pain rips through me as one of the razor edges catches the webbing between my thumb and forefinger. Blood wells up with the slow surety that comes only from a deep cut.

The man makes a *tsk* sound. "Tough luck, that," he says. His glittering eyes watch me with a strange, fishlike quality that reminds me a little of the mad bum at the bench. "You'll have to grab another," he says.

I'm shaking now. I grab a bar towel and press it to my bleeding hand. I look wildly about for anyone to help, but neither Eddie nor any of the cocktail ladies are anywhere to be seen. Where the hell is an old lady playing video poker when you need one?

"Today is my lucky day," he says, seeing my panic. "I can guarantee us a little time for a quiet chat." He settles into one of the bar seats and scoots in, crossing his arms at the elbows. Dust smokes from his shoulders. His brown eyes have a golden tint. "I'm Jasper," he says. "I work at the Avalon."

He waits, expecting me to introduce myself, but I'm still trying to wrap my head around how he stole all the dust in my bar, so I hold my bleeding hand and just stare at him.

After a minute of silence, he rolls his eyes. "And you're Lee. Lee Baker. The silent treatment won't get you anywhere, boy. I know every time one of us comes into this city."

"One of us?" I ask.

Eddie comes walking slowly down the middle of the casino, but he seems entirely unaware of anything happening around me.

Jasper leans forward. "What's old Eddie paying you? Not much, I suspect. This place has been hurting for a while now. I'm surprised they can afford a spinner at all." He reaches over the bar and plucks up a teacup and hands it to me.

Really, it's the reaching over the bar that clears my head. Nobody reaches over my bar—not even hopped-up wizards.

"Eddie!" I call, but just as I do, his attention is drawn elsewhere by one of the blackjack dealers calling him over.

He never even looks at me. Jasper watches the interchange without surprise.

"Now then. The tea."

I take the cup and pour the hot water slowly, trying to buy some time to think. This time, the dust he stole doesn't mess with me, although I feel it's waiting for the order. He's controlling it somehow, changing its form from its usual free flow to something he can command. Seeing the dust shaped and ordered like this gives me a queasy feeling, like seeing a big animal pace in a small cage. It's unnatural.

I set the teacup and saucer in front of him with more force than necessary. The porcelain rattles, and the water spills over a bit onto the chamomile bag. Jasper picks it up daintily and opens the tea anyway, shaking his head like a disappointed schoolteacher. He dunks the bag to let it sit, folds his fingers, and looks at me.

"What do you want?" I ask.

"I want to know what you can do," he says.

"With what?"

"With the luck," Jasper says, indicating the bar and the casino around us. "I took yours, so you take someone else's. Let's see what you can do."

I stay quiet, watching him as he slowly rotates whatever is in his pocket and the golden glitter in his eyes grows more malicious. I don't want to let on that I have no idea what to do with the dust—what he calls luck—and that until he walked in, I didn't think anyone could actually do *anything* with the stuff.

His smile returns as he sees through me. "Unless, of course, you *can't* do anything with the luck," he says, both to himself and to me. "In which case, you probably think you're losing your mind." He laughs, a deep, guttural sound. "And I can just pick apart this bar and this entire casino piece by piece if I want."

The dust streams from him then probes the bar like a charmed snake. I try to think what I can hit him with. The guy is a giant—something tells me a full-on attack won't go well for me. But he cracked the glass behind my bar. He's gotta answer for that.

Boiling water it is, then.

I grab a kettle then put it under the spout and press the

hot-water button, but it spurts out in fits and starts like a blown keg. I get more of it on my sliced hand than in the kettle.

"Tough luck," he says again, watching me like a rat in a maze. The dust he stole licks at the spigot and the kettle both.

Panic rises like a rash up my neck.

"Jasper Jones," someone says, loud and clear, from behind him. "You know you are not welcome here."

Jasper pauses midsip, a look of dismay flashing across his face, and the cold golden sparkle in his eyes blinks out for a moment, resetting itself before clouding again with color.

He sets his teacup down again into the saucer.

"Zja-Zja. I didn't know you still slummed it here."

Zja-Zja the Eye rolls her Rascal to the base of the bar stairs and stops, and the charms on her arms and in her hair settle like wind chimes in a soft breeze. She leans back and appraises him down the bridge of her nose. "You'll watch your tone, Jasper Jones. And you'll get up out that seat and get gone 'fore you regret it."

"I'm enjoying the company of your new bartender. And what little luck your bar has to offer."

The dust rises from him once again and snakes its way toward Zja-Zja. If he cracked the glass and sliced me up without breaking a sweat, I hate to think what he could do to a handicapped old woman.

"Be careful," I tell her, "he's got...." I don't know how to describe it. "He took the dust from the bar. He's—"

"He's a damn fool, is what he is," Zja-Zja replies, staring straight at Jasper.

The charmed dust is inches from her, probing and circling like a python looking for a hold. Just as the dust rears to strike, she pulls her amulet of the eye from behind a thicket of other necklaces and chains.

The dust pauses. Jasper scowls.

Zja-Zja spins the carved river stone at the heart of the amulet in a smooth, well-practiced motion. The dust loses all form and falls to the ground in a puff of glittering smoke. The dust's collapse rebounds back to Jasper, the thin line melting away until he takes his hand from his pocket. He holds something small and silver, a bit like a cigarette.

The dust that remains shapes up and retreats back to him.

Jasper pockets whatever he's holding before I can get a good look at it. His gaze is still golden but less intense. He sneers. "You always did love your baubles, Zja-Zja," he says, his voice a low growl.

"I got baubles for days, honey. Now get."

Jasper turns back to me. He sips his tea once, watching me carefully, as if daring me to say anything at all. When I don't, he sighs hugely then stands.

"Might as well. This place has never been the same, ever since the luck left. Or what was it you called it? Dust?"

I don't answer, afraid that any response might feed him further.

"Doesn't quite fit. Seems too dirty of a word for it. But you know, you're the second person I've met that calls it that?"

Jasper tucks the chair in neatly and walks to the stairs, where he pauses and turns. "Her name was Baker, too, come to think of it. Claire Baker."

My heart does a little roll, and the blood in my body feels like it reverses. I hold on to the bar tightly. Jasper's long, slow grin returns.

"Must be a coincidence," he says.

He steps down and walks around Zja-Zja, keeping a respectable distance. He doesn't look back as he walks down the length of the casino, through the foyer, and out the doors.

I turn to Zja-Zja, wide-eyed, looking for answers, but she shakes her head.

"Later," she says. She backs her scooter away and makes a slow, precise turn. The motor buzzing, she zips away to her parlor. She looks distracted, leaning back, lost in thought.

As she leaves, a kind-looking older couple steps up and sits down side by side at the bar. They plunk in their player's cards and tap away at the video poker. The man orders a whisky soda. The woman orders a skinny cosmo.

I excuse myself for a moment and crouch down by the cabinet under the sink. I rummage around with my good arm until I find what I'm looking for. This was always where we kept the first-aid kit back in Brooklyn too. I pop it open and give my hand a spray of Bactine then a quick wrap with an Ace bandage. I pluck out a blue surgical glove, shimmy it on, and flex my fingers. It'll do.

The drinks must flow. That's the one promise a bar has to keep. So I get to mixing. As I do, I notice just the faintest glimmer of gold surfacing from the worn wood once again.

By the time Eddie comes by to talk about the cracked glass, the Swan Song is back to about a quarter of the dust it started with this morning. I check the time clock on the register and am surprised to find it's nearly five p.m. The bar is a little less than half full, as is the casino. I've easily been able to keep up with the drinks, even lamed.

Eddie puts his hands on his hips and looks up at the jagged crack between *Swan* and *Song*. He shakes his head. "Zja-Zja tells me you had a little visit from Jasper Jones earlier today."

I don't know how much Eddie knows about the dust. He doesn't seem to notice it, but then again, neither does Zja-Zja. And she chased the big man away.

"He broke it," I say. "And sort of sucked the life from the room."

Eddie nods slowly. He busies himself with restocking the cocktail napkins and organizing the hanging glasses, meaningless jobs that tell me he may not want to talk about the dust. And he certainly doesn't want to look at the crack in his bar. He looks everywhere but there, as if it shames him.

"Jasper seemed to know his way around the Swan Song," I say instead.

"He should," Eddie replies. "He worked here for years. He was the bartender when I first took over as GM."

I try to imagine that cold-iron pipe of a man behind my bar, mixing drinks and pouring tea, arranging bottles and shining glasses to a sparkle. I can't picture it.

"He wasn't always like that," Eddie says, fiddling with his tie. "We had a few good years with him. The Avalon was the first megacasino to come along. Changed everything. They poached him, and I let them. I was younger. I thought he was replaceable. But we haven't really been the same since. For a long time, we've held on, but it's getting harder. Especially the last couple of months."

I try to picture this place full—tickets coming in faster than I could make them, lines two or three deep at the bar, the casino roaring.

I can't picture that either.

"We've had a bunch of bartenders since Jasper, but none of them with his... talent. Zja-Zja and I were hoping maybe you could change that."

I look down at the bar, grip the worn wood, and tap the brass swan fixture to my left like it's a light bulb I might be able to flick on. The golden dust is still faint, like a sparkling thing at the bottom of a lake, but it's there. I can see it. And I can feel it.

"I think this old bar has a lot of luck left in her," I say. "I was wondering if I could take a double tonight. I got nowhere to be, and I think I might be able to spring for a room here if I work a few more hours."

And a shower—a shower most of all. In fact, I think if I make enough to get a bed for the night, I might just sleep in the shower anyway.

Eddie appraises me and nods slowly. "Why don't you work until eight? Same-night discounts open up then. I'll make sure you get one."

I nod my thanks and move over to check in on the older couple playing poker and sipping drinks. Barbara comes over and drops off a drink order at the side bar on her way back out to the casino floor. She's the one with the bob hairdo. *Bob for Barbara.* I pick up the ticket and turn back to find Eddie still standing there, watching me and looking vaguely uncomfortable.

"Everything all right?" I ask.

"Make sure you take care of that cut," he says.

I doubt those were the words actually on his tongue. "I will."

"And be careful," he adds.

"It's already stopped bleeding. Just looked bad, is all."

"No. I mean Jasper isn't the only one. There are others like him. Worse, even."

I stop pouring and look over at Eddie. He's watching the older couple tapping at their screens and chatting away, oblivious. I think maybe he's distracted and has moved on, but then he speaks in a quiet voice.

"People think this town runs on money. They're wrong. It runs on luck. And the people who deal in luck are very powerful. And very dangerous."

He leaves me grasping the ice-cold shaker in one hand, trying to wrap my head around the thought of more people like Jasper.

More people like me.

At seven p.m., four of ten seats at the bar are taken. I guess this is what amounts to the evening rush at the Swan Song, not exactly a full-court press. The casino has a little bit of noise to it but mostly from a group of old men that have been betting quarters at the roulette table for hours, drinking light beers. That is why, when *she* shows up, she stands out even more than she did when I first saw her outside the airport.

She takes an open seat next to the older couple, who won a few hands early on and are pushing their luck until the next comp. The older man quickly shuffles to make room for her, and she even gets a polite smile from his wife. She smiles in return, that same slightly apologetic smile she gave me. Perhaps she's been apologizing for that Huxley fellow she was with for so long that it's become something of a habit even though he doesn't seem to be with her right now. Thank God.

I see the icy flash of her engagement ring for just a second as she pulls back her dark-copper hair and settles her skirt under herself. She's wearing a light blue that reminds me of a spring sky. She plops one tanned and freckled arm over the other, elbows on the bar. She's with another young woman, almost as beautiful, who takes the open seat next to her.

Both women look around as if surprised to find themselves here. That makes three of us. Not counting myself, these two are the youngest in the casino by a decade, easily. I busy myself with hanging glasses, my back turned to them for a minute. I feel I need to gather myself to ask for their orders like a normal bartender. I don't know why. I doubt she'd recognize me anyway.

"Interesting choice, Jillian," says her friend. "This place sort of reminds me of one of those old supper clubs back east my grandma belonged to."

So her name is Jillian. I lock away the name by saying it three times in my head.

"Fine with me," says Jillian. She sounds tired. Her chair squeaks as she leans back and lets out a long breath. "I just had to get out of the Diamond for a bit. It's all a little bit much right now over there. This looked like a place I wouldn't run into anyone I know. Plus, the little drunk duck on the sign is cute."

"It'll get better, girl. Trust me. You remember how it rained all weekend for my wedding? Rainiest stretch of August in the Hamptons in a decade. Week of my outdoor wedding."

"And we had a blast. Turned the bowling lawn out back into a Slip 'N Slide and told the band to play on. Not a single ball gown survived that day."

Her friend laughs. "My wedding dress sure didn't."

"I'd known you for twenty years even then, and I don't

think I'd ever seen you and Danny laugh so hard as you did the day you were married."

There's a pregnant pause, one in which I'm quite sure Jillian isn't smiling.

She speaks up again. "There's things going wrong like rain on your wedding day, which can make great stories, and then there's things going wrong like this."

"You and Hux will laugh about all this one day too. Just like Danny and me."

"Yeah, maybe." Jillian sounds unconvinced.

I can't justify organizing the glasses any longer, so I turn to them and set down two drunken-duck cocktail napkins. "Hi, there. Can I get you ladies something to drink?"

Jillian looks at me, and a single furrow appears between her light-green eyes. She's trying to place where she's seen me before. Her friend looks from me to her and back again.

"From the airport," Jillian says, snapping a finger in recognition. Then that apologetic smile again. "Hux thought you were trying to poach our car. Look, I'm really sorry about that. It's been a crazy couple of days."

I mean to laugh it off and suggest a couple of martinis— the good stuff on the shelf. But then I see the dust that she's brought in with her, and whatever words I have fall to the floor. It clings to her like a train of spiderwebs... and it's all wrong. Worse than the rigid way Jasper made the stuff dance to the beat of his drum, even. It looks like she's trailing shards of golden glass like the chains of Jacob Marley.

For an awkward moment, I can only work my jaw in silence. Then I dig deep and find words.

"No worries," I say, mustering a smile. "Good thing he stopped me. I'm always hopping in people's gorgeous brand-new Mercedes. It's a thing I do. I'm Lee, by the way."

She smiles brightly. Her friend laughs. I clear my throat and fiddle with a cocktail napkin, turning it clockwise then aligning it again. I think back to when I saw her outside the airport. Did she have these chains of dust on her then? I think I would have noticed. She's picked them up in the interim. Or maybe something—or someone—gave them to her.

"So you're a bartender," she says, trying to be polite and keeping the conversation moving even though she sounds like she's got a weight on her back—and to my eyes, at least, she does.

"Yep," I say. "It's a new gig. Just got it while I try and figure some stuff out." I catch myself thumbing the smooth curve of my wedding ring inside my palm and make myself stop.

Jillian nods, seeming to know when not to press.

Her friend chimes in, "So what's good here?"

"Well, we've got a hell of a tea collection."

As both girls laugh, the shards of dust that cling to Jillian shift uneasily. "I'm gonna need something a little stronger than that right now," she says.

"Well then, you can't go wrong with my cosmo. The pomegranate juice is an antioxidant. It's basically good for you. A health drink."

Jillian taps her lip in decision. "A health drink. Sounds up my alley. And one for Tessa, too. She likes being healthy," She looks in her purse for her ID, and her face falls. "Oh my God, I don't have my wallet."

"It's probably back in the room at the Diamond," says Tessa soothingly.

"Maybe," Jillian says. She scratches idly at a shoulder, as if she can perhaps feel a shadow of the shards I see nettling her there. "Or maybe it fell out of my purse on the walk. Or maybe I got pickpocketed. It's one thing after another. It's like I've got this cloud I can't shake."

I reach for the well vodka then pause, checking to see if Eddie is nearby. I can't see him, so I reach back for the good stuff. "This round's on me. Sounds like you need it," I say, pouring generously into the shaker. My gloved hand shakes a bit, but I catch the tumbler without accidentally knocking it over.

Jillian notices the near spill. "You don't want to get near me," she says, as if she's trying her best to joke. "I'm bad luck recently."

She doesn't know the half of it. I can feel the malice of the shards of dust hanging upon her, like they're making a little bubble of low pressure—a hurricane in a bottle. If the dust really is luck, Jillian is quite literally a walking ball of bad luck right now.

"All weddings come with their share of madness," I say. "With so much buildup, something's bound to go wrong."

"What's yours?" Jillian looks down at where I'm fiddling with my ring again, then back up at me.

I muster the fakest smile I think I've ever worn and say, "Car troubles. It's a long story."

Jillian looks carefully at me. "Well. At least it worked out in the end."

The smile is starting to hurt my face, so I move down the bar to check on my other guests. The sound of the car wreck is weaseling its way back into my brain with the consistency of a metronome. *Slam* and *pop*. *Slam* and *pop*. Again and again. Barely a second, but a second is all it took.

One second snuffed out everything.

I refill some tea, pop a beer bottle open, and refresh a cocktail. The old lady I give that to smiles at me and says she was on a bad streak for a bit, but her luck is coming around. I focus on the bar and see the light shimmer of golden dust grow brighter by a few degrees.

Jillian pulls out a small silver key, tarnished with age, and sets in on the table. "I don't even want this thing," Jillian says to Tessa. "Hux insisted on it. All of a sudden, he's getting all traditional on me," she says.

As soon as the key touches the wood, it locks up whatever small tendrils of fresh dust have been forming there in a freezing rictus. The dust slows and stops in a slowly expanding circle, like a growing patch of hoarfrost on a frozen window.

I want this key away from my bar before it rots the whole thing, and I speak up before I can think not to. "What is that?"

Jillian and Tessa both look at it like it's a dead bug. If they saw what I can see, they'd be backing away from the bar. They're not, but I wouldn't be surprised if they sense something off about the key nonetheless. The couple to their left get up and shift seats without a word. Maybe they sense it too. The body is weird like that.

Jillian answers, "You know that old rhyme for brides: something old, something new..."

I nod. "Something borrowed, something blue."

"Well, my dear fiancé has crafted a sort of scavenger hunt for me to pick up all these things before the wedding in three days."

"While he goes golfing," Tessa chimes in, rolling her eyes.

"This is the *something old* part, a silver key that goes way back in Hux's family. It's sweet, I guess, but I'm not really in the mood for all this. We're dealing with lost luggage and a whole crop of the centerpiece flowers dying and canceled flights galore. One of my bridesmaids is stuck in Miami. Another got the stomach flu yesterday."

"Maybe it's the key." I have a strong urge to cover the tarnished thing with a drunken-duck cocktail napkin like a piece of half-chewed food. It's old and no bigger than a paper clip. It might lock a jewelry box or something. A dark spot on the teeth looks disconcertingly like old blood and turns my stomach a little.

When I look up again, both women are watching me strangely.

"I mean, maybe it's bad luck or something," I add, trailing off.

Jillian narrows her eyes a little. She and Tessa look briefly at each other then laugh.

"I already told her I thought it was creepy," Tessa says. "A stained old key? Who does that, right?"

"Right," I say, forcing a hollow chuckle of my own as Jillian plucks up the key and chain and drops them into her purse. A faint circular outline stays behind in the frozen dust.

I'm happy to see the thing off my bar, but I don't want it in Jillian's purse either. Or anywhere near her.

"It's what Huxley wants," Jillian says, and that smile comes back again. "If it keeps him happy through this, then I'll do it." She sounds like she's repeating a mantra in a mirror. As Tessa takes an uncomfortable sip of her drink, Jillian throws the rest of hers back. "Thanks again for the drinks, Lee." She stands and looks around. "I like this place. It's different."

"It'll do," I say. "Come back around anytime if you need a break from your scavenger hunt. I'm curious what you'll find."

I'm trying to be casual, but I think I come off sounding

oddly personal, like I've got some skin in this game. Jillian nods politely, and Tessa waves goodbye before they both go on their way.

The rest of my double shift passes without incident. The customers at the bar come and go, and I fill all the orders in a daze, watching that ice-burned circle where the key sat. It takes a full half hour to fade completely.

My mind flips between Jasper, with the way he turned my dust against me, and Jillian, hobbled by what looked like shackles made of the very same dust. It's just starting to float around me again, and Eddie catches me in a daze, trying to touch the thin tendrils of gold with my fingers.

"You look like a lunatic," he whispers quietly, smiling genially at a couple I missed sitting down, who are staring daggers at me for a drink. Eddie sets a pair of drunken-duck napkins down and tells them, "We'll be right with you." He turns back to me and hands me a key card. "Get some sleep." He sniffs. "And a shower."

"Stress sweat. Sorry."

"Understandable. I've secured you a significantly reduced rate for the short term. So feel free to unpack."

*Unpack.* I snort laughter at that then stop myself and rub my face. I may be more tired than I've ever been, and I need to lie down before I make an ass out of myself. "Thank you, Eddie. Really."

Eddie nods at me but is already attending the newest customers. I wonder if he's the one who works when I don't, the one who took over the bar when Jasper left, juggling that along with everything else. Wouldn't surprise me. I get the feeling he's done whatever it takes to keep this place afloat for the past several years.

On my way to the elevators, I stop by the Parlor of the Eye. Jasper left a parting shot about my mom, and I want some answers. The lights are on, but a glittering poster board on a wooden easel just outside of the bead curtain says "Privacy Please. Reading in Progress."

I don't have the energy to wait, so I take a rickety ride up to the fourth of five floors and find my room. I'm not expecting much, but even so, I'm pleasantly surprised. The room is small but not claustrophobic. A neatly tucked queen bed fits snugly between two thin end tables. A small television sits atop a narrow chest of three drawers. A small writing desk with pen and paper faces the window. The view isn't great, but this far down the Strip, I'm not going to see much anyway. I can just barely make out the front turrets of the Avalon to my left. To the right sit derelict construction lots. The window lets in the moonlight, though, which is all I care about.

I plunk down on the bed and catch the faintest whiff of old cigarette smoke and am taken instantly back to our apartment. Before Mom quit smoking—a long and drawn-out battle if there ever was one—she'd steal a smoke every now and again on the outer stairway. A few whiffs always crept along the side and came through the open window there.

I know it sounds gross, but I miss that smell.

I "unpack," by which I mean I place my wallet, my mom's poker chip, and the card I got from Berto on one of the nightstands. My phone is dead, and I think the plan is cut off anyway, so I put it in the drawer next to a yellowed copy of the Bible, the last vestige of the luckless and lost in Sin City.

On second thought, I pick the Bible back up and rifle through it. Sometimes, people put a few bucks in these things. No luck.

The bathroom tile is a mixture of off-white and black

speckled with gold glitter, dated but clean. It's a tub step-in, and the water pressure isn't great, but it's enough to get the job done. I sit under a stream of hot water until my fingers prune up and the bathroom is rain-forest foggy.

I dry off and put on the thin black bathrobe hanging on the back of the door. I aim to watch some TV, but I fall asleep as soon as I hit the bed.

~

WHEN I WAKE UP, the first rays of sunlight are creeping through the hanging slatted curtains. The dust in the room is quiet, but it's still there. It fogs up the sunlight, refracting and glittering like lasers at a rock show.

I close one eye and look around. Still dust. I close the other eye and look around. Still dust. I swipe at a low-lying pocket that's settled itself on my bed like a sleepy cat swishing its tail. I think I make it move a bit. This has been my morning routine for a week now, to see if my brain was still bleeding. Not anymore. I know for sure that at least one other person lives in Crazy Town with me: Jasper Jones.

What a relief that is. Even if he is an ass.

I make a mental note to close the blackout shades next time, but this morning, I'm grateful for the light. The clock says it's already nearly eight. I've got some things to do before my shift starts at ten.

I stumble around the room, getting myself together. Having to put on my old clothes grosses me out, but they're all I've got unless I want to walk around Vegas in my pink-and-black Hawaiian shirt. I'd totally do it, but I don't know how many people in this city know about the dust or how many are like Jasper, so I figure the fewer that know where I work, the better.

I scrub my face with soap and water, work up as much of a lather as I can on my scruff, then get to work with the cheap plastic razor. Five minutes later, I've got a few bits of thin toilet paper patching up a few nicks, but I've won the battle against my neck beard, and I am presentable—as long as nobody takes a good whiff. I use all the tiny tube of tooth-paste, brushing my teeth for a good, long time, but I still smell like airplane, and I will until I can scrape together enough cash for a wardrobe change.

For the time being, whatever I make is going toward paying off this room. I pick up the bill that's been slid under the door. Holding my breath, I take a look.

I needn't have worried. It's cheap. Even for a cheap hotel, it's cheap. Eddie helped me out, but the thing I think I like most is that there's a check-in date but no check-out date. That makes me feel good.

The last thing I do before leaving is to take the meager wad of tips I got working my double and parcel out enough to cover the room for the night. I set that on the dresser. Then I think better of it and put it all in the little safe in the closet. I snort in laughter at the thought of storing such a small amount of cash in a safe in this city, but "rich" is all a matter of perspective, and when you think about it, what's in that safe is basically half my net worth.

The thought withers my smile.

I add the room key to my pocket with Berto's card and the chip from the Diamond, check to make sure the door is locked, and head out.

The casino is quiet. Only two of five dealers are work-ing, and their tables are half full. Barbara—*B for bob cut, B for Barbara*—is the only cocktail waitress working the floor, and she's moving at an unhurried pace, looking bored, carrying tea. Susan—*S for silver eyeliner, S for Susan*—is standing behind the bar, cleaning glasses. I don't see Eddie and hope he's at home, sleeping.

The old lady whose bracelet I found is settling in at the machine I mentioned at the back of the house again, the one drenched in dust. She's carefully positioning a glass of orange juice and counting the charms around her wrist. I wince a little, hoping she gets a nice hit or two and then takes a hike before Eddie gets back. Regardless, seeing her is a reminder to keep the dust to myself.

If nobody is gonna tell me what's going on with this dust, I'm just gonna go off what I know. And what I know is that this stuff hangs out around where the action is.

Las Vegas isn't a good city for broke people. That much is already clear to me. It's gonna be hard enough to track down whatever happened to Mom without also being broke. Maybe it's time I stopped being half terrified of this dust I see and started using it to my advantage.

I've got a few hunches about how the stuff works. Maybe I can put it to good use and make a few bucks.

I stop by the House of the Eye on my way out, but it's closed up. A glittering poster-board sign propped on an easel out front says the Eye will be in at noon. I should speak to her before going out—my guess is she'd try to talk me out of it. And she'd be right. Trying to cheat a casino is a dumb idea. My guess is things rarely end up working like they do in the movies, luck sight or no.

But without a bit of a bump, I'll be working double shifts for the rest of my life to keep a roof over my head instead of tracking down my mother and getting to the bottom of all this. I've got just about two hours to make some decent cash. And I'm gonna take advantage of it.

～

Vegas Boulevard is already radiating heat. I set a steady pace down the Strip toward the new properties, where the real hustle and bustle is, and my back is soon damp, my forehead beaded with sweat. I pause at the Excalibur. Worker bees are washing down the sidewalks and the hanging livery and fluffing up the wilting plants. The water seems to evaporate into the golden haze of dust as quickly as it hits the ground.

I don't need Jasper's kind of trouble, so I move on, falling in with a steady stream of tourists. They're mostly older folks and families with young children, trying to get in what they can before the truly fierce heat settles in.

The dust doesn't glow as fiercely about town as it did the first night, but I follow its stream easily. The stuff flows down the center of the street with the singular purpose of mountain runoff aiming for the sea. In this case, I'd guess the sea is the big casinos like the Diamond. But here and there, little eddies lap up onto the sidewalk, sending questing tributaries into smaller casinos, shops, and restaurants in gentle waves that remind me of the New York Bay at low tide.

Nothing compels me to turn off the path yet, so I keep walking out of the fringe and into the heart of the Strip.

I step out of the sun and sit on a bench underneath a huge sign for a casino called Metropolis. It's got a retro-futuristic vibe—spinning rings and sharp spires. A chrome rocket ship the size of a school bus rotates up top. I shade my eyes and look down the sidewalk. This place just keeps on going. The entrance is a block away, shimmering like a mirage. I wipe my brow with a forearm and my forearm on my jeans, then I get up and keep walking.

If an architect in the 1950s was asked what living in the twenty-first century might look like and then took a bunch of psychedelic drugs, he might come up with something like Metropolis: a skyline of spheres, crescents, and pyramids topped by needle-thin spires. Everything moves, as though the whole place is one big clockwork mechanism, all of it serviced by enclosed moving sidewalks that remind me of a suction tube at a drive-through bank teller.

Nothing about this part of Vegas is sleepy, even at this early hour. Shops blare retro music, and open-air diners are packed with tourists under misting fans, already getting drunk at brunch. I pass a row of booze-slushie machines designed to look a bit like old chrome washing machines, spinning lazily with a rainbow of frosty colors. I step on a moving sidewalk that takes me toward a building that looks like the retro rocket ship on the sign out front but propped standing, ready for blastoff. The six letters in the word *casino* rotate around one another in little orbits on the sign outside.

Where the sidewalk ends, I'm greeted by the manic chimes and dings of hundreds of spinning slot machines. Cheers spout up at intervals like geysers from at least fifteen full tables that I can see—craps, blackjack, three-card poker, pai gow. There's even a table for a game we used to call war back in the day—basically just high card wins. The table limits go from Golden Swan low to Diamond high. The crowd is younger and louder than anything I've seen at the Swan. Pretty cocktail waitresses wearing flared short skirts and bright-red lipstick zip back and forth in red high heels with plastic cocktail trays full of drinks. Nobody even looks at me coming in, which is exactly what I want.

I take a walk through, watching the dust snake in and out of the activity like a glittering gold ribbon, splitting, spreading, reforming. It clings to some people, ignoring others, skirting some tables and falling like sheaths of dripping silk from others. This close to the action, it's hard to follow. I can't see the forest for the trees. I need a better vantage point.

The check-in desk is humming with activity. Chipper attendants bring bottles of water to those waiting in line. Futuristic-looking golf carts whisk new arrivals to their rooms across the property. I take a seat in a bucket chair that curves over my head like a pod and gives me a good view of the casino floor. I take a few deep breaths and look for what the dust is telling me. If I can make it work for Agnes, I can do it for myself too.

I case the slot machines. Golden potential is spread all over this place, but from afar, I see just how indecisive the dust is. It's far more changeable than I thought, pulled this way and that, not just by people but also by things and sounds. Following the natural flow of the stuff is hard when a giggling cocktail waitress takes it one way and a brooding gambler with a cigarette and a handful of black chips takes it the other. Just when I think I find it, someone hits something on another machine, and the bells and whistles draw the dust away.

The longer I watch, the more frustrated I become. How Jasper ever managed to control this stuff is beyond me. Whatever book he's been speed-reading, I'm looking at upside down. For about half an hour, I watch, but no slot machine calls me more than any other. Maybe it's time to cut and run, work another double, and let another day pass with my mother gone in the wind.

As I maneuver my way awkwardly out of the sitting pod, something catches my eye.

Not a slot machine—a blackjack table in an offset cluster of table games that are a bit hard to see from the front entrance. This table has two spots open, but one of them is drenched in gold. The more I look at it, the more the whole table seems to glow because of this seat, like a bright light in a cluster of dim bulbs. The players there seem happy too. One of them—a man in a black ten-gallon cowboy hat—nods with slow surety at his hand.

I stand and maneuver my way through the center of the casino, passing a raucous craps table and huge main bar setup with a do-it-yourself Bloody Mary station almost as big as the Swan Song.

When I get to the table I spied, the golden seat is still open. I slip between the cowboy and a young couple—the husband standing behind the wife. The dealer nods politely at me.

"You picked the right table," the cowboy says, sizing me up. He takes a sip of red beer and looks forward again.

"Hope so." I lay out my entire wad on the table to chip in. All forty bucks. The dealer gives me eight chips in return. My stack looks silly compared to the rest of the table, especially the cowboy's chunk of change.

I place the table minimum in play: five bucks.

The dealer signals bets are off with a quick swipe of the felt then deals the cards, one face up to each player and one face down to herself. As soon as my card hits the table, the dust moves, pulling away from the deck and dealer and toward my seat.

She deals the second card to each of us, face up. My hand isn't good: I've got a thirteen when the dealer is showing a nine. Players are supposed to hit in this situation, but the way the dust is pulling away from her cards gives me pause. I stay. The cowboy looks at me sidelong and shakes his head but says nothing, taking another sip of red beer.

A little Asian woman sitting in the corner spot barks

with laughter. "She's probably got nineteen," she says. "That'll beat you."

"Maybe," I reply.

"Rule book says you should hit."

"I know what the book says," I reply.

When the dealer comes to her, she hits, taking the card I'd have had. It's an eight. Would have given me a perfect twenty-one, but it causes her to bust. She curses in Chinese and glowers at me.

"Tough hit," I say.

"You ruined the flow of the table," she snaps.

The dealer flips cards for herself. A two to make her count eleven, then a three to make it fourteen, another two for sixteen. She pauses with the next card... then flips a face card to bust. Players win.

The cowboy laughs, taking another sip of red beer as he gets paid out. He had a big stack in play. Looks like that dealer's bust made him at least five hundred bucks. She pays me my measly five and winks. Everyone gets paid except for the little Asian lady, who is crossing her arms and staring at the empty air behind the dealer, muttering little curses.

The next hand plays out the same way. With each card dealt, a little bit of dust moves from the deck to the table—not just to my seat but to the others, too, even the angry lady. I stay again on a hand when the book says I should hit. The dealer busts. The cowboy laughs again and orders another red beer.

The dust changes on the third hand. More of it flows from the dealer's deck to my seat in particular. I double down on a ten and get a twenty. The dealer flips a nineteen.

"The kid can't lose," says the cowboy, tipping his glass

my way. The little Asian lady scoffs. She's down to her last chip.

"Ruined the flow," she mutters again.

I ignore her and ask the cowboy what time it is. He looks at his big gold watch and tells me nine thirty. The dust is still flowing heavily in my direction. I've got time for one more hand.

I put my whole stack of chips in: a hundred bucks. My heart pounds as the dealer calls off bets and starts turning cards. The cowboy hits to a twenty. The dealer swings around to me and drops a jack of spades then an ace of spades.

Blackjack. Instant winner.

Everyone at the table claps while the dealer pays me one hundred fifty dollars on top of my one hundred. Everyone except the little old lady. She hits on a ten then a thirteen then a seventeen, all while watching me. She busts. Then the dealer busts, for another table win. I gather my chips, thank the table, and get a final nod from the cowboy and an ugly scowl from the old lady.

"Good riddance," she says and thumbs her nose at me.

I bite back a retort. She's not worth arguing with, and this is not the time to draw attention to myself. The dust is changing again but in a way I don't understand, pulling away from me like a low tide. Something tells me I need to get out of here.

I can feel the lady's eyes on my back as I ask an approaching cocktail waitress for directions to the cashier's cage. She points down the hall and around the corner. I thank her and walk off, eager to get out of sight of the table. Some people get weird about gambling, superstitious and sour, when the cards turn against them. Emotions can run high when money and chance are involved.

No wonder the dust loves this city.

I turn the corner to a quiet hallway and keep walking. I look for signs to the cage, but I can't find them. Maybe I took a wrong turn. I take another few steps forward until the dust around me quickens—a tiny tick in resistance, barely stronger than a passing breeze but enough to give me pause. The little hairs on the tops of my hands are standing straight up.

The doors ahead of me are closed. A sign above reads No Exit. I mutter a curse. The dust that was swirling around my feet is moving like molasses.

I turn around. The hallway I just walked down is blocked by two hulking men, arms crossed to make big rock shelves in outline. A third, much smaller outline steps from behind these two and takes a step forward. Her outline is different from the heavies.

Her outline has a faint halo of gold.

"I thought I catch a cowboy," she says, and I recognize the clipped tone of the little Asian woman at the table. "Turns out the cowboy just had dumb luck. I catch something much more interesting instead."

"I'm just trying to cash out—"

"You steal from my casino, luck junkie."

"Luck junkie?"

"A thief. You play with magic you don't understand."

She takes another step forward. In her hand she thumbs what looks like a Buddhist wrist bracelet. She slowly rotates it as she speaks.

"You know the rules, junkie," she says.

"I have no idea what you're talking about, lady," I say, the panic rising in my voice.

She spins the beads—spin... spin... spin. With each touch, the bracelet glimmers brighter, like a light bulb gathering power. "In my casino, the luck answers to me. And only me."

I back up, turn to the first door, and try to open it—locked. The second door isn't locked, but it seems jammed on something. Or maybe it's the dust, oozing and slow, gumming up the works. Maybe it's that damn bracelet.

When I turn back, her two goons are already on me. I duck under the first and try to make a run at the second, but I slip on the marble, which has suddenly grown slick. The second goon pushes me easily to the ground, and the first picks me up by my hair. For just one second, I'm too proud to cry out in pain. The second quickly passes.

I open my mouth to scream, but the goon jams the meat of his palm into my mouth. I bite down, more out of surprise than anything, but he doesn't seem fazed, not even uttering a word as he and the other heavy drag me to the door I thought was jammed. But it's not anymore. The lady opens it easily and steps through.

I'm dragged behind her into an industrial laundry facility. Huge dryers packed with white sheets and towels spin and spin dizzyingly to my left and right. The air is hot and damp, and the smell of gallons of detergent and fabric softener is cloyingly sweet. Any sound I make in here will easily be drowned out by the combined roar of the machines, even a scream.

One of the big boys doesn't like me looking around, so he pushes my head down. All I can see are the petite velvet slippers of the little old woman. They have golden heels and golden tassels at the toes. My own toes drag as I'm carried down the aisle of machines until the lady stops. The men drop me like a sack of potatoes, and I scramble backward until I press up against a warm dryer that rumbles against my back.

"Please, I don't want any trouble. I just wanted to play some cards."

The woman looks at me placidly. She could be forty— could be sixty. She seems oddly timeless. "Right, right, right," she says. "And you just happened to find a seat at that table and hit when you hit and stay when you stay, and you got lucky, right? Just dumb luck."

I nod vigorously, pull my chips from my wallet, and hold them out to her, my hands trembling. "Here, take them back if that's what you want."

She slaps the chips from my hands and scatters them across the hard concrete floor. They roll under machines and out of sight. I quest desperately after them with my fingers.

"What I want is to know what you're *really* doing here, luck junkie. You look clean. You get hired from out of town? You a mule for one of the big boys? What?"

"I have no idea what you're talking about," I say again, my voice squeaking a little. "How about I just get out of here and never come back?"

"Oh, you're never coming back," she says, nodding knowingly. "But I'm not done with you yet. Because you lie."

She nods once at the big men, and they both grab me by the arms. One pops open the door to the huge dryer, and together they throw me in on top of warm sheets then slam the door. I turn back to the glass and pound on it, but one of the big guys is leaning against the handle. I watch in disbelief, my heart hammering, as this crazy woman presses the start button on the machine. The spinner slowly shifts underneath me.

I'm helpless, paralyzed by fear as I'm upended, flipped and turned and bounced within a suffocating sea of hot whiteness. My screams are muffled. I try to reach out, to orient myself against the scorching metal of the basin, but I'm flipped again and again and again. My head slams intermittently against the glass. My bad shoulder lights up with fire then goes numb.

Just when I think I'm going to pass out, the door opens.

"Who sent you, luck junkie?"

"Nobody sent me! Please, no—"

She slams the door and starts the cycle again. This time, I think I do pass out. When I come around again, the door is open, and she's looking at me, her gaze flat. My head is pounding. My shoulder throbs. I feel sweaty and battered.

"Who sent you?"

"The Golden Swan!" I cry out, desperate.

She furrows her brow, then she starts to laugh. "The Golden Swan?" She laughs more loudly, the sound harsh and cackling. "No wonder. Makes sense. Eddie can't afford good spinner help, so he hire junkies now."

She nods once to the goons. One pulls me from the dryer by my neck and flops me on the mercifully cool concrete. I'm limp and dizzy and feel like I might puke. But the air on my face is one of the best things I can remember having felt in a long time.

They drag me, an arm each, between them. I don't even care where they're taking me, as long as it's out of this room. She opens one door then another, and suddenly I feel the dry heat of the open air on my face. I look up for the first time. We're in a back alley somewhere.

The big men throw me down. I land squarely on my back and just stay that way, staring up at the rectangle of blue sky between the high alley walls on either side. I hear her voice, but I don't have the energy to turn and look.

"Nobody steal from my casino. Not even a no-good luck

junkie like you. Tell Eddie I pay him a visit soon. Then he see what a real luck spinner can do."

I hear the door slam. After lying on my back for a moment more, I turn onto my side and puke all over the ground.

I'M SITTING in the back of a vintage Lincoln Continental in the tuxedo I just got married in. Alli sits next to me, her wedding dress splayed out perfectly beneath her like a lily pad of bright white. She's looking out the open window as the little church on Fourth and Pleasant recedes in the distance, along with the cheers of our small party. She smiles like she's already going over each memory of the day, locking it away, squeezing my hand like she's never going to let go. The sunlight catches a sparkling pendant holding back her cherry-red hair. The car smells pleasantly of polished leather and clean sweat and the champagne toast still lingering on our breaths.

I know the date by heart: Friday, June 1st. The time too. 4:45 p.m. Five minutes before disaster. And this is a dream.

I try to speak to her, to squeeze her hand back, but I'm trapped as a set piece, as if I'm watching a movie in the driver's seat of my own body. The driver pulls out onto Main. Gets stopped at a red light. Decides to make a right-hand turn to get around some construction. Turns on his signal.

"Everything was perfect," she says.

The sunlight strikes the tiny diamonds encircling her brand-new wedding band, and the star-shot reflection sparkles on her face for half a heartbeat.

I try to scream at the driver to sit still, to tell him we've got all the time in the world, construction be damned. I want to jump over the console, to keep him from turning that wheel. My body doesn't respond. I can't do anything but hold her hand. My own wedding ring feels heavy on my finger, like a weight pinning me to the back seat.

I've had this dream every night since Alli died. Every night, it's been the same.

But something is different this time.

This time, I can see the dust. The Lincoln is coated in it. The back seat seems to vibrate with it. I feel like the nearby traffic is mired in gold dust like molasses.

But the dust under the delivery truck is as slippery as wet ice. Its brakes lock up just as the Lincoln tries to pull out of traffic. The truck's brakes squeal terribly, but it has no prayer of stopping. It's a ten-ton weight sliding helplessly down a shuffleboard sanded with glittering gold, a comet that sloughs off a trail of bad luck behind it.

Alli sees none of this. She's looking at me, smiling like she's won the lottery. She's blissfully unaware of the truck barreling down upon her.

My scream is cut short by that terrible sound, the one that haunts my days as well as my nights—the violent slamming of metal on metal as the car caves in where she sits.

I've heard it so many times in my dreams that I can pick out the sound of her window popping.

Every time, I scream, and every time, my scream wakes me. But this time, it's different. This time, the scream is my mother's scream. I'm sure of it. It's as if she's right there in the car with me.

I turn to try to find her, to see her face. But my bubble of unconsciousness pops with the sound of my wife's obliteration, and I wake up to find a man bending over me, prodding me gently in the chest.

"Hey. *Hombre.* You gotta get up."

I recognize that gold tooth. Aqua-blue eyes are wide with worry. Berto. Slowly, I come back to myself. I'm back in an alley out behind the Metropolis, my vomit still wet on my cheek.

"What time is it?" I ask, trying to sit up. I wince. Everything hurts. I lift my shirt with my good arm, expecting to find blood, but I see nothing. I feel like I've been beaten like a rug on the line, but I've got nothing to show for it, only jumbled-up insides and aching bones. Something tells me that crazy Asian lady has done this before.

Berto checks a beat-up digital watch. "Almost ten."

I push myself to my knees and stagger at the pain that blossoms in my shoulder.

So... jumbled-up insides, aching bones, and one redislocated shoulder.

Berto helps me to stand.

"I'm gonna be late for work," I say staggering toward one end of the alley.

Ahead, a beefy guy in a tattered orange vest, whom I recognize as one of Berto's card-slapping associates from the corner, shakes his head quickly. Berto grabs me by the arm, yanks it outward once then pulls me close. I scream at the horrible clicking feeling then melt as the joint settles in place again.

"Gotta fix busted-out shoulders quick," Berto says. "It never goes right if you have warning, you know?"

I take two deep breaths and swallow a hint of bile. I check the stitches. One is seeping blood, but the rest have held. *Small miracles.*

I don't know whether to thank Berto or collapse, but I do know if I collapse I'm probably not getting up again for a couple hours. I stagger back to the end of the alley, but Berto stops me, gently this time.

"*Perdón, cabron.* Can't go that way."

"What? Why not?"

"Not safe."

He turns us around and helps me gently but firmly along. At the other end of the alley is another young Mexican man in a tattered orange vest. Berto pauses. The man looks left and right then ushers us forward with a quick tick of his head. Berto moves me along again with a hand flat on my back. When I tilt too far one way, he steadies me with his other arm.

"Not safe? What's the problem?" I ask, still dazed. My words feel like cotton in my mouth.

"The problem is you got it in your head to step to Lady Chang," he whispers. "That was stupid."

"That's the Asian lady? Chang?"

Berto shushes me, still moving me along. At the end of the alley, the watchman points us to the left, and Berto leads me without hesitation. I'm in no shape to second-guess.

On the sidewalk to the main drag, he changes his body language, keeping his head down, and tells me to do the same. I do but not before I see some rough-looking characters watching us. One man starts to cross the street to our side. He's thin and tattooed and wears a black T-shirt with the sleeves ripped off. Berto mutters a curse and pushes me to go a little faster.

"She called me a luck junkie," I say. "What's a luck junkie?"

Berto lets out a snuffle that probably would have been a laugh under other circumstances. "Thieves, mostly," he replies. "They can see the luck flow. They get high on it. Do bad things."

"She threw me in a dryer," I say in disbelief, as if I have to remind myself that actually happened and wasn't a part of some horrendous dream.

Berto sucks air through his teeth. "The dryer thing. She likes to do that when she wants people to talk," he says. "Did you talk?"

I stretch out my neck, working at a crick that won't leave. Then I stop in my tracks, and Berto almost walks past me.

"Oh God. I told her I work for the Golden Swan."

Berto mutters another curse and prods me along once more.

"She said Eddie would be seeing her soon," I say.

Berto shakes his head. "Maybe," he says flatly. "Maybe not. Maybe you get lucky and she moves on to a bigger fish."

I hear Berto's point man start slapping his nudie cards a little ways behind us. Without turning around, I'd say it sounds like he's trying to run interference on the skinny tatted guy.

"What's the deal with the meth head?" I ask, remembering the crazy that tried to eat my finger, and shudder. I bet the two are related, symptoms of the same sickness.

Just ahead is another orange vest. The man wearing it shakes his head, and Berto ushers me quickly to the right and down the nearest alley.

"The big casinos offer cash for luck junkies," Berto says. "Junkies can cheat the casino if they're good enough. They're like card counters but worse."

"How much?"

"A lot."

"Pay who? Who's after us?"

"Other luck junkies," Berto says. "Desperate for cash. Desperate for the flow."

"The flow? You mean dust?"

Berto tests the word out. "Dust. I like that. Yeah, it's the dust. You watch your ass around that stuff, *hombre*. It'll ruin your life."

We come out of the other side of the alley and make a quick left. I'm totally lost, but Berto seems to know exactly where he is. Ahead, another orange vest shakes his head then disappears. Berto stops and turns around to look back down the alley. He takes a deep breath then leads us back the way we came.

The two of us are alone in the alley. Berto starts trying random doors. I follow his lead, rattling handles, leaning into crossbars with my good shoulder. Nothing opens.

The gaunt figure of the tattooed man appears at the end of the alley. He stands stark in the contrast. Something shiny and sharp glints in his hand. Berto and I both freeze when we see him. I'm still trying to process the knife and what it means when the thin man runs right at us without saying a word.

When I try to turn tail, Berto grips my arm and holds me in place. "We'll just attract more of them with a scene out there. He wants the bounty for himself. Maybe we can take him."

I've only ever been in a few fistfights in my life, all of them dumb drunk nights out that devolved quickly and ended even quicker, but the bartender I used to work nights with said that while guns caused a scene, the guys with knives were the ones you really had to worry about. *Guns for show—knives for a pro.*

Thin man looks like a pro. He holds the knife in one closed fist, blade down, and runs at us with both hands up guarding his face. On instinct, I step around to his left, away from the blade, but he swings at me with his left fist anyway, connecting solidly on my ear. I'm thrown off balance to my knees. Everything sounds like I've been dunked under water.

He stays on me, which gives Berto a chance to duck low and get behind him. I regain my senses in enough time to see him flip the knife point side out and close on me from above. I expect his eyes to glitter with gold like Jasper's did, but they're a brittle yellow, bloodshot and manic. His eyes race all over me, looking for something. He pauses when he sees my wedding ring and breaks out into a crooked, yellow smile. He flips the knife around again and rears back like he wants to hack my whole hand off. Just before he's able to lunge, Berto swings the wooden handle of an old broom into his exposed ribs from behind.

The thin man grunts and spins around just in time to get the broomstick to the side of his head. He staggers, and Berto rears back to land a top-down finishing blow, but the thin man lashes out at his stomach with the knife, and it connects. A thin line of blood wells up through a neat slit in Berto's crisp white T-shirt. The broomstick clatters loudly to the alley floor, and Berto slumps to sitting.

The thin man stands over Berto, watching. I think he can see what I see: the dust running away from Berto like a stream of water. The thin man stands in the flow and breathes haggardly. The dust plays around him, and bits of it stick to him in clumps like pollen. His eyes go dull, pupils dilating. He looks like a man who just took a strong bump, and he smiles stupidly, weaving where he stands.

My voice shatters the odd silence. "How bad is it? Can you move?"

Berto presses his hand gently against his stomach, and it comes away red... too red. "I don't know," he says quietly. He sounds as scared as I feel.

Looking at him, I start to panic. The alley feels like it's caving in over me. The ringing in my ears feels like it's getting louder. Louder. Suddenly, I hear that awful sound again. The *slam* and *pop* that snuffed out Alli's life. It comes at me again and again and again. Alli in the back seat. Holding my hand. Watching me while the truck bears down behind her. The smell of her. Clean, exhausted, alive. It's like I can taste the air in that car.

Since then, the only good thing that has happened to me happened because of this guy sitting on the concrete, clutching his gut. I don't want to lose him. He's a good guy, and dammit, he doesn't deserve to bleed out in a back alley.

I feel a strange sense of power lurking at the edges of the pain that soaks my last memory of Alli. It's calling me. If I dive deeper, I might be able to grab it and freeze it before the truck comes.

Focusing on the pain, I slow down the *slam* and *pop* until it's everything and nothing, and I dive into the moment.

I run my thumb along the smooth, beveled gold of my wedding ring, slowly spinning it around my finger. I see the flow of dust in the alley with remarkable clarity. Gold glazes everything, but it's pooling more and more around the thin man. He laps it up like a dog, sloppy... greedy.

In my mind, I'm holding Alli's hand. I hold it for hours in the span of a second.

In the alley, Berto is bleeding.

I run my ring around my finger. The dust pools around the thin man, but it's slowing. His head lolls around to me as if he sees me for the first time. His eyes slide down my body and stop at my ring.

In the Lincoln Continental, Alli turns to me, blue eyes sparkling. The sunlight sifts through her hair, exploding off the crystal that holds it up, threading through the ringlets of red that fall to her shoulders.

*"Everything was perfect,"* she says.

I hold the moment and dig... dig deeper. I feel warm, like I'm bleeding myself.

The thin man takes a staggering step toward me. He finds the knife in his hand again and grins stupidly, then he licks the flaking skin on his lips.

In the Lincoln Continental, I let Alli's words hang in the air between us for a moment.

Then I let the truck hit us again.

The otherworldly scream of brakes. The slamming of metal like mountains colliding. That final pop of glass that changed everything. A sound so brief and powerful yet so final that I wonder how anything could continue after it.

I know now that sound marked the moment I started seeing the dust. In a way, nothing did continue after that sound. In another way, it marked the beginning of everything.

My heart breaks open all over again. A hole rips through me, dreadfully cold. I open my eyes, expecting to be staring at the hospital ceiling again, but I'm still here, still in the alley. And all the dust is coming to me.

The dust pooled around the thin man streams toward my left hand. The dust that lingers in the doorways and sifts from the bricks comes to me. Even a cloud of dust on the main street comes to me. I am a blast zone in reverse. All of it is streaming into my ring and from my ring into this chasm I've torn open inside myself, coating the hole I made.

And it feels wonderful.

A golden lens seems to slide and click over my eyes. Everything glitters. Everything is gold. I find the thin man as his manic grin falls from his face.

"No!" he screams, the first word he's spoken. He lunges forward with the knife, but I see the angle like it's written in the air before he swings, and I easily dodge the thrust. I snatch his wrist out of the air like it's a lazy mosquito and bend it back and around. He drops the knife but struggles still. I use his momentum against him and break his wrist with one sharp push, easy as snapping a wishbone.

He screams and crumples to the alley floor. I step over the thin man and crouch next to Berto, who's looking at me, wide-eyed with a little bit of fear.

"Let me see it." I reach for his hands as they clutch his gut.

He shakes his head furiously and applies more pressure. I can't tell whether the bleeding is getting worse or if his white shirt is just making it look that way.

"Let me see it, Berto."

"I been cut before. If it's bad, I don't wanna know. I can't exactly walk into the hospital, *ese*. They'll send me back to Sinaloa, where I'm a dead man anyway."

I gently place my left hand over his, already stained red to his cuticles. Dust pours from my ring, and my fingers are obscured by the flow, like I'm reaching into a golden bog. Dust falls in waves down either side of him. Berto winces at my touch but allows it, mostly because, I think, he's too terrified to move. His normally sharp blue eyes are sad with acceptance. He turns his head away and watches the alley like a wounded wolf sizing up the last tree he'll ever lie under.

The way I see it, we've got two possible scenarios here. Maybe the thin man's knife swiped deep. Maybe two inches of metal cut through muscle like butter and opened his stomach lining like a zipper. Maybe Berto's hands are the only things keeping his guts in.

Or maybe Berto got lucky.

I think of that old paradox of Schrödinger's cat, shut up and silent in a box. You can't tell whether the cat is alive or dead without looking in the box, so while it's in there and you're not looking, it's both. When you open the box and look inside, you make it one or the other.

Berto's blank stare tells me one thing, but the dust tells me another. The dust tells me that maybe, just maybe, what kind of cat I find is up to me.

I hold his hands in mine for a moment more, then I gently lift them away. The dust falls away with them, and underneath is a thin red line, long but not killer deep. Blood seeps more slowly even as I watch. It's already coagulating on the edges.

"I don't think you're gonna die today," I say.

Berto looks down at his stomach as if surprised to still see it there. "*No es posible*," he says quietly. He looks up at me. "I been cut before. I know what bad feels like. This one felt bad."

"Guess it's your lucky day," I say, helping him slowly sit up then holding him under the arms to stand.

"My lucky day or yours?" he asks, looking at me carefully.

I'm guessing he can see the change in my eyes just like I saw the change in Jasper's eyes. The alley looks like it's in the golden hour. The dust moves around us in a slow whorl, snaking between the fingers of my left hand and flossing in and out of my ring.

The thin man whimpers and pushes back against the filthy wall of a dumpster, trying to make himself small. He clutches his broken wrist and watches in open-eyed terror as I pass, Berto on my far side.

A rusty flatbed delivery truck pulls up to the sidewalk

just as we exit the alley. Two young men wearing tattered orange vests hop out and tend to Berto, muttering rapid-fire Spanish that he replies to with a calm shake of the head.

"I gotta lay low for a bit, *ese*." he says, wincing as his friends help him into the seat.

I grasp him by the shoulder and exhale slowly, willing more and more of the dust into him until he pushes my hand away.

"I'll be all right," he says. "Save some for yourself. You're gonna need it. All of Vegas will know about you soon."

"Know what?"

"That Lady Chang was wrong. You're no luck junkie at all. You're a luck spinner. You're the real deal."

One of Berto's friends steps up into the driver's seat and closes the door, while another hops up onto the bed and holds on. Berto nods a farewell that strikes me as strangely sad—it's in his eyes and the way they take in my own. Like he feels sorry for me. His truck pulls away with a throaty roar, leaving me in a cloud of exhaust.

I WALK into the Golden Swan fifteen minutes late for my shift, wearing a new pair of black jeans, fresh underwear, and a sharp white undershirt. Nobody even looked my way when I lifted all of it from the mini-mart down the block. All I left was a trail of dust. I shrug into my uniform in the break room, wincing at every move, then button up and look at myself in the mirror. The golden film that blanketed my sight has faded. The dust I gathered is long gone, left with Berto or lost on my trip back. My right ear is bright red where the thin man landed a punch, and I look like I could use about a week's worth of sleep, but all things considered, I could look a lot worse.

Eddie is standing behind the bar with arms crossed and mustache twitching in annoyance when I get there. He's glowering at me, although I catch a flicker of relief when he sees me.

"Sorry I'm late. Won't happen again." I step around him to prep the bar, but he's already done most of it, which makes me feel even worse.

Come to think of it, I'm not feeling so good. Even the brush of the bar towel against the wood makes me cringe a little, like nails on a chalkboard.

"What happened?" he asks.

Something tells me now isn't a great time to lie to the man.

"I went to try my luck at one of the casinos," I say, stacking and flaring the napkins he's already stacked and flared.

Eddie lets out a small hiss of breath through his nose. "Which one?"

"The Metropolis."

Another longer hiss of breath.

"I assume I should be expecting a visit from Lady Chang, then?" he asks.

I clear my throat, wipe down the bar, then wipe my brow. Everything seems amplified, harsh: the lights, the sounds, even Eddie's voice. "Yes," I concede. "She said that. In so many words. And not a social visit, either."

Eddie's mustache looks like it's about to twitch off.

"Listen, I'm sorry, Eddie. I didn't know about her. I didn't know—"

"Of course you didn't know," Eddie grumbles. He turns to me with genuine anger in his eyes, which, more than anything else has, makes me realize I'm in deep. "Here's a tip, Lee, from an old man who's been around here a while. When you don't know what you're doing, *don't do anything.*"

He lets those words linger between us for a moment then takes his bar towel off his shoulder and shoves it toward me. He turns and walks off without a word.

My shift begins. The tea starts flowing. Barbara, Nancy, and Susan each comment on my throbbing right ear, which feels like it's at least twice the size of the left. I pour a scoopful of ice into a clean bar towel and ball it up. In the spare moments between serving up drinks for the waitresses' rounds, when the bar is still empty, I try to ease the swelling by icing down the right side of my face.

I brew some tea for myself, pour it into a tall glass of ice, and suck half of it down. I feel like my heart is racing, but a quick check of my pulse tells me it's not. Maybe this is what an anxiety attack feels like, the world screaming at you when everybody is just going about their business.

The morning is slow, which makes this weird hangover worse. The one bright spot is seeing the old lady I helped on arrival, Agnes, wearing her newly recovered charm bracelet and sporting what looks like a fresh perm. She asks for an orange juice. No, she hasn't hit the jackpot yet, but she says the numbers are lining up more than they ever have before. She hustles back to her machine after leaving me a nice tip.

The afternoon drags, and I drag along with it. I pop a few bottles of beer for a lonely-looking smoker camped in the corner playing video poker, mix up one skinny cosmo and one whisky Coke for Barbara, and worry about Lady Chang walking through the front door. I can't get enough water. My body feels like hollow and raw, like a rooted-out stump.

The more time I get to reflect, the more down I get. I don't mind getting roughed up myself. I was trying to game a casino, after all, a risky proposition no matter which way the luck flows. What bothers me is the fact that I put Berto and Eddie—two of the three people in this entire city who actually took a chance on me—in danger.

I'm digging around below the bar, restocking tiny water bottles—one for the fridge, one to hold against my forehead —when I hear the subtle electric whine of a motor scooter on approach. I stand and see Zja-Zja parked at the base of the steps. Her cherry-red lips are pursed, and she's drumming her inch-long purple fingernails on the console loudly enough to be heard across the bar. I wave at her sheepishly. She gives me a slow shake of the head that says everything loud and clear without her having to say anything at all: *"Lee, you a damn fool."*

Barbara passes by with an empty cocktail tray, and Zja-Zja pauses her with an upheld finger. They confer, and Barbara comes up to the bar.

"Zja-Zja says to take your ten. I can pour tea for a bit."

I thank her and hand over my bar towel as we pass. At the bottom of the steps, I stop in front of Zja-Zja like a child caught peeing in the corner. She watches me in silence for a moment then lets out an enormous sigh that rattles her charms against one another.

"Walk with me," she says.

She pulls back the throttle on the scooter, and it rolls out at a leisurely clip. I keep pace beside her. The slot machines in their rows chirp and flash at us as we pass, burning my eyes.

"How badly are you hurt?" she asks quietly.

"Could have been a lot worse," I say, pulling at my stiffening neck. "But she made her point."

"Let me guess—she threw you in the dryer."

I try to roll out my shoulder and wince at the memory of the dryer drum crunching hard against my shoulder blade while I was awash in a spinning sea of white. "I don't think I'll ever be able to smell fabric softener again without puking."

"You're lucky that's all she did."

"She called me a luck junkie."

"But you ain't a junkie," Zja-Zja says. "You a spinner."

I stop, surprised, but she just keeps rolling. "Ain't for nothing that they call me the Eye, honey. You think I just play at this shit? Please. Try to keep up."

I scramble back to her side. "Berto tried to explain it to me, but I don't get it."

Zja-Zja straightens the charms hanging around her neck and scratches lightly at her chin with one of her bejeweled fingernails, as if trying to find the right words.

"You ever know anyone who's just lucky?" she asks after a moment.

I think as hard as this hangover will let me, but most of the people I find myself with aren't exactly what I would call *lucky*. Lucky to be alive, I guess, after decades of drinking. Lucky to get out of the rough end of the service industry without a raging cocaine habit, maybe. However, now that I think about it, certain bartenders and servers always seemed to catch the best tippers. Shifts just seemed easier around them. I wonder what the dust looked like back at that bar when they were around.

Zja-Zja keeps talking. "I knew a man once. Luckiest man I ever knew. Came to Vegas a few times a year and always fell ass backwards into free things. Upgraded flights. Free tickets and meals. Not comped, either. He hardly ever gambled. Although one time, I saw a high roller at the roulette wheel ask him red or black. My man says *red* without blinking. The high roller, she plunks thirty grand in chips on red right then and there. Guess what comes up?"

"Red?"

"Black."

I wince.

"Then she gives my man ten grand in chips anyway. Says she's had a good trip. She's way up. Tells him to have some fun. He's that kind of lucky."

We're near the back of the casino now, and Zja-Zja pauses to take in the room. I do the same. The casino is meant to seem big from the front—an illusion of mirrored walls and patterned carpeting—but from the back, I can see just how contained it all is. Not small, exactly, but simple. Square. Nothing like the sprawl of the Metro or the Diamond.

She scans the room until she seems satisfied. She scooters on and keeps talking.

"Course, it works the other way too. Everybody knows someone who's always in the wrong place at the wrong time. Flat tires. Fistfights. Jury duty. IRS got their name on a list. You name it. They can't explain it either. They just got bad luck."

We come upon Agnes at her slot machine drenched in gold. She's smiling and chatting with a friend sitting next to her, sipping orange juice and tapping the Ante button with a slow and steady regularity, like a metronome. She doesn't notice us. Zja-Zja narrows her eyes at the old lady.

"My friend who got the ten grand for losing has no idea what luck looks like. He's just lucky. Same with most folks that can't catch a break. They're sensitive to the luck, what you call dust. They just don't know it."

Agnes hits some sequence, and the slot machine chatters and blinks for a bit. Her eyes light up. When she claps, her charm bracelet jingles softly. Zja-Zja watches it carefully. It's drenched in dust, but other than that, I can't say how it's any different from my ring. Zja-Zja, however, looks like she's reading a book. I wonder what she sees in these trinkets and talismans that I can't see.

We continue our walk, rounding the far corners of the casino floor. Zja-Zja's eyes flicker from table to table, machine to machine, even as she speaks.

"So my lucky friend is at this level," she says, flattening one bejeweled hand just above the handlebars of her scooter. A collection of polished stone rings stacked half the length of her middle finger glints in the casino lights. She moves her hand up a tick. "Luck junkies are here. They know just enough to get killed." Then she moves her hands up a couple of feet. "Luck spinners are here. They can use the dust. Shape it. Make it do things."

We're rounding the back side of the Swan Song now. Barbara is leaning back against the back bar, arms crossed, looking bored. The polished wood in front of her is slowly seeping with dust, like water filling a hole dug in the sand of a beach. Here and there, streams of dust trickle down to the floor. She looks like she couldn't care less.

"It's rare to be able to see the luck," Zja-Zja says. "Even rarer to spin it, like you."

She follows my gaze to the bar, squints hard, then shakes her head. "I can't see it myself. My specialty is with objects. Charms. Totems. Cards. I see them differently. But I don't see the dust you see. At least not like Jasper explained it. And I sure as hell can't move it like a spinner can. Sometimes, I wish I could. Most times, I'm happy I don't."

"Why's that?" I ask.

"That luck junkie you ran into with Berto—"

"You know about that?"

She gives me a look that says, *"It's literally my business to know."* "How'd that junkie look to you?" she asks.

I remember his manic eyes, like he was drowning in water but dying of thirst. I remember the way he looked at my ring, like he would eat my finger off if he could.

"He looked terrible," I reply.

"Junkies can get addicted to the flow fast. They can't control it, but they can steal it. Get little tastes here and there of what it can do. But little tastes are never enough. They want more. And more."

Our rounds take us down the length of the casino, past the Swan Song and toward the foyer, where the gold-tinted glass of the front doors filters the sunlight and the marble reflects its soft glow, almost indistinguishable from the small but steady streams of dust that vein the floor... most of it going out the door.

"Well, spinners got access to more. And they can control it. More of what kills you is never a good thing. Spinners and junkies ain't too far removed, honey. Both deal with the dust. Too much can fry you just like a junkie. I've seen some go mute. Others blabber nonstop. I've seen junkies end up in the crazy ward or dead in prison. Some wander off into the desert and die. Others walk into traffic." She stops rolling and looks at me carefully. "It burns up their souls like flash paper. And they're addicted to it."

In that alley, when I ripped afresh the wound left by Alli, the dust rushed in to fill the empty space in my heart, and I found a warmth and a confidence I thought I'd never find again. I knew that every move I made would be the right one. I felt complete for the first time in months. And just like a drug, the comedown is brutal. The wound is rubbed raw and aching, and all I want to do is plug it up again.

A man could get addicted real quick.

"I get it," I say, itching awkwardly at my neck. I feel ants tromping in a line up and down my spine, but it's just the fabric of my shirt.

Zja-Zja looks at me carefully then sighs softly. "I hear sugar helps with the hangover," she says as she throttles forward, leading me. "If you can see luck in Las Vegas, you're like a card counter on steroids. No casino wants you anywhere near them. Competition between casinos is fierce. Everyone wants to control the flow. It brings in people and money. Some junkies, the ones not so far gone, hire out as spies. They'll sneak in a casino for you if you pay them, tell you what they see. Which way the luck flows. They'll even take a swipe at the house if the pay is good."

I thought about the look in Lady Chang's eye when she called me a luck junkie, as if she was personally affronted. Like my presence was a slap in the face. A deadly fire lay behind that hateful glitter.

"The things people do for money," I say.

"They'll take money. But it's dust they really want," she says, nodding at my wedding ring. "They want things that attract the dust. Totems. Ornaments. Keepsakes. Baubles." She brushes her long nails gently across the necklaces she wears—her river stone hidden within today's selection of woven leather and beads. "For a junkie, something that can call the dust is worth way more than money."

We round the casino and proceed down the center, back to the Swan Song. Zja-Zja checks each table perfunctorily, like a cop on the beat. I get the feeling that this path is well-worn for her, a way to keep tabs on the casino as much as she's able.

"Lady Chang's job is to steer the flow toward the Metro, just like Jasper's is to steer it toward the Avalon. Part of that means keeping junkies and anyone else with the sight out. With force, if they have to. Chang set a trap. It's a common tactic. She changed the flow of a table somewhere in the Metro. Made it seem like a sure thing to someone who can see the dust. Then she waited to see who would show up."

"And I fell right in," I say, shaking my head.

"You fell right in. And then you told her you were from the Swan." She shakes her head and *tsk-tsks* me under her breath. "Soon, all the casinos will know. They'll start looking. And when they find a spinner instead of a junkie, they won't like it."

We roll up on the bar. Barbara nods at me as we swap places, and she gives Zja-Zja a little fist bump as she passes on her way back to the floor. I run my hands across the softly glowing wood like a security blanket.

"I'm sorry, Zja-Zja."

Zja-Zja looks up at me through narrowed eyes, fingers fiddling with her stone. I think she's going to turn around and leave for a moment, but then she settles back into her chair.

"I forgive you, honey. You're like a child in this, and you can't fault a child. But that was your one pass. You must be careful." She flips the river stone thoughtfully, eyes distant. "I'll take a chamomile tea."

I set about serving the tea, relieved to have something routine to put my hands to while my mind tries to make sense of everything I've heard. I bring the cup and saucer around to Zja-Zja, and she takes them daintily in both hands, one long nail threading the small handle of the cup as she sips. She looks out over the Golden Swan like a mother hen settled uneasily over her coop while foxes circle outside.

I'm reminded of the way she stared down one of those foxes just yesterday, until Jasper backed off and left.

"Why is Jasper afraid of you?"

Zja-Zja sips quietly for a moment before speaking. "Jasper didn't want to know the things my sight tells him. I suspect Lady Chang don't either. That's the way with hard folks. They got hard stories that the cards ain't done writing yet. But that won't stop them for long. Especially once they find out how green you really are and that you're all we got. They don't want to risk the Golden Swan returning to what it once was. They'll strike at you first."

"So what am I supposed to do? Just wait for them to come after me?" I ask.

"Work," she says forcefully. "You work. And you watch the floor, like we just did today. Those rounds are yours to make now, so you make them. And you pray that Lady Chang or Jasper Jones or any other true spinner doesn't walk through those doors."

She calms herself and takes a sip of tea then a deep breath. Her free hand disappears into the throng of beads and crystals hanging over her bosom and pulls out a tattered business card. "And then," she adds, "before you do anything else stupid, you go see this man."

She hands me the card. Three lines of text are printed on the front in faded purple.

The Marvelous Max
Magic and More
On Fremont Street

I flip it over and back again, puzzled. "Is there an address, or what?"

"You'll know him," says the Eye. She takes one last dainty sip of tea and sets the cup on a nearby table. "I need to be alone with my cards for a time. I feel like something has been set in motion that I cannot quite see, but I hear the dominos falling from far away."

She turns her chair around with deft flicks of her hand on the stick.

"Walk softly, Lee Baker," she says as she rolls away. "And whatever you do, don't go into any more damn casinos."

∾

I watch the doors. I tend the bar. Time drips in fits and starts like cold honey.

Every small woman I see turns my stomach. The outline of every tall man gives me pause. I can't get back to work until they pass by.

The Swan Song is slow. To keep myself sane, I clean all the bottles, flare and reflare the stacks of cocktail napkins, and wash out the traps and drains with scalding water. I clean and rebandage my cut hand. Every hour or so, I scan the room like Zja-Zja told me to, but I don't even really know what I'm looking for. The dust moves and flows, more of it around the bar than anywhere else, pools here and there near tables and machines. Most of it sifts slowly out the front doors to join that flow heading down to the heart of the Strip. Nothing is any different from what I saw this morning.

Maybe twenty people total are in the casino. Half came off a small bus from a local retirement home. A few of these old folks glitter more than others, but no Lady Chang or Jasper Jones is among them.

My vision is blurry, and my head aches. I'm on my third cup of coffee. That awful hyperawareness is fading, but in its place is a relentless exhaustion that creeps back in as quickly as I try to shake it off. Just when I'm thinking of asking around for some ibuprofen to beat back the dull throbbing in my head, someone taps on my shoulder. I nearly jump out of my skin, spilling the last few drops of my coffee.

It's just Eddie. He steadies me with a hand on my shoulder.

"Clock out," he says. "You look like you're about to drop."

"Who'll keep watch?"

"We fended for ourselves for years before you came around, hotshot. I'll manage," he says, a sardonic smile on his face. He passes behind me and busies himself at the bar, counting, straightening, organizing things already organized. He manages to clip short a sigh. "Empty bar anyway," he says quietly.

He's putting on a game front, but I see he's worried. He's trying to keep it together for the sake of the Swan, but Eddie is worn thin. The casino just isn't getting the foot traffic. He doesn't need to see the slow exodus of dust from this place to know the Swan is dying a slow death.

Up in my room, I spend longer than I care to admit staring at the Avalon down the street. The setting sun drenches the turrets and towers in rose gold, and when the shadows lengthen, the lights turn on in sequence, from bottom to top. The nightly fanfare reaches a crescendo with a roar from the animatronic dragon atop the main gates, which comes to life, shooting a great gout of flame to the delight of tourists below.

Lights blink on in windows high atop the towers, and I wonder where within this fake castle I might find the real wizard, the magician that knows where my mother is and what has become of her. Streaks of gold dust vein the tallest tower, shifting ever so slightly, like charmed ivy.

The urge to go straight to the Avalon is strong. I have a vision of grabbing Jasper by the lapels of his track jacket and demanding, *"Where is she? Where is my mother?"* In my mind, my righteous anger gives me strength. I reality, I know he'd just humiliate me, turning the dust against me in ways I don't understand and playing me like a fiddle again.

I still feel the aches and bruises from Lady Chang's punishment, but the lingering hangover from pulling in all the dust in that back alley is even worse. Now that I've had the dust, I feel its absence terribly. I'm left with a hollow sensation. The ring on my finger feels tarnished and old, and I feel like a fool for still clinging to it—a relic from a time that never was. I'm here to find my mother, not to get caught up in this strange, glittering power struggle. I'm failing her.

*That's just the golden hangover talking*, I tell myself, but the anxiety lingers. I dig around in my pocket, find the chip, and pull it out.

*The Diamond.*

*"Don't go into any more damn casinos,"* said the Eye.

I can't imagine the type of spinner that watches over that glittering monstrosity. If the Avalon is dangerous, the Diamond is suicide.

*Not yet. But soon.* Just holding the chip makes me feel a bit better, giving a bit of direction to the flows of depression that seem to have enveloped me.

I pull out Berto's card and think about calling the number. I even go so far as to pick up the old, fat-numbered room phone to dial, but I pause. I'd be calling out of a selfish need to hear the voice of a friend when what he really needs is rest. I know he'll recover. The dust saw to that.

Plus, I shouldn't assume Berto is on the other end of this number. The card is still for an escort service, at least on the surface. God knows who might pick up.

I pocket Berto's card and pluck out my most recent acquisition:

## The Marvelous Max

I've never been to Fremont Street, but I've heard of it. I worked with a bartender who was a habitual gambler and swore by the place. He never even set foot on the Strip and called it a gaudy tourist trap. He preferred Old Vegas, with Fremont at the heart—said it was vintage, more action, a bit shadier. More alive.

Maybe this Marvelous Max can set me straight with the dust so I can find my mom, help me make things right for the Golden Swan, teach me what I need to know not to get killed around here.

Or maybe I'll end up wandering the streets of Old Vegas until I drop.

A long night's sleep would do me good, but long nights of sleep are reserved for people with quiet minds and calm lives. Folks sleep well surrounded by family.

I set an alarm for three hours from now and stand Max's card against the dusty bedside clock.

# CHAPTER FIVE

Vegas Vic, the iconic neon cowboy sign, looms large over my head as I step off the bus. He winks at me and shuffles a cigarette in his mouth, thumbing the way to Fremont Street over and over again. I think he's supposed to look welcoming, but that wink looks a little conspiratorial for my tastes.

The walking mall that cuts through the heart of downtown is crowded and loud. People move in and out of casinos and bars and stop to shop at kiosks or to watch the buskers. A group of tourists flies overhead along a zip line, whooping like monkeys. Packs of people gape at technicolor LED light shows hung high above them. None of them notice the streams of gold flowing at their feet like windblown rain across a windshield.

I stick to the center of the mall and keep my head down as I walk, as far as possible from the doors of the casinos. Somehow, I have to find one person in all this bedlam. I'm miles from Jasper and Lady Chang, but I still feel a vague sense of unease, as though other eyes are watching me from behind the mirrored windows and doors.

I maneuver around food stalls that sizzle with the smells of spiced meat and fried dough. Street vendors sell cheap plastic toys that zip into the night sky and float softly down again. Knockoff glasses and purses sit in rows on colorful blankets underneath neon lights. The chimes and dings wafting through casino doors clash with musicians covering hair-metal hits of the eighties and nineties on their outdoor stages. I could easily get lost in this place and end up wandering until deep into the early hours of the morning. With no better plan, I look at the dust.

I follow the glittering tendrils, stop where they stop, and move where they move. The dust eddies in and out of the casinos, but more often than not, it pools around the people outside. I pay special attention to the buskers and musicians. Marvelous Max has no address on his calling card, which strikes me as something a street performer might do.

I pass one every few minutes. Jugglers, balancing acts, human statues—these I expected to see, but others are there, too, all sorts of odd people doing strange things for money. A contortionist wearing a thong maneuvers his body through a hoop no bigger than his head. A tiny girl in a tinier bikini swallows flaming swords that look half her height. Some men and women have resorted to straight-up exhibitionism, writhing inside painted circles with nothing more than a few carefully placed pieces of tape covering them.

Then there are the street magicians.

I pause at the cordoned-off stage of a fat man in a rumpled tuxedo. He's proclaiming loudly about a dove that he's made disappear, reassuring a group of concerned children that the animal will return—with the crowd's assistance, of course. He solicits a loud applause and, with a snap of his fingers and a puff of smoke from the wrist, he produces the dove out of thin air right above the kids. They scream with delight as the bird does one small, flappy loop around the stage before landing on the sweaty brim of the magician's top hat. He pops off the hat, flips it around to allow the dove to settle again on the rim, and holds it out for donations—a few dollars here, a few there, some spare change—then people disperse.

The man takes a deep swig of something from a water bottle and cleans up his act. Although the dove seems certainly to like him, the dust nearby is ambivalent: it flows right through the stage, moving on. I follow it.

A little ways down, a man dressed in a billowing silk shirt is holding out a deck of cards above a throng of people. He coaxes a young woman up on stage and asks her to pick a card, show the crowd, and return it to the deck. He moves her to the center of his circle, dances around to the beat of the band playing nearby, then tosses the whole deck over her in a shower of playing cards. When everything settles, he points at her backside. She pulls her card from her own back pocket and laughs wildly.

The magician holds out a bowler hat for tips and gets a few dollars here and there, maybe just enough to justify picking up a whole deck of cards twenty times a night. The people move on, and the dust moves on.

I follow the snaking patterns of gold for hours until my eyes blur and everything looks gold to me. The dust is fickle, changeable stuff. You might as well try to understand the shifting of the open ocean.

Water, water everywhere, but not a drop to drink.

I sit down on the concrete sidewalk between casino properties and massage my aching neck. Closing my eyes, I try to pull myself together. I suppose I could always come back tomorrow although I don't know if I'd find anything different. Something tells me Zja-Zja can't help me much beyond the business card, or she would have.

I look at all these people that are not my mother and think about the hard numbers with missing persons. Every day that passes takes her farther away from being found. After a while, the math turns exponential. The odds are stacking quickly against me.

"Pick a card, my man."

I open my eyes. A few strides down the street, a home-less man has set up a folding table on which he's placed three playing cards, face down. He's short and thin, wrin-kled by age and the sun. A lady's sun hat with a floppy brim sits askew on his head despite the night, tufts of white hair sticking through broken holes in the straw crown. He wears a paint-stained T-shirt and tattered cargo shorts too big for him.

He gestures with one sunbeaten, calloused hand over the cards and speaks again in a twitchy stutter. "Pick a card, any card."

Strange that I didn't notice him there when I sat down. Although he stands out when you look right at him—espe-cially with the lady's sun hat—at a glance, the eye wants to pass him by.

I look at him carefully, longer than is polite. He rocks back and forth with a twitchy smile on his face, waiting patiently. My sleep-deprived brain takes longer than it should to realize what doesn't quite make sense about this picture.

No dust.

The dust that billows and streams throughout Fremont is nowhere to be seen on or around this man. A golden stream tests the corner where he sits before rolling away, as if blown back by a gentle breeze. In its absence, the corner is quiet and dark, strangely peaceful. Forgotten.

"I don't gamble," I say.

"Everybody gambles every day. Even if they don't know it. You took a gamble getting up in the morning."

Can't argue with that.

I turn toward him and survey the table. The playing cards are creased down the middle like tiny tents. The designs on their backings are faded, but the drunken duck is unmistakable. These are old house cards from the Golden Swan. I look at the homeless man anew. His eyes find mine, and they're briefly as clear as day. For a moment, he doesn't look that old at all, maybe midforties underneath all the additional years the sun and this city have piled onto him. He's a handsome man with a confident gaze, sure of himself and his business, such as it is. In that moment, I know we're sitting in this quiet and forgotten corner of Fremont because this man wants it to be that way. Somehow, he's made it so.

He turns away and points one trembling finger at the each of the cards, doing some strange math in his head.

"Max?" I ask.

"Don't know a Max," he says, still figuring in his head. "No *ordinary* Max. I might know a Marvelous Max, though. If you pick a card."

I cross my arms and suppress a grin. "Three-card monte is always rigged. It's a sucker's game."

He winks at me several times. "Every game in this city's a sucker's game," he says, falling over his words a bit. "Play it anyway."

I sigh, reach over, and tap the middle card. Max picks it up: queen of hearts. He looks up at me, pops his bushy eyebrows, then sets it down again. He picks up the other two cards: the black jacks of clubs and spades. Then he flips all three over again exactly where they were.

"You already picked her once. Pick her again and win double your money."

I shake my head. My dustup with Lady Chang and the industrial dryers of the Metropolis has put me in the hole again.

"I don't *have* any money."

"Well, what *do* you have?"

I reach into my pocket and pause. If I want to learn more about the dust, I need Max's help. And I get the feeling that, in order to get Max's help, I gotta play.

Time to take a gamble.

I pull out the chip from the Diamond and set it on the table with a thunk. Max looks at it blankly for a moment, then his eyes widen. He takes a closer look and flips the chip to the side that says one dollar.

He frowns. "One buck?" He grows distant and pats himself down like he's looking for a cigarette. For a second, he seems to forget I'm there.

"It's all I got," I say, bringing the conversation back around again. "If I win, you tell me about the dust."

The tic at the corner of his eye abates momentarily as he stares at the chip. His gaze is narrow and flinty, as if he's angry at finding it on his janky card table.

"What you wanna know about the dust?" he asks quietly.

"How about what it is, for starters?"

"Fine." He tears his eyes away from the chip and begins to toss the cards. "Keep your eye on the queen. Eye on the queen."

The shuffle is a show. The cards seem to float over one another, first fast, then slower, slower, until he settles all three cards. I followed the queen as best I could, but that hardly matters. In three-card monte, what you see ain't what you get. I might have a shot if I could see how the dust plays off the cards, but there's no dust to be seen. Max made sure of that.

Or maybe that's the whole point. Bring in the dust to find the queen. Maybe that's the test.

If I want the dust to break through whatever barrier Max has set up here, I'm gonna have to call it like I did back in the alley. And that means I'm going to have to pick at my scar again.

I take a deep breath and try to work some moisture into my mouth. Max waits patiently, watching me and rocking back and forth.

I close my eyes and run my thumb lightly along the golden curve of my wedding ring. The ring spins freely, calming me and taking me back to that hollow place inside where I've frozen the exact moment that marks the last time I was truly happy. The pain is still raw from yesterday, when I remade the memory, more vivid than ever.

I don't want to take the pain full bore this time. I just need a bit of the dust. So I settle into my seat in the Lincoln and focus on a tiny part of the moment: a single, cascading ringlet of Alli's hair, the way it glows in the dappled sunlight from the window, the way it seems to bounce off her shoulder as she turns to me.

*Everything was perfe—*

I open my eyes, ripping myself out of the seat before I get in too deep again. The reality of our quiet little corner of Fremont is cold and dark in comparison, and I want to go back inside, to live in that old Continental forever. I'm a little surprised at the anger I feel at finding myself back here, on this dark little corner of a seedy city, sitting next to a stranger.

The hollow spot within me twinges. A tendril of dust pauses on the street nearby like it has caught the scent of the memory too. Slowly, it snakes toward me.

The dust reaches the outer edge of Max's little slice of shadow and pauses. That same unseen wind kicks up and scatters its form. Max stares at the spot where it was. His twitch is back.

I run my finger along the edge of my ring and focus on the gouge I've made in that part of my soul where the memory lives. I picture it like a fingernail dragged through sand. I know the dust wants in.

The tendril reforms, pulling together the way wind-blown snow gathers in the passing wake of a truck.

The dust tests the shadow again, this time pushing through, and although it looks buffeted, it holds. The tendril inches closer to me, losing a bit of itself with each snaking movement. By the time it reaches my left hand, it's barely a hair.

But a hair is all I need.

I can feel the dust threading the thin space between my ring and finger. A few drops of it seem to ride up and into me, pushing the pain away. I hold my left hand over the table, ring finger twitching slightly.

The dust is drawn to the leftmost card. Whether or not that's the queen, I can't say for sure. All I know is it's the one the luck favors. What that means is still a little foggy to me.

And here I was gonna pick the center card. Shows what I know.

I flip the left card, and when I see the red queen, I let out a breath. The dust is blown from the table and my finger in an instant, scattered in an invisible wind. An instant later, that rubbed-raw ache hits me—a fraction of what I felt in the alley yesterday but noticeable nonetheless.

Max nods, rocking rapidly. "Okay, okay, okay," he repeats.

I plop the card back down on the table and straighten, stretching my stinging neck.

"So what is this stuff, really?" I ask.

"You already know that. It's luck."

I shake my head. "But it's more than that. It's like..." I look down at the empty space between my hands, struggling to find the words. "Like it sees potential. Like it knows the future."

I think of the way I cleaned up at the blackjack table before Lady Chang caught me. And after I sucked in all the dust in the alley, I knew all the right moves.

Max slows his rocking and stoops over to pick up a half-smoked cigarette from a crack in the sidewalk. He looks it over as he talks.

"Somebody got good luck, they a bit quicker than everyone else. A step ahead. Got all the right moves. Some-body got bad luck, they still a step ahead. They just got all the wrong moves. Time. Luck. Potential. Sight. All of it's the same to me." Max's words spill out so quickly that I have to focus on his mouth to understand. He pulls a faded lighter from one baggy cargo pocket and lights up the nub of a cigarette without a second thought.

"How do I control it?"

"That's t-two questions," Max stutters. "You gotta play me for it."

"All right." I spin the chip on the card table for a few seconds before pressing it flat.

Max looks at it distastefully. "What about that ring you got on?" he asks, pointing at my wedding ring.

I cover it protectively without thinking and shake my head. "No way."

"Wife'd kill you?" he asks slyly.

"Probably. If she wasn't already dead."

Max pauses for a moment at that. He takes a big drag of the half-spent cigarette, pulling it nearly to the filter. Then he either twitches or nods once—it's hard to tell for sure. If he's surprised to hear about Alli, he doesn't show it, which makes me think he's not surprised. He spits the filter from his mouth.

"You think it's the ring that's doin' it," he says.

"That and..."

"And a memory." Max quietly finishes my thought for me. Spoken like a man with experience of his own.

I wonder at the shape of the hole in his soul. Is it like mine? Is it deeper?

"All right then. We'll play for the chip again." He picks up the three playing cards and shows them to me again— two black jacks and one red queen. "Find the queen," he says, a small smile on his cracked lips. "And this time, you can have all the dust you want."

My ears pop as the barrier holding back the dust around us falls away, and an ankle-high cloud of glittering gold tumbles into the empty space at our feet. It flows around me like a dust devil, taking brief notice of my ring and the chip on the table then spreading out under the tented playing cards before slamming itself into Max.

Max doesn't flinch. He picks at a fleck of ash that landed on his tattered black shirt. The ribbon of gold seems to go through him then takes up a slow, swirling motion around his body like a slow parade of fireflies.

He ignores the dust and shuffles the cards over one another briefly, and I have a hard time even wanting to follow the red queen. I've never seen the dust act like this before, never seen it move with such purpose around anyone. I have to force myself to focus on the game.

The cards are shuffled. Max leans back in his swirling globe of gold and gestures at the table with his calloused hand. "Pick a card," he says. He coughs into the crook of his elbow then waits, watching me.

The streams of people walking by don't even spare us a glance. They can't see that this entire corner of Fremont is lit up like a Christmas tree.

For the first time, I feel bad for everyone else without the sight. They're missing this: an old man with a twitch in his hands and a spark in his eye, a scuffed card table, three cards—all in a snow globe of gold.

I try to focus on the cards, to watch the way the dust plays on them. But it's like reading the flashes of sunlight on the open ocean. I can't make out any pattern at all. I look at Max and know he sees the lost look in my eyes, but his gaze never wavers from mine.

I close my eyes and tap into the memory with the tiniest of pricks. Dust rushes in like a shot of ice water, numbing me. I open my eyes and hold my hand over the cards, but I can't focus. I can't find where my dust ends and the rest begins.

"Pick a card, L-L-Lee."

It's no use. I choose the left card for the hell of it, close my eyes, and flip it over.

Queen of hearts. Clear as day.

I laugh breathlessly and turn the card toward Max. "I win."

"You sure?" he asks, and his eyes flash quickly with gold before going even darker.

"Yeah. Queen of hearts. Look."

"I don't see the queen of hearts," he says quickly and quietly.

I frown and flip the card around. The face is blank, a misprint.

"What is this?" I stammer.

"Looks like nothin' to me," says Max.

I rub the card stock between my fingers. I can feel the grain, the heavy weight. This card is as real as the concrete I'm sitting on. It's just blank now.

"How did you do that?" I ask.

Max reaches and flips the other two cards: jacks, both. He giggles like a schoolboy. "Double or nothin'. You shuffle."

I put the blank card back down, flip the jacks, and shuffle the cards in a slow leapfrog, watching Max the entire time, looking for any sign of how he's working. The dust around him moves differently from the dust around me. It billows and crashes around my legs and arms like I'm a buoy in a storm, but it moves like a gyroscope around him, as if it's keeping him standing.

I stop the shuffle.

"Now find your card," Max says. "I know you know where it is."

I made sure to place it dead center. I flip it. There it is.

"And the others?"

I flip them too. Blank. Blank.

Three blanks.

I check the table, looking underneath and all around. Max is wearing short sleeves. Nothing hiding anywhere on him. No trick of the toss that I can see.

"Pretty slick," I say to myself. Then I ask, "How'd you do it?"

In a blink, the dust is all blown away, as if Max flipped a tablecloth with a full dinner set upon it to leave the table spotless. When the afterglow recedes and the night is dark once more, I find Max with another half of a cigarette butt, smoking plaintively, looking out onto the street of tourists. The dust quests our way now and again but meets the same invisible blockade as before.

"If you can read the luck, you can pick the right card on the table," Max says, speaking out into the darkness, his cigarette a soft, glowing red. "If you *know* the luck, know it like I do, you can change the cards that are dealt."

He twitches a nod at the cards and blows a thin stream of smoke over them. "Pick 'em up."

I pick up the cards again and find the two jacks and queen. I've seen parlor tricks, street magicians too. This feels different. I want to ask more, but when I look up again, Max's attention is elsewhere. He's looking carefully down the street. I follow his gaze, and the crowd briefly parts to reveal a man and woman, hard-looking people, ropy and thin, with fists balled loosely at their sides. They're glancing down each alley they pass and peering into each busker's circle, scanning the crowds. They're working the street in silence, with the deliberate, herding slowness of dog catchers looking for a stray.

They have the same barely concealed mania about them as the man that stabbed Berto in the alley and the one that surprised me on the bench. *Luck junkies.*

"Time to go," Max says.

A thought occurs to me. "You keep the dust away so they won't find you."

"I don't worry about the rats I see." Max stands up

slowly, favoring his back, and the cards disappear into his pockets. "I worry about the rats I don't see." He pulls the card table up and folds it in one motion. Just like that, he's packed and ready. He makes to walk right by me but seems to think better of it. "The luck tells me things," he says, pulling down the wrinkled skin under one eye and giving me a bloodshot stare. "And it's telling me I'm not done with you yet. Keep yourself alive until tomorrow night... maybe we keep talking."

He shuffles straight into the nighttime foot traffic of Fremont and disappears before my eyes, hunching over, lower, lower until he's gone. One moment, he's there—the next, I've lost him.

I turn back down the street. The junkies are close now. Maybe they were looking for Max, what with all the dust he was slinging about, but I think they'd be happy to find me and my ring all the same.

I can't melt into a crowd just yet, so I gotta make myself scarce the old-fashioned way, by scurrying away and hiding.

An alcove behind some scaffolding four strides away gives me good cover, although it's damp and smells like piss. I lean against the warm metal and watch the luck junkies approach through thin gaps in the slats.

They're oblivious to the flesh-and-blood world around them—pushing the crowd aside like hanging coats, sometimes shouldering into people too preoccupied to get out of their way. They follow the movement of the dust like lizards flitting from shade to sun, lingering for a time wherever the dust pools to soak it in. Only then do they seem to come to themselves, scanning faces and sizing up bodies.

When they don't find Max, they flit away again, back to the streams of dust.

I notice a little too late that one of those streams leads right to me.

The dust snuck up on me. I swear it wasn't anywhere near me a minute ago, but here it is. In a panic, I try to kick it away, to snuff out the glowing trail with my shoe as if it was a burning line of gunpowder, but that does nothing. My shoe passes right through, hardly stirring the dust at all.

I should have seen this coming—would have seen it coming, perhaps, if Max hadn't blinded me by comparison. I might not be the dust magnet he is, but the luck still likes me. Or my ring. Either way, I'm screwed. I wish I knew how that crazy old man repelled the stuff. I bet that little trick has saved his life a time or two.

I push off the stairway and move away, but the dust follows me—not a lot of it but enough to get noticed if one of the junkies happens to look up at the wrong time.

Panic rises in me. I want to bolt, but that'll get me noticed for sure. I walk as quickly as I dare right into the biggest crowd I can find—twenty or so people drinking at an outdoor bar called the Gin Mill. I insert myself into a line for drinks. Everybody is watching the bartenders flip bottles and spin cups, turning every order into a show as they pour.

Everybody except the luck junkies.

When I glance behind me to get a read on them, they're staring right at me.

To those with the eyes to see, I still stick out like a sore thumb. The dust flows differently near me, bubbling and swirling. I think I'm still wearing some residue from the three-card monte game in the snow globe. I certainly feel light-headed enough. I might as well be wearing a Kick Me sign on my back.

The man moves around wide, probably trying to get behind me to pin me here. The woman moves straight toward me. As she closes in, I get a good look at her: gaunt face, sharp cheek bones, greasy hair pulled tightly back and braided into a whip that lies off her shoulder. Her eyes are wide open and a hungry black. I'm reminded of the mangy coyotes that used to get driven into the outskirts of NYC, hungry and desperate.

I edge closer to the bar and get a few nasty looks. I even consider making a run for the casino behind, a nautically themed place called the White Isle, but when I look toward the entrance, the bouncer at the front door makes eye contact and crosses his meaty arms in warning.

The woman now has her right hand inside the pocket of her ratty jeans and definitely appears to be gripping something there. With nowhere to run and nothing to defend myself with except my fists, I turn toward her and square up with my hands low and open.

She runs into me quietly but with force enough to push us both back slightly against the crowd at the front of the bar. I hear some grumbles and a half-hearted shout, but then the bartender lights a long line of drinks on fire, and everyone's watching the show again except the two of us.

She presses up hard against me and tries to pull her hand from her pocket, but I hold her wrists still. We face each other like this, straining in silence, surrounded on all sides by oblivious tourists. Her breath smells sickly sweet, like she's been chewing sugar cubes. Her hair smells like an unaired basement. A long, thin scar runs across her ear and down one side of her jawline.

I bet I know what she wants to pull from her jacket.

"I don't know where he is," I say tersely. If she came for Max, maybe she'll leave when she doesn't find him.

"Give me the ring," she hisses in reply. "Give it to me, or I cut it off."

I hear a quick snapping sound and feel the stinging bite of a blade on the skin of my knuckle. She popped the switchblade right through her pocket. The pain is bright and brief, but she's close to driving her point home right into my liver. She's stronger than she looks and slippery, and she's trying to shift her weight to get me off-balance. I'm starting to shake with the effort of pinning her close.

I feel the tip of the knife like a pinprick through my shirt. The scale is tipping in her favor. A bump from the crowd pushes me a hair closer to her, and the prick starts to sting.

"Lee?"

At first, I think she's saying my name even as she tries to kill me, but the tone of voice makes no sense.

"It *is* you." A woman's voice, relieved, then concerned. "Are... you all right?"

The voice is coming from my left, away from the bar. The luck junkie and I turn our heads at the same time.

Jillian is walking hesitantly my way, a look of confused concern on her face. She's trying to place the luck junkie's face and hasn't noticed the knife yet.

Shards of dust are clinging to Jillian's every surface. Luck that should be flowing freely around her instead clings to her like the quills of a porcupine, forming and reforming in spiny clumps that won't let her go, even as she walks toward us. Her easy smile was waning when I saw her last at the Swan Song, and now it's completely gone. She looks deeply weary. The change is so shocking that I let up on the knife.

I realize my mistake a second after I make it, tensing instantly and waiting for the gut punch of steel, but it never comes.

The luck junkie is literally falling over herself to get

away from Jillian. She stumbles backward, bouncing off the crowd and tripping over her own feet. She falls to the ground and scrambles back with the knife out and in front of her as if to ward Jillian off. "Get away!" she yells. "Don't touch me!"

That gets some attention. A young woman screams and points at the knife. The crowd surges away, taking Jillian and me with them. For a moment, the luck junkie is left in a little pocket of empty street all her own. She seems to have completely forgotten about me as her manic eyes slide all over Jillian, taking in the shards of dust, which terrify her.

In an instant, her partner is there, pulling her to her feet in one sweeping movement then yanking her alongside him at a trot. She stumbles once then outpaces the man at a run. He follows without looking back.

A slow, pervasive cold is creeping up my right arm, like I've dipped it in a bucket of ice water, and I notice Jillian is holding my right hand. She doesn't seem to even know she's doing it, watching the luck junkies disappear in the distance along with the rest of the crowd. She must have grabbed me on instinct when the crowd surged away from the knife. But her touch is starting to sting.

Jillian turns to find me watching her. She gently lets go and looks down the street again, but she can't hide the blush that briefly darkens her neckline.

The sting lessens without her physical touch, but the numbness doesn't go away completely. I slowly turn my hand front to back. Nothing looks amiss to the naked eye, but a thin layer of frozen dust remains where she touched me. Its golden color is tinged with the icy white of frostbite. I rub carefully at the dust blisters with my ring until I feel warmth there again.

Jillian is watching me, looking embarrassed, and it

occurs to me that I must seem disgusted by her touch. Which I am—but not the way she thinks.

"Sorry," she says. "I was just startled—"

"Totally fine," I interject. "Everybody was startled."

"Did you know that woman?" she asks.

I shake my head. "I think she might have been trying to razor my pocket—cut it without my noticing to grab my wallet or something."

Maybe she doesn't buy the lie, but it's enough for now. I can see that she's playing the events back in her head and the facts aren't quite lining up.

"Do I know that woman?" she asks, partially to herself.

"I doubt it very seriously."

"But she looked straight at me. Like she was horrified by me," she says. When I start to shake my head, my mind racing to come up with some excuse, Jillian begins to cry softly, barely noticeable in the buzz of the crowd but heartbreaking nonetheless. Her eyes well up, gleaming with reflected neon light. "Maybe I deserve it," Jillian says quietly.

I furrow my brow. A few people that were close by are looking at us curiously. From their perspective, we just thwarted a knife attack. The bouncer at the White Isle is standing very close to the door now and staring at us both.

"You wanna take a walk?" I ask.

She nods. "Might as well."

I reach out to grasp her hand, hesitating for only a split second. I think she notices the pause, but her hand grasps mine. As I guide her through the crowd, the burn starts to build again.

On the edge of the street, we get some space, and I gently release her hand, which falls limply to her side. Thin rivulets of tears glisten on the scattered freckles bridging her cheeks. She sees me looking and gently blots them away with the back of her hand.

"Sorry. It's just that everything is falling apart. For the wedding. For me and Hux. For me in general."

"What happened?"

"You name it, it's a disaster," she says, shaking her head. "Earlier, I got into a huge blowup with Tessa. Somehow, it ended with my best friend packing her bags and heading to the airport."

She looks up at the light show above us while we walk as if entranced. I see a strange malice in her eyes as they reflect the glow of the night. The hardness looks out of place. "She's never liked Huxley. She's just jealous. Can't stand that I might be as happy as she is someday."

The shards of dust clinging to her flare out like a blowfish. More needles of dust plunge into her. I wince, but she doesn't seem to feel anything—at least not as a specific pain. Otherwise, she'd be running screaming down the street by now.

After a moment, she lets out a breath, and her shoulders slump a little. She shakes her head minutely, as if coming to her senses. "I said some horrible things to her, things that were not me."

As we walk, she absently adjusts a thin silver chain around her neck. As she lays it flat again, the source of all this new corruption becomes clear. The necklace threads that awful silver key—her *something old*. She fingers it absently as we walk. The shards of dust are all somehow connected to it, like strands of frozen gossamer spiraling out from the center of a spider's web.

And she still has no idea.

"I thought you hated that thing," I say, trying to keep my voice even.

"I did, yeah..." she says. "But Huxley took it and shined it all up, turned it into this necklace for me. Then he gave it to me with this new bracelet, as a set. Something old, something new. It was really sweet. This is what he does. He'll seem like he couldn't care less about the wedding... then do something like this."

She jangles her new bracelet, a thin band of silver studded with soft pink diamonds that sparkle wetly in the light. The bracelet corrupts the dust just like the necklace does. Sharp shards jerk along with the movement of her wrist.

"They make quite the pair," I say.

"Not sure they're exactly *me*. But I'll wear them through the wedding."

The corrupted dust spreads slowly from her wrist, testing at me again, staining the space where we stand a muddied yellow, like winter sun on a dirty windowpane. It raises the hackles of everyone we get near. A man selling counterfeit purses on a blanket nearby tells us to keep moving if we ain't gonna buy. A man selling sausages from a cart to our left looks up at us with a slight grind of his teeth. Two young men shoulder by me without comment. However, they seem to forget us as soon as we pass.

"I spent months planning this wedding. Years picturing it. Now, I just wish it was over. Isn't that crazy?" she asks.

"You just hit a string of bad luck," I reply and think of the story Zja-Zja told me about the man who flipped the script on the roulette wheel, turning a thirty-thousand-dollar loss for some rich stranger into a ten-grand gain for himself.

Bad luck. Good luck. It's all the same dust. What matters is how you use it.

I get an idea.

"You ever been to Fremont before?"

"I've had some good times here, yeah."

"What's the luckiest thing you can think of on Fremont?"

Jillian thinks for a moment. "Well, I mean there's Vegas Vic, the neon cowboy sign that waves. He's supposed to be pretty lucky, I think."

I remember seeing that sign, and the dust did circle it more thickly than elsewhere, but I bet the junkies circle it too. That's not quite what I'm looking for.

"To everyone else, maybe it's Vegas Vic, but what about only to *you*? Something you've come across down here that just felt good."

She crosses her arms in thought as we walk. The shards of dust shift and glint like broken plates of armor. I try to steer us to the edges of the sidewalk. Those we pass pause for a moment, slightly stunned, as if Jillian wears a perfume that brings back the memory of a heartbreak.

"The absolute best trip I had here was a girls' weekend the summer after we graduated college. Tess was there, plus three other close friends," she says then pauses. "I don't keep in touch with them anymore."

The dust crystallizes further over the slim curve of her right shoulder in an opaque shell, and she scratches at it idly, her hand passing through. "We ended up down here looking for some cute boys we were trying to meet up with again. We never found them, but we had a blast walking the mall anyway."

She's lost in the memory now, and the faraway smile looks good on her face. She stops in her tracks and cocks her head, panning down the street until her gaze stops at a casino a block away on the left with a glittering gold sign. The lettering has a waterfall effect.

"There," she says and laughs once. "We ended up there, at the Golden Gate. Out *way* too late. There was this old man doing card tricks on the opposite corner there, really crazy ones. Pulling cards we pictured in our minds from cracks in the sidewalk and things like that. He told us about this brass statue of Elvis in there that's good luck if you rub his hand. The night just got better from there."

A lot of street magicians flip cards on Fremont. But somehow, after all that happened earlier, I can picture Max taking some time to dazzle a group of pretty women.

"Elvis, huh?" I say. "How about we pay a little visit to the King? Maybe he's still lucky."

"Why the hell not?" she replies, a little desperately.

The Golden Gate doesn't look like anything fancy from the outside. Up close, the neon sign is missing a few bulbs here and there, chopping up the waterfall effect in a dizzying way. The golden paint on the front entrance is chipped, and the gold-tinted panes of the front doors are scuffed from years of use.

It's jammed with people anyway. I stop Jillian while we're still across the street.

Elvis is just inside the door, in the center of the foyer. He's life-sized and frozen in time, one hand in the air after thrumming the guitar slung low on his hips. His lips are locked in a playful snarl.

A security guard keeps careful watch over the statue while pretending to do nothing of the sort. I can see why. Dust flows liberally over and around the King, especially his outstretched hand, which is discolored from touch. His ass is burnished from rubbing too. My guess is he's been a conduit for dust for years, like the bar at the Swan Song—a luck charm.

He probably also attracts more than his fair share of

luck junkies. Thus, the security guard watching everyone going in and coming out.

Jillian moves to cross the street, but I pull up.

"What's wrong?" she asks.

"How about you go in? I'm gonna just take a second here, get some air."

She looks at me strangely but doesn't prod. She walks over and inside while I shuffle out of direct sight of the guard and anyone else that might have an eye out for a luck spinner—even a half-assed one. A rough-looking man leaning against a porn shop across the street looks at me a second too long after I catch his eye. He puts his cigarette out on the wall and walks inside the shop.

Or maybe I'm just being paranoid.

I thrust my hands in my pockets and turn back to find Jill across the street, smiling sadly at the King. Her arms are hugging her body, and she has a faraway look on her face. I know that look—I've worn it a time or two myself. She's thinking of a snapshot of life gone by, a time when the weight on her shoulders didn't exist. When she was with people who lifted her up. When she floated instead of dragged.

The wellspring of dust surrounding Elvis and the corrupted dust clinging to Jillian want nothing to do with one another. The shards on her have all shifted—away from the statue so that they jut from her back like the plates of a prehistoric animal.

She looks back at me. I mime that she should rub the sacred backside of the King. She blushes and shakes her head.

I urge her on, pantomiming that she should at least shake his hand.

She walks up to the statue. The security guard spares

Jillian a distasteful glance then busies himself with keeping a herd of young men from leaving the casino with glassware.

I hold my breath as she takes his fingers in a weak grasp, like he's the queen of England. She even curtsies, which breaks my heart a little.

Weak grip or no, the shards of dust on her back want nothing to do with the King. They are smoking, stirring like ants just put under a magnifying glass. She winces but holds on.

I try to will the corruption off her. *C'mon. C'mon, you evil shit. Leave her alone.* But the bad dust is hard to kick. She's clearly in discomfort. After five seconds, she snaps her hand back, and the evil shards surge around her protectively. The faraway look returns to her face.

I mutter a curse. She's gonna need a little help.

I look at the guard. He's still transferring beers into to-go cups. I hesitate one moment more, thinking how stupid this is and wondering how getting tossed around in a dryer somehow *still* didn't manage to get the point across about *not going into casinos*. Then I open the doors.

"For a second, it's like I felt the way I did before Vegas," she says, looking at Elvis in awe. "Back when everything was on track."

"I know." I approach the King, telling myself not to look at the guard, but I do anyway, and he's staring bullets at me, walkie-talkie already in his hand.

"Do you trust me?" I ask her.

"Not really, no," she says.

"Understandable," I reply. "Just let me try something."

I close my eyes and take it as a good sign that she hasn't run away yet.

I try to call up my memory of Alli, but I'm experiencing some performance anxiety. A group of men inside the casino are scampering toward us at a funny half trot, coming as fast as they can without noticeably disrupting the casino floor. Two are clearly thugs, large men with slack jaws and putty faces. Between them is a squat young man wearing a tight gray suit and stroking a well-coiffed red beard. He has a golden gleam in his eye and a snarl on his lips.

That would be the Golden Gate's luck spinner.

He's maybe a hundred feet away when he meets my eye. I try to cut open the memory again and focus on the pain. The sound is there, always there, but it's not at easy to hear this time. *C'mon c'mon c'mon.*

No dice. I peek again.

The spinner throws open the doors to the foyer and steps in. His hand moves from his beard to a golden fleur-de-lis lapel pin threaded through the buttonhole of his jacket. As soon as his fingers touch it, they grow sticky with glowing dust.

Running seems like as good a plan as any right now. I turn us around and reach for the door.

The spinner flings something at me like a street punk flicking a cigarette. It zips through the air with humming-bird speed and buries in my bad shoulder just as I pull the door handle. My arm twinges horribly, and the ball and socket pull apart slightly under my skin like wet paper.

The door falls closed again as I cradle my arm and stifle a cry.

"Old war wound, Lee?" the spinner says with unearned familiarity. "They act up at the worst times. Tough luck."

He pulls another string of dust from his lapel then rolls it briefly into a thin toothpick and takes aim behind me. "That door has a wonky lock. With a little luck"—he flicks the needle at the top hinge, and I hear a metal *thunk* down at the foot—"I can lock it from here." Smiling wickedly, he coaxes another string of dust from his lapel, longer this time. "Now we can talk properly."

I rattle the door—shut tight. The goons start circling. We're trapped.

Jillian's voice is thin with panic. "What are you doing to him?" she asks.

I'm not sure whether she's asking me or the bearded bastard.

The spinner takes the cue anyway. "I got a knack for making bodies remember things. Pain, especially. Everybody's got old war wounds. It's basically a patch job after thirty, am I right?" He laughs alone. "You wouldn't believe how easy it is to tear something again once you've done it once." The dust needle he's pulling from his lapel is half as long as his arm. "All you need is a little bad luck," he says.

Jillian's hand slips into mine. I almost don't feel the sting, so shocked am I by the simple comfort of her grasp. In an instant, I'm taken back to the Lincoln. I'm holding Jillian's hand like I'm holding Alli's—effortlessly, without affectation, resting softly across the center seat. Jillian's sting fades entirely, and I sense only my wife. The sunlight dapples her neckline. Her fingers entwine with mine. The smell of her hair as she leans into me is clean, like a watered rose.

*"Everything was perfect,"* she whispers.

I dig a little deeper than before to find the good stuff, to feel that fissure open in my core, two sides of my heart slowly pulled apart. The *slam-pop* of metal and glass gets louder and louder until it hammers into me with a shock like jumping into cold water.

Before I dive too deep, I open my eyes and take a shuddering breath. Then I slap my free hand on the shiny brass

ass of the King, and my wedding ring *ting*s softly with the impact.

The rush is electric, a silent sound wave rolling up my arm, gathering strength through my core. Dust surfs through me like spume atop a wave, gathering until it roils down my other arm, foaming as if my heart is the shattered and strewn breakers on which it gathers strength.

It passes like a current across our clasped hands, rocketing from me into Jillian.

Her eyes widen like the aperture of a camera. Light is reflected and fragmented to rainbows in the copper color of her eyes. She squeezes my hand fit to break it.

"Oh" is all she says, short and clipped.

What I see looks like a woman standing in the backdraft of a jet engine but somehow immune to the blast itself. The spinner isn't so lucky. He falls back, his newly crafted needle shredded by the razor fragments ripping off of Jillian. He's sandblasted, screaming in pain, wiping at his face and arms like the dust is acid, and in a way, it is. I'm on the good side of the blast, but the burn goes more than skin deep. My eyes are watering as if the whole foyer got bear maced.

The goons rush to him. They seem far less affected by the bad air than the spinner is, but I have my exit—for the moment.

"Time to go," I say, echoing the words of Marvelous Max.

Jillian straightens, unfolding each vertebra as if for the first time in months. She's taller than I thought.

"*What* was *that*?" she asks, popping each word.

"I'll explain later. We have to get out of here," I say, coughing and pulling her toward the exit.

She drops my hand like a hot plate. "What did you do to

me?" A disturbing note of hysteria tinges her voice. "I feel good. I feel—"

Time's a wastin', so I jump in. "You feel like yourself. Like you're supposed to feel if you weren't cursed."

She moves back toward the statue—away from me, away from the doors.

Words pour out of me: "Those things you're wearing —*something old, something new*—they're cursed. They poisoned you. You gotta get rid of them. And for God's sake, don't take anything *borrowed* or *blue* from Huxley either."

She shakes her head, a wan smile on her face. "There's no such thing as curses."

"Yes there is," I say, "and you know it."

A heartbeat passes. Two. Her face falls. She does know it. She knows it because she remembers what it felt like, even if it's already fleeing her like the remnants of a bad dream. I see in her eyes that she knows how bad it was. She's trying to account for lost time.

A dark spark blooms anew at the center of the key she wears around her neck.

"You have to get rid of them," I say again, pleading.

"But Hux bought me these..."

The spinner is pulling himself together again, helped up by the two heavies.

"These guys are dangerous," I say. "They can make things happen—bad things—by shaping the luck around them. Now c'mon, we gotta run."

"They won't hurt her."

This is a new voice, cold and aggressive. I instantly recognize the East-Coast snap.

Huxley Betancourt steps through the open doors on the casino side and walks around the spinner, still gathering his wits on the ground. He doesn't even spare the man a glance.

"Hux?" Jillian looks at me then at the ground, ashamed of being found with me, as if we were on a tryst, not trying to shed cursed dust.

Then I remember the look in her eye when I held her hand, and I wonder if I'm lying to myself. I wasn't *just* trying to free her from the dust. I wanted to see her, wanted to extend the night with her. And I think part of her wanted to see me.

Hux sees her shame and smiles with the grim confidence of a man who knows he has the upper hand. "They're not after her. They're protecting her," he says, turning to me. "From men like you."

Hux holds out a hand, beckoning to Jillian. His gold watch peeks out from beneath the crisp white cuff of his shirt. Gold dust smokes evilly off the watch face. "Come here, sweetheart."

She goes to him. As she touches his hand, the evil gleam at the center of the key grows. The red diamonds of the bracelet well up as if with blood. The razor shards will soon scale over her once again.

"Baker. So you're the prodigal son?" he asks, appraising me like a butcher. He nods almost imperceptibly at my ring. "That's interesting," he says, nodding. "I mean, I've seen better, but it is interesting."

His rolling gaze stops again, transfixed on my left pocket. His eyes widen for an instant, hungry. As he takes a step forward, the last residue of gold dust around my ring flares for an instant. I doubt I have enough luck to move a fly, even if I knew how. But Huxley still pauses.

I press my luck.

"Stay back," I say, waving a hand in what I hope looks like an ominous fashion. I feel like an idiot, but Huxley watches the ring carefully, eyes flicking back to my pocket then up to the ring.

He takes a hesitant step forward. I shoot my fingers out and wiggle them around for effect. A weak stream of dust jumps from the tip of my ring finger and scatters quickly into nothingness.

"You have no idea what you're doing," Huxley says, smiling. He takes another hesitant step forward, his eyes on my pocket again, gleaming with greed.

I take one last, desperate look at Jillian. She's looking at Huxley as if he was a stranger and won't meet my eye.

The heavies have the Golden Gate spinner up on his feet. One of them turns toward me. My window is closing. Huxley takes another step forward.

I wish I had even half a minute more to explain myself to Jillian, to tell her I'm as confused as she is. But I don't have half a minute. I press at the door with my good shoulder and find it open once more. I give Jillian one last look and take off running into the night without a word.

I'm not proud. But I am alive. That hungry look in Hux's eye scared me worse than the spinner's needles. My left pocket has the dollar chip in it.

And he wanted it bad.

## CHAPTER SIX

When I get up the next morning, I swing my legs off the bed and just sit there in my underwear and take stock of myself. I thought I would sleep off most of the dust hangover, but I was wrong. My body is an old jalopy, and I'm in the driver's seat, turning the engine over and over and over again. Right when I'm about to give up, the engine limps to life again.

My sheets are all on the floor, kicked off during the night. I had a fever dream, but the specifics are already fleeing my brain. All I remember is the cards: the Fool, dancing obliviously to his death; the Magician, spinning dark magic from dust; the Tower, raining fiery destruction.

The deeper I get into this world where luck flows fast and loose, the more convinced I am that my story ain't ending well. Zja-Zja's three-card draw said as much. I wonder whether I was always heading this way or if her reading set me on this path.

Either way, the train is chugging along.

I stare at the smoke-stained ceiling above my bed, and for a brief span of seconds, I convince myself that the spinners and the junkies and the dust don't exist. They're a good couple of seconds, but soon enough, my body betrays me. My throbbing headache surfaces again. My shoulder stings like I have a thistle buried in my skin somewhere I can't reach. Then there's the dust itself, insidious, two-faced stuff that moves in to cloud my vision.

I hate the dust, and I want the dust.

I want to use it to help people like Jillian and Berto. I want to somehow use it to find out what happened to my mom.

But I know enough about myself to know that ain't the whole truth. I also want the dust because it helps me deal with the pain I feel every morning when the truth of Alli's death settles over me with the all-encompassing assurance of a shroud.

The deeper I dig at that memory, the more the dust pours in. The more the dust pours in, the more distant and gilded that moment feels, like I'm looking at a picture of the memory in a museum, nodding at Alli, unseen at my side. *What a tragedy.*

That numb distance scares me.

I take a long, hot shower, barely able to lift my right arm to wash my hair, and taste sweat before the soap whisks it away. I put on my black jeans again and slap off the dirt where I can. I shrug on a fresh white T-shirt from the pack of three I lifted from that bodega. When I brush my hands quickly back and forth over my head, my hair spikes out wildly. It's gonna take more than one wash to get the grease out. My stubble is looking less *rugged* and more *lazy* by the day.

I pluck the dollar chip from my nightstand and stare at it hard. Although it clearly glitters with dust, I'm not seeing whatever Huxley saw through my pocket that made him home in like a bird of prey.

I tuck the chip safely in my front pocket and pluck up Berto's card next. Maybe I should call him and check in. Then again, I'm not sure what I would say. *"Sorry for getting you stabbed"?* He needs rest more than a lonely call from me.

I tap my back pocket to double-check for the room key on my way out and put the Do Not Disturb sign on the outer handle. For whatever its worth, the little room has felt more and more like my own with each passing day. I don't want anyone in it without my knowing just yet.

Zja-Zja isn't in yet. Her glittering placard says Coming Soon. The black beads and scarlet bolts of fabric hanging behind the glass move ever so slightly in the darkness.

I'm not gonna miss her this time. I've got an hour before my shift starts and more than a few questions I'd like to ask the Eye. I sit right down and rest my back against the locked doors. And I wait.

And wait.

Thirty minutes later, I'm still waiting. The hot shower probably wasn't a good idea. I'm sleepy, despite having gotten a good six hours. I should have known better. Hot showers are for a job well done. Cold showers always kept me sharp when I had to show up to work doubles back in Brooklyn. I should have taken a cold one.

I think I doze in fits and starts, for suddenly a memory from the night before jogs loose—something Huxley said.

*"Baker. So you're the prodigal son?"*

He's come across my mother somehow.

Maybe Mom is a junkie. Maybe she came here looking to snort dust just like the other hollow-eyed and broken souls I keep running into. Maybe she was fiending so badly she left me in a hospital bed. *"I'm so sorry, Lee. This is all my fault..."* Or maybe she's dead. Maybe she wandered into traffic, her mind wiped from dipping too far into the stream. Maybe she got knifed for her earrings or something. I should check the morgues for unidentified bodies. That was the first thing I should have done. What the hell am I doing traipsing around Fremont? My mother could be in a freezer somewhere.

I open my eyes and straighten up.

Zja-Zja is looking down at me from her moving throne. Her eyebrows are painted dark purple, and her lashes sparkle with glitter. Her pursed lips look like a lacquered plum. They peel apart when she speaks.

"You look awful, honey," she says.

"This town is trying to kill me."

She nods knowingly. "It'll kill all of us in the end."

"That a prophecy?" I ask.

"Just common sense. Anybody who thinks they can live in the flow of Vegas forever is a damn fool. This town will eat you. Now, my guess is you aren't here for the comfort of my floor, so come on in."

She reaches over my head and unlocks the parlor then presses the access button to open the door. After she backs up and rolls around me, I get up, brush myself off, and follow.

"Take a seat," she says.

The reading table isn't set up, so I flop down on one of her couches. I'm enveloped in plush pillows and the vague scent of incense. It's wonderful. I could easily fall asleep here, too, but I force myself to sit up and plant two feet on the ground while Zja-Zja works behind her curtain with what sounds like a teakettle.

When she comes rolling out again, I cut right to the

chase. I dig out the chip and hold it up. "What the hell is this thing?"

She pauses in her tea service and nods to herself as if she expected the question all along, then she plucks out two bags of our famous chamomile from a private stash. She plops a slightly yellowed mug with a faded drunken duck in front of me. Hers reads You Had Me at Tarot across it.

She pours us each a steaming cup and settles her hair about herself. "It's a dollar chip that says the Diamond on it."

I take the cup without breaking my droll gaze. "C'mon, Zja-Zja. If I do die in this town, it's gonna be because of this"—I point at my wedding ring—"or because of this." I hold up the chip. "I know it's worth more than a dollar."

"And you're probably right. On both accounts."

I wait. Eventually, she sighs. She takes a quick sip of tea then holds the mug as if to warm her hands.

"Funny thing is, if you were to go to the Diamond—if they didn't kill you as soon as you set foot in the door, that is —you'd find that the chips they actually use on the casino floor look nothing like that one," she says.

"So it's not a chip from the Diamond?"

"It is somehow. As soon as you put it down on my table, I saw it was significant. Maybe the most significant thing that has crossed my parlor in years. So I started digging, but..." She peers with frustration at the chip in my hand. "The short answer is I don't know exactly what it is."

"And what's the long answer?"

She takes her river-stone necklace and spins it. The etched markings on either side move and shift, forming new signs as they blur. Dust that slowly sifts around the floor perks up.

"What did Max tell you?" she asks.

I set aside how she knows I found the guy already. The things Zja-Zja knows are coming as less and less of a surprise to me. "He sort of mumbled about luck and time and potential all being the same thing. Something about being able to change the cards that are dealt. He did this impossible trick where he turned three playing cards blank. Smoked a few trash cigarettes off the ground. Disappeared into the crowd."

Zja-Zja laughs softly, eyes distant. "You keep finding him, and you keep listening. He's the only one around here that understands the luck for sure."

"The only thing I know for sure about him is that he's crazy," I say.

"Marvelous," she says, correcting. "He's Marvelous Max. But being marvelous comes with a price. Maybe that price is madness." She spins the stone again. "He gave me this." Though I wait, she offers nothing more.

"I played three-card monte with him," I say and sip my tea, savoring it. I think I'm sweating out the dust hangover because I'm freezing—gooseflesh all over. The tea helps.

"That's a sucker's game."

"I know. It was the only way to get him to talk to me. I wagered the chip."

She sucks in a breath, eyes wide. She looks at me like I'm a lost cause. "And you callin' *him* insane?"

"So far, this thing has been nothing but trouble. Everyone wants it, but nobody can tell me what it is."

"It's a key," she says quietly.

I pause. I sip my tea. I wait.

"That's all I know for sure, all that has been revealed to me. I wish I could tell you more. Even figuring out that much put Berto's network in danger."

In a flash, I'm taken back to the alley, to Berto clutching

his stomach, to the prayer on his lips as I washed the dust over him. I remember the way I had to pull his hands off and, when I could see the skin held, the way I told him through tears. This man that I hardly knew risked his life for me.

I hang my head and shift my cup uselessly in my hands.

"He's okay, by the way," she says, her tone softening. "Wondering why you haven't called him."

"He got knifed on account of me. I'm beginning to think I'm bad luck." I sink deeper into the couch and press the teacup to my chest.

"I've seen bad luck, honey. Berto has too. You ain't it. You know he's a luck junkie himself? Ex-junkie. Hasn't dipped in the flow for going on ten years now. But he can still see it, read it. And the way he tells it, you saved his life."

I think about how he always knew which way to go, how his people were always there in the nick of time, how he found me—first thing off the plane—and steered me toward this place.

Zja-Zja starts to prep her parlor. She motors over to her reading table and brushes it free of lint, picking up some more stubborn flecks of dust with her long fingernails.

"Fluff those pillows. I got a client coming in five minutes."

"I got one more question," I say.

"Figure you did. Make it quick."

"People seem to know me before I ever meet them."

Zja-Zja pauses for just a split second in her brushing, but I notice.

"That's what you get for trying to pull one over on Lady Chang's casino. Word about you went out on the wire."

"No." I shake my head. "It's more than that. And I think it has something to do with my mom. It's like wherever I look, she's just out of sight." *Hidden somewhere. Or trapped. Or dying. Or dead.* I force myself to derail that line of thought. "Did you see her in my cards?"

The Eye clears her throat and backs up the scooter.

"Zja-Zja," I say again, "are you ducking my question?"

She starts messing with things behind her curtain, clinging and clanging around. The water turns on and off... then on again.

"I'm not leaving until you answer me. I'll sit here breathing heavily through your entire next reading if I have to."

The water turns off.

"I shoulda never let you in the door, young man. The way you dredge up ol' business I thought long put to bed."

"You don't believe that," I say, smiling. "Not really."

She sighs audibly. "No. I suppose I don't."

She pushes back through the curtain as if appearing on stage then settles her bangles and jewels and pulls up to her table. She pulls out her satin bag of tarot cards and removes the deck. Then she shuffles through them, looking at each face in turn like an old friend until she stops, her face falling. She flops the card onto the table.

Bricks burning. Bodies falling. Flames reaching high into the air over faces frozen in pain.

The Tower.

"This card and I do not get along," she says simply, tapping it gently in the center. "For one, it's hard to read. Could mean death and destruction. Could mean a bad day. But I'm scared of it regardless because I've only pulled it twice in my life during readings. Twice. Out of however many thousands I've done. So many I can't even remember."

"I was one," I say.

Zja-Zja nods. "Jasper Jones was the other."

I'm not sure what I was expecting—my mother, I guess —certainly not that tree of a man who ordered tea and then nearly broke my bar in half for fun before Zja-Zja stopped him.

"He worked here too," I ask. "Maybe it's an occupational hazard."

"Maybe," she says. "The Golden Swan has a lot of history in this town, among the luck folk. Back in the day, Jasper Jones ran the Swan Song. He was top dog in Vegas, or near to it, back when this place swung its weight around. Then he left us. Going on ten years ago now."

"You've had no luck spinner at all for ten years?"

"Not until you came in. It's been bad. The junkies came in and gamed us for thousands before Eddie wised up. He don't got the sight, but he knows the signs now. Worked like a dog to understand as best he could. He's a savvy man. And he has me."

Zja-Zja adjusts her bosom and turns one bracelet so a charm faces forward.

"When the big resort developers came in, they took most of the foot traffic. The Diamond is just the latest. The Metropolis before them. Owned by companies with tons of money and clouded ambitions. Some of them dark. I feel it. I've read it in the cards."

She waves off her words as if they were lingering cigarette smoke.

"The way Jasper tells it, he left for the Avalon to strike while the iron was hot. They were the first big casino to come into Vegas in a decade. They needed a spinner, and he had a reputation as one of the best. I'm sure they paid him well, too, offered him a cut of the action, maybe. Just business, right?"

Zja-Zja shakes her head, a sad smile on her lips. Her bangles clink with the sound of wind chimes heard from a distance.

"The night of his last shift, I found him drunk as a skunk here in my parlor. All alone. Right there where you sit. He was staring at the reading table and mumbling to himself. I'd had about enough of him by then, so I told him to sleep it off somewhere else. He said he wouldn't leave until I read his fortune."

Her sharp gaze grows distant with the memory, and a little sad.

"In all the years he worked here, he never let me read him until that last day. He was always distant, even during the good years. But that day, he took his charm from his pocket and set it down on the table for the significator."

I remember the way Jasper's hand moved, clutching something silver within the breast pocket of his track jacket. The dull red line stretching from my fingertip to the crease of my first knuckle will keep reminding me for a while. It stings something awful whenever I wash my hands.

"What is it?" I ask. "His charm."

"A little silver spoon. A baby spoon."

I was not expecting that. I had the odd notion that he was fingering a silver bullet in there. Maybe a skull key chain or a weird tooth. "A baby spoon?" I ask, incredulous.

She shrugs. "I don't know what it means to him. But it's very powerful. I sensed the weight of it as soon as I laid eyes on it. He didn't explain it, and I didn't think it my place to ask. I remember the soft way he brushed the hollowed scoop of the little thing. How shined it was there from years and years of thumbing. All my readings matter—all have the truth to them—but some matter more than others. That was one of them. That one was like yours."

She flips through the deck with the surety of a master chef chopping onions for a meal. Finds three cards and sets each on the velvet in turn, her eyes distant with the memory of that day.

The first card shows a man and woman standing naked in a garden, eyes only for each other. A winged angel with eyes of fire looks down upon them.

"The Lovers, for his past."

The second is an old man, head bowed, draped in tattered rags. He carries a staff in his left hand and holds out a lantern in his right.

"The Hermit, for his present."

The third, the castle tower being destroyed. Flames gout from windows. Two figures fall, burning, to the ground under a jagged scar of lightning.

"The Tower, for his future. Same as you."

I don't like looking at the Tower card. Instead, I focus on the other two. "What do they mean?"

"I believe that Jasper was happy once. Carefree and deeply in love. For a time. But that ended. Badly. When he came to us here, he was already running from something. Wanting to disappear. But there's more to the Hermit than hiding away. The Hermit waits. Knows things. His lamp is the Lamp of Truth. He watches for signs."

"Signs of what?" My eyes are fixed on the Hermit, and I have a hard time reconciling the humble image with the imperious and cruel man I met.

The Eye taps the Tower card but says nothing.

I sit back, rubbing my temples. I've found few answers. More questions.

After a moment of silence, she speaks. "I don't know what the Tower means, other than destruction. But I do believe that Jasper's Tower and the one I pulled for you are the same card in more ways than one. Whatever event this signifies, you're both in it together."

I let that sink in for a second, not knowing what to make of it, but if I had to be in a two-man boat headed for a waterfall, I'd rather it wasn't Jasper Jones holding the other oar.

"And over all of it, I sense a woman," she says. "The same woman for both of you."

"Mom?" I ask.

"I can't say. I've never met your mother. But I know a common thread when I see one. Now, that's plenty for one morning. I got to get to work," she says.

I push myself up from the plush couch with effort. Zja-Zja watches me carefully, her gaze pushing me through the bead curtain and out into the casino as surely as a finger in the small of my back.

Opening the bar for business takes a long time when I've got only one good arm. I pop the caps off the spigots of each liquor bottle methodically, lost in thoughts that keep drifting back to Jillian. *Refresh the ice bin. Drain and then top up the washing stations.* I even spot check the wine-glasses, as if I'm gonna have a run on chardonnay at ten in the morning. None of it helps. I can't shake her.

The way she looked when I blew those chains away... only to have them creep back over her like English ivy.

My wife stands silent as ever in the corner of my mind, a quiet presence watching every thought I have of Jillian like a slideshow before her. I'm finding it harder to remember Alli's face the way it was day in and day out, as we lived and laughed and loved together... and easier to remember exactly how she was in that one second on that awful day. The *memory*.

But that's not her. Not all of her. Every time I draw on that day and bring the dust to me, I feel I'm losing something real while sharpening something painful, lacquering it, preserving it.

I feel like we're sitting together in the dark, watching this happen. *Incredible how someone can be dead and gone, but you can still feel like you're failing her... cheating on her*.

I decide to dust off the often-neglected top shelf, and when I turn back around, Huxley Betancourt is pulling out a chair at my bar. He unbuttons a navy double-breasted suit as he settles in. The gold buttons look purposely mismatched and very old, and they drip dust. The pennies in his polished loafers also trail a fair amount of dust. The gold watch on his left wrist is tucked under the cuff of his linen shirt, but a deep golden glow emanates from within the sleeve, and dust streams out in a thick gold line, dropping to the bar like a line of fire with every movement as he sits.

He scoots his chair up and settles on his elbows and peruses the wares, his face carefully composed. The cruelty in him last night seems contained, masked by a congeniality that somehow turns my stomach even more.

He holds up his hands in peace. "Too early for a drink?"

I'm still too stunned to reply, bar cloth hanging in one hand, tequila bottle in the other.

"Who am I kidding? It's never too early in Vegas," he says. "How about you pour me a sipper of that *añejo*? That's a good one."

I don't know what else to do, so I slowly move over to the tumblers and pluck one up. I flutter a cocktail napkin down in front of him and set the glass upon it. Then I pour Huxley Betancourt a drink.

He spins the glass slowly on the bar. "I think you and I may have gotten off on the wrong foot," he says.

"Before or after you hired the junkies to knife me?"

He smiles as if fondly reminiscing. A sharp pain in the still-healing slash on my palm tells me I'm unconsciously balling my hand into a fist.

"Look. You're in love with Jillian," he says, as if to say, *"These things can't be helped."* When I start a half-hearted protest, he cuts me off. "I get it. She's gorgeous. Eager to please. Rich."

I feel I should defend myself, defend Jillian, defend Alli, and tell him he's all wrong. I was only trying to save Jillian from *him*, and love has nothing to do with it. But I know in my heart that he's not wrong... not exactly. I am in love with Jillian or some part of her, at least: the part that held my hand in the face of the Golden Gate goons, the part that reminded me what human connection is like.

Huxley waits for a response I'm not gonna give him. Even assholes are right sometimes.

"What the hell do you want?" I ask instead.

Huxley takes a slow sip of the tequila and swishes it around in his mouth, looking at the honey coloring. "I think you know what I want."

I think about playing it cool. Then he sniffs the bouquet of the tequila, and his pretentiousness tips me over the edge.

I pluck the chip out and hold it between my thumb and forefinger. "This ol' thing?"

Now, he's the one trying to play it cool... and failing. His eyes are hungry even though he takes another slow sip to try to hide it. I roll the chip back and forth over my knuckles, a coin trick I perfected long ago on my slower days behind the bar.

"That's the one," he says, clearing his throat.

"And what, you think you can just waltz in here and take it?" I ask with more confidence than I feel. I'm still fried from my electric connection to the King that cleared Jillian's hexes. I feel sunburned inside and am not sure how many more times I can mine my broken heart without seriously hurting myself. If Huxley uses even an ounce of the dust he's dripping with, he'll be able to bowl me over.

"No," he says simply, eyeing the way I'm priming my wedding ring. "I'm not a luck spinner. I'm a businessman."

I try to keep the relief from my face. "Well, then you can just piss off."

He doesn't piss off. He smiles and sets the tumbler down. "I'll take another."

I don't like that smile. It's thin lipped and far too knowing. The longer he's here, the more uncomfortable I get. I look around for Eddie, Zja-Zja, anyone—no help to be found, most likely a by-product of all the charms he's wearing.

"Why do you want it so badly? You've already got gallons of luck on you. And anyway, the dust around this thing is—"

"Strange. I know." He nudges the tumbler at me.

I grind my teeth, weigh my options for eighty-sixing him, and find them just as lacking as they were five minutes ago. I pour him another dram, and he watches the glass fill.

"I guess I am a bit of a junkie," he says, "although not like the trash I hired to tail you. I gave them a penny from my shoe as payment." He laughs. "It was an old penny. Minorly charmed. I just told them to rob you, but they'd have killed you if I asked. For a penny!"

His laugh reminds me of a scumbag I used to work with who got his kicks drowning rats caught in the traps in the alley behind the Brooklyn bar. Last I heard, he was doing three years out at Rikers Island. A cop rolled up on him pissing on a homeless guy.

"I deal in antiquities. I can see a charm—totem, object of power, whatever you want to call them—from a mile off. As it happens, I have a buyer for that chip, a buyer willing to offer a substantial sum."

"And what, you want to split it with me?"

Huxley laughs, a high and sharp sound that would raise the hackles on a cat. "That's cute. No, Lee. You'll be giving the chip to me."

"Listen, jackass. If you can't take it and I won't give it, we've reached a bit of an impasse, wouldn't you say? And as fun as this has been, I think our time together is about up—"

"I'm sure that Jillian told you about our upcoming nuptials? In one of your long walks on the beach?" he asks, catching me off guard.

"Yes. A wedding at the Diamond. Very fancy. You'll be lucky if she can still walk down the aisle with all the shit luck you've saddled her with."

He waves me off. "Oh, she'll be fine. In the short term, at least. I test many of my pieces on Jillian. She's wonderfully susceptible to bad-luck charms in particular. It helps me price them."

My jaw drops, and my healing palm splits opens again with a sharp stab of pain that I ignore. I can feel the blood running, but I don't care.

"Relax. She has no idea. Or didn't until you came around."

The bar seeps gold, tendrils seeking out my wedding ring. I don't care how beat up I am inside—time to dig a little deeper. I'm gonna make sure Huxley doesn't walk out of here the same way he walked in.

But he shoots his watch hand out and snatches mine in midair. He clamps down, smothering my ring, heedless of my blood, now running down his thumb and spattering on the bar.

"Now, now," he says. "None of that."

The dust from his watch snuffs out what little luck I was gathering to my ring. The charm is like a repellant, oil to my water. Luck flees from where his arm rests on my bar, puffing away from his wrist like blown sawdust.

I watch his grip in horror, ignoring the pain.

"Nice watch, isn't it?" he asks. "I took it off a very wealthy and very crooked businessman in a Greenwich cemetery. It was his luck charm." His small smile turns toothy. "I dug him up myself."

He lets go, and my hand drops to the bar, lifeless. I steady myself against the wood, light-headed. He straightens his cuff and distastefully wipes my blood from his hand with a cocktail napkin. Then he adjusts his watch fondly.

"I had it refurbished, attuned to me. Now, the ice that ran in that old man's veins drips from my wrist. When you deal mostly with luck spinners but can't spin the stuff yourself, it's nice to have something that levels the playing field a bit." He takes an even breath and sips his tequila. "Now then, where were we? Ah yes. Jillian. I've decided I just can't wait to seal the deal, so I've moved the wedding up. To tonight. And once we're married, I'm going to test every evil and nefarious and draining hex I ever come across on her beautiful body for as long as she lives, starting with her wedding ring. You should really see this thing. It is quite the piece, a shipwreck antique. One of my finest."

The little shiver of glee that hits him makes me sick, but at least it stops him from talking, so I try to think for a second.

"Or you could give me the chip," he says.

I work saliva back into my mouth and manage to find my voice. "And then what? You'll leave forever?"

"I'll drop her like a sack of potatoes."

"And how do I know you'll keep your word?"

"You don't," he says simply. "But for what it's worth, I will. To be honest, she's tied to me mostly through charms and hexes as it is. Maybe a little whiff of affection from our past, memories of young love between two people who don't exist any longer. And once I get the chip, I don't even need her money anymore." He dismisses the thought with a flick of his wrist. "Waste of my time, really."

He pushes back from the bar, and I take a step away. I feel like I need a shower after having heard all this.

"Those are my terms." He shoots his wrist out and checks his watch. Dust flicks from the dial onto the bar and practically hisses where it lands. "You have five hours to make your choice. We're having an intimate little ceremony at the Love Tunnel, just down the road. It's one of those round-the-clock places. A step down from the Diamond, to be sure, but I'm so eager for things to begin, and it's all I could find at this hour."

He straightens his jacket and turns to leave. "Choose wisely, Lee," he says over his shoulder and walks out.

I stand stock-still until the doors close behind him, then I lean heavily on the bar as little starbursts fleck the edges of my vision. They fade after a few deep breaths.

I straighten. Very slowly and methodically, I make myself a cup of tea, and I think.

By the time I finish my tea, my shift is in full swing. By

that, I mean I'm actually called upon to make a few drinks, and two customers actually sidle up to the electronic poker and ask for bottled beer with their comps.

I'm not very chatty with them, nor with Barbara, Nancy, or Susan, who work the floor. Nobody seems in the mood for conversation anyway. The Golden Swan has that awkwardly sad feeling of a poorly attended party. More dust is flowing out the doors than my bar can replenish.

When the time to clock out comes, I've made up my mind.

# CHAPTER SEVEN

The Love Tunnel is a twenty-four-hour roadside chapel in a dilapidated strip mall about a mile southeast of the Swan. Even at seven in the evening, the place is basically a ghost town—the only signs of life are a handful of junker cars in the shared lot and one or two people walking quickly down the sidewalk. After the bus pulls away, the block is so quiet that I can hear the neon sign buzzing like an angry bee. The last *l* is burned out.

I step over littered leaflets for hookers as I walk up to the chapel—if you can even call it that. The Love Tunnel looks like a repurposed bank. A sign hangs over a drive-through that reads Get Hitched from Your Car! The place has no exterior lights, but a deep whorehouse red emanates from somewhere within.

The front door is blocked by an easel with poster board that reads Closed for a Private Event. Beneath the script is an image of two turtledoves holding opposite edges of a single heart.

This is definitely a few steps down from the Diamond. I was expecting bad vibes, but this is a horror show—devoid of dust but not in the way that slice of Fremont was devoid of dust because Max blocked the stuff. The dust wants absolutely nothing to do with this place.

It occurs to me that someone should really know I'm here, in case this turns south quick. The Parlor of the Eye was closed when I checked on my way out, Zja-Zja gone home. I could have told Eddie, maybe, but Barbara said he's been holed up in the office, crunching numbers all day, trying to keep the Swan open for another month. I didn't want to bother him, but maybe I could have left a note or something.

*Too late now.*

I open the doors and step into a nightmare of red lace, fake flowers, and stale cigarette smoke. A plastic fountain of a baby angel to my right sounds like an old man trying to pee. I push through a tangled bead curtain into a small square chamber that looks like a storage unit. Huxley stands at the front of a short aisle that splits two groups of empty folding chairs. The only other person in the room is an ancient man wearing what looks like an old pirate shirt underneath a brown tuxedo. He has a Bible in one hand and a lit cigarette in the other.

Huxley pumps his fist in the air when he sees me. "Lee! Welcome, welcome! We're about to begin!"

I walk awkwardly down the aisle underneath the simmering red lights.

"Please, take a seat," says Huxley.

"You're not really going through with this, are you?" I ask. "Here? What happened to the big party? Where is everyone?"

"A series of unfortunate events over the week kept the wedding party away," he says with a knowing smile. "My parents are long dead. Her parents are oblivious. We're going to surprise them in the morning." He turns to the crusty officiant. "Gang's all here. Shall we?"

The old man stubs out his cigarette in an overflowing ashtray on the pulpit to his right and flips some sort of switch there that starts piping in tinny organ music. The bead curtain rustles behind me, and I turn, horrified, as Jillian walks in.

She wears a beautiful classic gown of creamy white silk that fits her upper body like a glove and flares gently below her. It's a gown meant for a grand affair, not this outhouse. She carries a bouquet of soft pink lilies limply in her hands.

She's not herself—that much I can see right off the bat. She's deflated and glassy-eyed. The charms that chained her have returned and are almost back to full scale. I see two new additions as well: a silk ribbon threaded through her hair, as well as earrings with center stones of a dark blue that reminds me of the ocean at last light. *Something borrowed, something blue.* Both curdle and crack the dust as evilly as the key necklace and the blood-diamond bracelet. Shards trail behind her, a wicked counterpart to the creamy white train of her dress.

The charms have sapped her. She's halfway here at best. But the worst part is that the half still with us is looking at Huxley like she wants to make him happy.

As she walks past me, I see confusion in her eyes. Conflict is written plainly on her face. She mouths my name as if to tell me something—what to do, perhaps, or how I can help her. But there are no good moves here. No matter what I do, I feel like she'll hate me for it.

And then she's stepping up to the altar aside her fiancé. He looks at her hungrily. The officiant is talking—"Dearly beloved, we are gathered here..."—but I tune him out. I'm watching Jillian. My mind is racing, and my window is closing.

Then Huxley brings out the ring.

It's fair to say I'm new at this game. I have little to no idea what I'm doing with the dust, and I understand how little I know. But I do know this: the ring Huxley is holding out to Jillian is evil. Whatever happened to it, whatever story is locked within the stone and the metal, has corrupted it completely.

Even Huxley refuses to touch it. As he holds the opened box out to her, the ring paints the air around it black, like its very existence is erasing what little light there is in this place.

And she's reaching out to it. She's going to put it on and wear it forever. Or as long as it takes to kill her.

"That's enough," I say. "Stop this. Stop all this. Close the box, Huxley."

He looks expectantly at me, suppressing a smile into a thin white line. The bad luck on that ring nips at me though I'm twenty feet away, a damp and invasive cold, like someone left the door open in a snowstorm.

I sigh as I reach into my pocket and pull out the chip.

"Close the goddamn box. And shut off that terrible music. Get away from her, both of you. And it's yours."

"Deal." Huxley snaps the box shut.

Jillian flinches at the sound and shakes her head as if she's lost her place in the book of her own life, skipped ahead on accident, and come across a passage that makes no sense at all.

Huxley holds out his hand. "Give it to me."

I take one last look at the chip. Zja-Zja called it a key. Max said it wasn't something to be wagered. Yet here I stand with no solid idea of what it is, other than a lost opportunity. And when the flip side of keeping this chip means saddling an innocent woman with a lifetime of cursed burden, the decision is easy.

I flip it to him, and he catches it in midair, looks at it with ravenous eyes, then squeezes his hand shut around it.

He turns to Jillian. "Wedding's off, sweetheart. Sorry."

Big tears are rolling down Jillian's face, glittering drops that catch the evil red of this place within them. "I don't understand," she whispers.

"And I don't have time to explain. Got to run. Business to attend to." Huxley reaches into his breast pocket and takes out some bills that he throws at the officiant without even looking. His eyes are on his own clasped hand.

Behind me, the bead curtain shuffles again. And again.

That would be the other shoe falling. I should have known better. I *did* know better. I just didn't care.

When I turn around, I see four new guests, three men and a woman. None of them is dressed for the affair. They have the torn, stained, and hungry look of luck junkies gone too long without a fix.

"We had a deal, Huxley," I say flatly.

"And I upheld my end of things. The wedding is off. I'm not lifting a finger against you. Of course, what these fine folk do to you is none of my affair."

"Oh yeah? And I suppose they just happened by? Out on an evening stroll through the strip mall?"

Huxley shrugs. "I may have let slip that your ring there is quite a powerful totem imbued with a good deal of sorrow. The luck seems fond of it. I bet I could find a buyer for that piece quickly. And I may have mentioned that the one who brings me that ring will be supplied with enough quality luck to pleasantly bake their brain for eternity."

The junkies are already fanning out. One is a fat guy

with a keg for a chest, two are tall and rangy older men, and the woman is short and lean, with half her head shaved. She scares me the most. Her face is totally vacant.

"I'm *almost* positive they'll leave Jillian alone," says Huxley. "Ta-ta. Pleasure doing business with you."

He turns away from Jillian without another word and exits stage right, through a rusty fire door that closes heavily. I hear a rustling from outside, as of moving furniture. There'll be no out that way. Jillian holds out one sad, limp hand after him, which hurts me physically to see.

The officiant takes one look at the four arrivals now spread out evenly among the folding chairs, picks up the cash Huxley threw at him, and plucks his half-smoked cigarette from the ashtray on the podium. He books it down the aisle and out the front doors, leaving the stench of stale tobacco in his wake. The junkies don't even turn to watch him go.

I *really* should have left a note.

"What happened?" Jillian asks. "What is happening to me? Is any of this real?"

"It's real, all right." I back up the steps to where she stands, shaky on her feet. I turn toward her, hesitant to get near. The key around her neck, the awful blue stones in her ears, the blood-diamond bracelet, and that evil ribbon layered throughout her hair—she's as dangerous as the four junkies coming at us.

She tugs at the necklace like it's choking her. "Where did Hux go?"

"He left you," I say.

The junkies are closing in, hunting in a disconcertingly silent pack. I wonder if they made a promise to split the bounty.

"Why?" she asks.

I don't have a good answer for her right now, so I say the first thing that comes to my head.

"Because of me."

The accusing weight of her eyes falls on me. "Is this about those curses? I thought that was a dream. Is all this a dream?" The hope in her voice cuts me to the quick.

"No dream. Maybe you can still get out, though. They want me, not you. My ring."

She moves over to the podium and leans heavily on it, breathing quickly. The junkies follow her with their eyes, but they're wary. They see the poison on her as clearly as I can.

"Go for the front doors," I say. "They'll leave you alone."

"What about you?"

"Don't worry about me. Go for the front doors."

She looks back at me, indecision splitting her face, but she's so weak and pliant that she takes a step forward anyway.

The half-shaved woman pulls a butterfly knife from her waist and flicks it open with a flourish. The snap echoes in the unearthly silence. I hear the echoing click of a switch-blade from one of the rangy scarecrow brothers. They don't want to touch her, but they don't want to leave witnesses either.

"Wait, wait, wait," I say. "Hold up. Come back."

Jillian stumbles back up the stairs, her breathing shallow. She leans heavily on the podium. "All I have is bad luck."

"No such thing as bad luck. No such thing as good luck," I say, trying to channel Max as best I can. "There's just luck, period. It's about how you use what you got.

Huxley gave you those things because they corrupt the luck all around us. He's using them against you."

She shakes her head. "I don't ever want to hear about luck again," she says weakly and collapses into a silky, sitting heap. The luck junkies take the opportunity to tighten their hunting circle.

I know I should be doing something to defend against them, throwing something or picking one out to take down in the hope it might deter the others, maybe buying me some time. But I can't take my eyes off Jillian, the way she hangs her head, tears cutting down her cheeks. None of this is her fault. She doesn't deserve any of it. Her visible pain tugs at my heart, ripping open the scab there, and if any dust was nearby, it would gather to my ring, but this place is a barren wasteland.

*A bad place to die.*

Jillian looks at her limp hands nestled in the puff of silk at her lap. "All I wanted was to marry a man I loved. A man I first met when he sent me a glass of pink champagne across the bar. A man that once flew across the country to give me soup and crackers when I had the flu. Who used to carry me home on his back from late nights out when my feet hurt." Her voice gains strength as she speaks. "And now I'm getting none of that because of you and your goddamn luck!"

"He may have been that man once, but he's not anymore," I say. "He's spent too much time around things like that key, the earrings, that bracelet, and the ribbon in your hair."

She looks down at the key hanging around her neck then tugs at it. She looks at the fat man, now mere feet from us. His sleeveless tee is stained with tobacco juice, and he smiles hungrily around a big wad of chaw.

"You want this stupid necklace?" she asks, her voice rising in pitch. "Take it!"

She rips the key from her neck and throws it at the fat man, and his wicked smile falters. When the key hits him, he stumbles backward as if whipped and grunts as he sits heavily in a folding chair, staring meanly at where the necklace falls in the aisle.

A thought occurs to me—a half idea to use the poison Huxley gave her to turn the tables—that is instantly blown from my mind as I'm tackled low from behind by one of the scarecrow brothers. I fold over like a clipped marionette. Jillian screams somewhere right behind me. The man rolls over atop me and starts to choke me. I dig a knuckle right into his sternum with all the strength I have, and he backs off. I squirm out from under him only to be pinned by the second one, the bastard with the knife. He raises it high. I roll hard and connect with my elbow across his face. He's stunned enough that I can kick myself free even as the first scarecrow scrabbles at my ring finger, tearing at the webbing between my middle and pointer. I give him a full rollover slap in the face that knocks him off the dais altogether.

I kick back to where Jillian is trying to stand up, but the reams of silk and lace catch her heels, and she tumbles to the ground again, right next to the man with the knife. I crawl toward her, looking to pull her away from him, but the man practically leaps away all on his own. His fearful eyes flutter from her ears to her wrist.

The idea is back.

"The bracelet, Jillian! Give me the bracelet!"

She's shivering hard, looking at the scarecrow with terror in her eyes.

I clap my hands. "Hey! Wake up and look at me!"

She blinks like she's been spat at. Then she turns to me,

looks at her wrist as if it was something foreign to her, then rips at the blood diamonds. I expect it to break like in the movies, sending a cascade of stones down, but she can't seem to get the damn thing off. She works at the fine clasps with shaky hands as the scarecrows gather themselves again. One lunges at my neck while the other slams my left hand flat against the floor. The switchblade is in his teeth.

I try to scream for Jillian, my voice hoarse and strained. Reaching out to where I know she is, I slap the back of my free right hand on the floor, grasping at air. The world is closing down around me, turning foggy and black at the edges.

A cold, stinging lump falls into my free hand. Checking the urge to toss it like a snake, I pull my hand in under the dog pile instead. The man on top of me has his teeth clamped, his face is red and splotchy, and his loose skin is bunched up at his furry neck. Purple veins like earthworms pulse at his temples.

I shove the bracelet at his face.

He rears back instantly, opening his mouth, so I stuff it in. His eyes roll in fear, and he grabs at his face, screaming. The sound is jarring, the first real noise that comes from any of them. His brother is distracted from my ring for a moment, and I snap my left hand in to my body, taking a huge and wonderful breath. Before anyone can react, I reach up and snatch the bracelet from the man's gaping mouth, turn toward his scarecrow brother, and sock him in the face with my bejeweled fist. He rolls over like a log, and I scramble after him. I hit him solidly in the kidney twice before the sting is too much for me and I drop the bracelet. My hand feels like it's been whipped with a ruler, and I shake it out. Then, gritting my teeth, I pick up the bracelet again and sand the bastard's face with it for as long as I can stand the freezing touch, until his cries turn to whimpers and the dais rumbles under me.

The fat man Jillian hit with the key is back.

I roll over just in time to see him falling over on top of me like a building. He lands crosswise right over my upper half, and every ounce of air I have inside of me shoots right out my mouth.

I try to call for Jillian's help again, but my lips flap like a limp balloon. The fat man is grunting or laughing, and I feel as if I'm being ground into the floor. I try to move my arms, but I'm pinned tight. The dais groans like it's gonna collapse, which is all the same to me. I ain't getting up from this one. My vision is shutting down from top to bottom like a set of busted-up shades. He might as well plop the both of us right through the floor and into hell.

*Cause of death? Fat man.*

Then he screams and rears up like a hooked sailfish, and I roll out from under him just before he crashes down again. I heave air and blink my sight clear. Either the lack of oxygen is getting to me, or Jillian is riding this fat man like a horse with a bridle fashioned out of that rotten ribbon.

Her silk train is splayed out majestically behind her. The milky-white ribbon is looped around the fat man's neck. Underneath her, he stomps about like a horse spurred bloody.

She steps off him and guides him headfirst off the dais and into the folding chairs. He hits the concrete floor with a wet *thunk* and lies still.

The one scarecrow still conscious has pushed himself as far from the bracelet on the floor as possible, whimpering at the edge of the stage.

In the brief pause, Jillian and I just stare at each other.

"That was incredible," I say.

"I ride horses. Back home."

"Damn right, you do."

Our moment is ruined by the snap and swish of a butterfly knife licking the air. The short woman with the half-shaved head is walking down the aisle with the soft and sure steps of a thief. She holds the knife lightly out to one side like a magic wand, flipping it open and closed as she surveys the damage done to the other junkies.

She seems unimpressed.

She reaches the fat man and pauses, pulling a stained black kerchief from her back pocket. She gathers the ribbon inside the kerchief then does the same with the key neck-lace, which sits in the aisle. As she approaches, she also loots the scarecrow I kidney-punched unconscious with the blood diamonds, all with unsettling and practiced ease.

Jillian has a bit more pop to her, which I'd expect as she's shed three of the four wedding gifts Hux gave her. She unfastens the brackish-blue earrings. Smart woman. Mom always said if you ever get robbed, just give them whatever they want. Every *thing* is replaceable.

Except when that thing is a wedding ring, the only gift left on earth from the woman I loved. And it's how I can call the dust, which means it's the only real hope I have at staying alive in this town.

"I can't give you my ring," I say, breaking the strange, reptilian silence of her approach.

Her response is to spring forward.

I step between her and Jillian and try to keep my eye on the knife. One lucky kick would dislodge the thing, but luck has deserted this place. She feints a lunge straight at me but dips down and around my kick, raking the knife across my shin and plunging it into Jillian's dress.

Fabric rips, and Jillian screams. I flip around behind the

woman and pin her knife arm to her side, pulling her back from the folds of the gown. I wrap my other arm awkwardly around her face and try to pull her away from Jillian. The junkie barely weighs anything, but then my ring finger goes white hot with searing pain, and I scream.

She's trying to bite my ring off. I panic. If I let her go, she'll have room to use the knife. If I keep holding on, she's gonna take a chunk out of my finger with her gross teeth. It's like I'm holding a pot of boiling water in my bare hands, and it's searing my skin, but if I drop it, it'll drench Jillian.

I tell Jillian to run, but instead she limps right up to us, coming face-to-face with the cold fury of the junkie. She takes one blue earring and pops it past my wedding ring, right between the woman's teeth, and shoots it down her throat like an aspirin.

All the fight is snuffed from the junkie's body. I drop her and step away as she holds her throat, eyes bulging. She starts hacking, and I wonder if I'm actually going to have to perform the Heimlich on a woman that tried to bite my finger off, but no, she's not choking. She's sticking her own finger down her throat.

"Can you run?" I ask Jillian, looking at where she was stabbed. I expect to see a lurid seepage of red within the folds of white silk.

She presses carefully down where the knife went in and feels around the slash. Then she nods. "I'm okay. It's three layers of sculptured silk." She turns to the junkie heaving on the floor. "This is an Alexander McQueen, you bitch," she says, ripping the skirt of the dress lengthwise to free her bare legs. She takes the second earring from her ear and pegs it at her as she heaves. "You might as well have the full set."

We run out the doors and through the parking lot, over

trash and dirt and little chunks of concrete, across patches
of fine sand blown in from the desert and caught by the
abandoned parking lot. The moon is huge and creamy
white, and it bathes the streets in a ghost light.

"You got any money?" I ask, looking for a cab.

"I don't have anything. No phone, no purse. It's been a
weird day."

I hear the rumbling of a city bus coming from out of
town, our first bit of luck all night.

"C'mon." I take her hand as we cross the street. Good
ol' regular luck flows by our feet, heading to the strip. I
never thought I'd be so happy to see the stuff.

The bus pulls over, and the door pops open. The driver
takes a long look at the two of us as I hand him my return
ticket then count out just enough change to get Jillian a one-
way. I look back at the chapel and detect no movement
—yet.

We hurry to the back. The few passengers we pass don't
seem to want to meet my eye. We've become *those* people.
The door hisses shut. The bus jerks along.

I sink into the bench seat at the back, and Jillian sits
next to me. She drops my hand and pushes herself away,
against the window. She sits that way—in silence, just
looking out the window—all the way to her stop.

When the driver calls out the Diamond, she gets up and
pauses as she passes me. The corruption of Huxley's charms
is leaving her, bit by bit. Without their sources, the shards
are sloughing off. But silent tears have cut rivulets down her
cheeks.

She squeezes my shoulder. "Thank you for getting me
out of that place," she says. "I'm leaving. Don't take this the
wrong way, but I hope I never see you again."

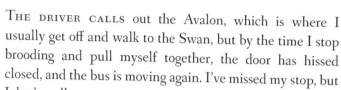

THE DRIVER CALLS out the Avalon, which is where I usually get off and walk to the Swan, but by the time I stop brooding and pull myself together, the door has hissed closed, and the bus is moving again. I've missed my stop, but I don't really care.

The faded digital clock above the driver reads fifteen past midnight. The next stop blinks several times on a display above the windshield then solidifies: Fremont Street.

The passengers riding along with me are dressed in livery, pressed shirts, short skirts, or fancy vests, with name tags on uniforms and glitter and makeup on tired faces. The evening shift is just getting off and riding home to the more affordable tenements and flats downtown—the working army of Las Vegas. Nobody talks. A few people sleep.

I lay my head back and close my eyes. I'm exhausted, but my body vibrates. I feel ants marching up and down my legs. Without the chip in my pocket, I feel even less substantial than normal. I'm not sure what I expected to happen after I gave it up. That Jillian might stick around? That we'd get to know each other? Become best friends and get married, and she could shuffle in and somehow fit perfectly in the Alli-shaped hole inside me? Foolishness, all of it.

The ride to Fremont is long. The dust snakes about the interior of the bus and whips by the windows outside—drips forming drops forming trickles forming streams. It looks like we're driving in a blizzard of gold, all of it shooting behind us, toward the heart of the Strip, where the Diamond sits.

My tether to this world seems tenuous, and my head is heavy with existential dread I can't quite define. Part of me wonders if I'm still somewhere in my mom's house back in Brooklyn, gone stark raving insane.

When we pull up at Fourteenth and Fremont, I'm eager to get out and feel the ground beneath my feet. I breathe deeply, smelling stale heat and gasoline, cigarette smoke and desert dust, and it somehow steadies my head a bit.

Vegas Vic waves at me in the distance. A neon wink. A shuffling cigarette.

I tuck my head down and put my hands in my pockets. Giving every casino a wide berth, I keep an eye out for luck junkies, spinners, anybody in the dust business. Nobody looks my way. My guess is those junkies on Huxley's payroll either got their due and are nodding off in some alley in a face full of the stuff, or they've moved on to easier scores than my ring.

The dust is acting odd, flowing away from sources in casinos and landmarks with speed. It tumbles along the sidewalks and gutters, spilling from rooftops and windows and merging to join into one stream that rushes along the streets. Down a block, Elvis is visible through the glass window of the Golden Gate. Dust streams from the King like snow blown from the summit of the Matterhorn.

I have the unsettling feeling of being on a river during a rising. I'd like to be done with dust for today, so I look for high ground. There, across the street, in an alcove underneath a loading dock, is a curious peace from the rush—an eddy where the dust swirls only lightly, barely there. The place seems to say, *"Move along. Nothing to see here."*

I cross the street.

Once under the dock, away from the lights and sounds, I see an old man completely unnoticeable from the street. He wears a faded mesh trucker's hat that reads Sin City and is dressed in a ratty cardigan with a zigzag print open over a bare and mostly hairless chest. Max is wearing the same old cargo shorts and the same taped-up flip-flops. He doesn't look up as I approach but just smokes his nub of a cigarette.

"Pick a card, any card," he says, stuttering a bit.

"I got nothing to wager, Max," I say, slumping down in a heap across from him.

Max pauses his card-over-card shuffling. "The ch-chip?"

"I had to give it up."

Max sucks the rest of his cigarette down with a sharp intake of breath then lets out a thin stream of smoke. He dabs the cherry out gently on the concrete and puts the butt in his front pocket.

"B-b-boy, I hope it was worth it."

I think of the way Jillian walked down that aisle, her body a hexed prison, part of her screaming to get out, another part helpless to stop herself.

"It was," I say.

Max chuckles and scratches behind his ear. "Easy for you to say. You don't know what you traded."

"Well, then, tell me."

Max flops out three well-used cards in a row. "Pick a card. No wager."

I'm in no mood for Max's games tonight. "Zja-Zja said it was some sort of key. But a key is no good without a door. And a girl might have died."

Max twitches back and forth for a moment in thought. "High price for *might have*," he says. "Pick a card."

Getting pissed, I snatch a card and flip it. The face is blank—nothing at all, a misprint. "What the hell is this?"

"Whatever you want it to be."

I'm not in the mood for this. My hand and my head hurt like a bitch. I stand and walk to the edge of his eddy to watch the roaring river of dust beyond. "What is going on with the luck flow?" I ask.

His eyes flicker as if he's trying to follow millions of individual specks within the rushing river. He looks at the dust longingly, not the way a junkie does. It's more like nostalgia. "Spinners' card game," he says, turning back to the card table with a snap. "Happens every year 'round this time."

"Game? What game?"

Max pats at his breast pockets, pulls out the nub of a cigarette, and frowns at it before putting it back. He idly calls a thin stream of dust into the alcove from beyond, teasing it with a finger until it weaves around him and through the pocket of the cardigan, then it snakes away again. He reaches into the same pocket and this time plucks an unsmoked cigarette from within, which he pops in his mouth and lights. His tarnished army Zippo shakes in his hands.

He exhales a thin stream of smoke and settles a little. "It's how they divvy the dust."

He leans down to the table and inspects the blank white face of the card I pulled as if the face was hidden somewhere. He scratches at it then sniffs.

"The luck spinners play a game for all the dust?"

"Spinners of the big houses do. It's how the rich get richer. The rest of us take what's left."

Max holds the blank card limply in one hand. His eyes are flickering again, following the river, stuck in a loop.

"Seems like a lot to risk on a card game." I say, loudly, to snap him out of it.

He taps out ash that isn't there. "This ain't a regular card game. It's one hand. Five-card stud."

"Well, that's even dumber. One hand?"

Another sliver of dust snakes through into our eddy and wreathes the blank-faced card in Max's hand, dancing like a charmed snake. He doesn't seem to notice.

"It's a long hand. The dust flies everywhere. The luck changes constantly, with every card dealt. More of a war than a card game, but instead of bullets, you get hit with luck. And you hit back."

Max scratches at the curly gray scruff on his neck with the edge of the card and pulls more dust in through his firewall. The card is fairly smoking with the stuff.

"That chip you lost is a ticket to the game. It gets you a seat at the table."

A few pieces of this great puzzle click together, settling to make a solid corner. No wonder Huxley wanted it. His buyer was probably some spinner looking for a shot at the dust.

I ache a little with the lost opportunity. A part of me that didn't exist a month ago wants to show up, kick some ass, and grab all the dust for the Swan. The rest of me knows I'm too green. More of a war than a card game? If I wanted to stay standing, I'd have to dive into that rift in my soul and see just how deep I could go—too deep, and I might not come back. The thought holds a sick appeal, like the edge of a cliff, where that tiny voice in your head urges you to jump. I shiver a little.

"Probably for the best," I say. "I'd get eaten alive at that table."

The weathered crow's-feet at the corners of his eyes give Max's smile a sly look. "That's what I thought too. Until I showed up."

"You?" I can't manage to keep the shock from my voice, thinking Max would be out of place in a McDonald's, much less a high-stakes poker game.

He snaps the old Zippo open and closed a few times. "I used to represent the little folks. Small shops on Fremont with a few slot machines in them. Saloons with one or two tables. Little poker parlors. Most of them here in downtown Vegas. Years ago. Was good at it too."

"Why'd you stop?"

Max spits on the ground. "A luck spinner named Jack Short came to town. He took over the card game. Started deciding who could sit at the table."

The card hanging limply in his hand is glowing like a golden coal now. Wisps of dust are leaking from his eyes. I scoot back a little.

"I was good. B-b-better than him, maybe. So he threw me out. Said I was a cheater."

"And are you?"

Max eyes me dangerously, dust smoking from him. Then he takes a deep breath and closes his eyes. His twitchy mouth settles into a calm smile, and his entire presence changes, from the way his shoulders relax to the stillness that settles over his limbs. When he opens his eyes again, the anger is gone, but the golden glint remains. The card he flicks in measured time between middle finger and thumb is almost too bright to look at.

"All I do is tell the cards what to be. Sometimes, the luck listens."

He flips the burning card onto the table, and as it hits the tabletop, its inner light is snuffed out like a match in the wind. It's not blank anymore. In fact, it's not even a playing card anymore.

It's a tarot card—the Tower.

"That's not possible," I say, pointing at it.

"Is what it is," he mumbles.

"How? How can you do that?"

Max yawns hugely. His demonstration seems to have taken something out of him. "I think about my granddaughter," he says, smiling distantly.

The kind of trauma he must have tied to that memory, the sheer size of the wound within to be able to call on the dust like that—not just to change the way a thing acts, like the other spinners, but to change the way a thing *is*... His pain must be horrendous.

"What happened to her?" I ask, not sure I want to hear.

Max looks at me strangely. "Happened to her? Nothing. She lives in Indiana. Just got married. She always liked me." He smiles again.

"But... but that's not how it works."

"You tellin' me how it works now?"

I get a good look at his old army Zippo as he shuffles it around the table. On one side, it says:

VIETNAM 72-75
SAIGON
WHY ME?

The letters look hand gouged from the burnished steel. On the other side is a crooked peace sign. I try to feel it out for luck power within, but it looks like nothing more than a lump of metal and a wick to me.

He plucks it up and looks at it fondly before tucking it away in his pants. *Strange.* I'm no history major, but I know if you lived through Saigon in '75, you probably don't remember it fondly.

"Is your lighter like my wedding ring? I can't see a speck of dust on it."

"Like I said, I don't work like that no more." He pauses to look carefully at my wedding ring, and his fond look sours

as surely as if he'd come across a dead bird on the sidewalk.
"Time for me to go to sleep," he adds, as if that were the
natural progression of the conversation.

He tucks the cards carefully into his ratty front pocket
and collapses the card table in a single motion. He leans it
against the concrete and seems to lose his train of thought
while rooting around in his bulging backpack before he
finds what he's looking for: trash cigarettes.

"You know, I can get you a pack," I say. "Put it on my
tab at the Swan."

He grunts, shouldering the pack, then wobbles a bit. He
pops in one stubby and somehow lights it up. "These are
better."

"Bye, I guess?"

"You should go to that c-c-card game," he stammers. "I
hear tell of a second spinner doing a stint at the Diamond. A
woman that Jack is training up. She came into town a few
months ago."

My world momentarily goes out of focus, turns upside
down for a second, then rights itself. I have to hold myself to
the concrete I'm sitting on. "No."

Max looks like he's already lost interest. His cigarette
butt hangs limply from chapped lips. He looks up the street,
then down, like he's lost.

"There's no way."

Max takes a few steps in one direction then reconsiders.
"I just say what I hear."

"When's this card game?" I ask, my mind racing.

"Tomorrow night. Sunset," he says, passing me while
going the other way.

The full magnitude of what I had and what I lost is
slowly dawning on me, like a flower that blooms overnight.
Mom gave me the way to find her. I was just too wrapped

up in this new world to see it for what it was, too wrapped up in Jillian...

Hot shame courses through me, both for the way I let Jillian get to me, and for the way I'm not altogether sure I wouldn't still give Huxley that chip again, even knowing what I know now.

"I gotta get a seat at that table," I say.

"You can't get a s-seat without the chip. You won't make it through the f-front doors. They'll k-k-kill you," Max says the last in a stuttering singsong.

"Then I gotta get a chip." But even as I speak, I know how impossible that is. I traded away my chance—not just to find my mom but to put the Golden Swan back in the mix, to keep the Parlor of the Eye open and keep all the ladies with odd granny names serving drinks... and to save what's left of Eddie's fingernails.

Max pats himself down as he walks away. He stops when he finds that Zippo. It seems to have somehow migrated to his breast pocket though I swear he put it in his pants.

"You know what I do whenever I don't know what to do?" he asks, just walking away as he smokes.

"What?" I ask. My voice cracks.

"I check my pockets," he calls back.

For half a second, I think the crazy old man managed to magic a chip into my pocket without touching me. He can change the face of playing cards, after all. Hell, he can change the cards themselves. Why not?

I check my pockets. No chip. Of course. I've got nothing left. I spent my last red cent on that bus pass for Jillian. Ain't nothing in my pockets but lint. And Berto's card, blunted at the edges and creased down the middle.

Memories march unbidden to the front of my mind—

Berto's words as he handed it to me on that first day, a hundred years ago now: *"If you need anything, give me a call,"* then Zja-Zja saying, *"I'd hold on to it. Use it when you need it."*

I look around for a payphone. If there ever was a place for a payphone—even the last one in all of Vegas—it would be here somewhere on Fremont. This was a dirty payphone type of place.

Sure enough, I see one tacked on to the side of a shuttered bodega down the street, on my side of the river. The phone is in an open booth with scratched and graffitied plexiglass on either side and the brick around it whiffs of urine. I pick up the phone and set it down twice, adding my greasy fingerprints to the mix, but on the third time I dial the number collect. The phone rings once before it's picked up.

"Girls direct to you!" says the voice on the other end, a woman with a Hispanic accent. Her enthusiasm sounds forced. "What girl do *you* want?"

"This is Lee, calling for Berto," I say quickly. A recording from the operator asks if they'll accept charges.

A pause on the other end. "No." She hangs up.

I stand there, looking at the phone. I check the card—number's the same. Maybe I had Berto all wrong. I step out and back into the full force of the night. Walk slowly back toward the spot Max vacated.

Whatever voodoo he did with the dust to create his quiet little corner is wearing off. The rushing river of luck is slowly but surely eroding whatever peace this corner had to offer. Swirling dust laps up against my shoes. I wonder what it might be like to just give in to the stuff, to rip open the wound in my heart and dive into the beautiful pain of that memory, to let it consume me, just taking in as much of the stuff as I could.

Zja-Zja said that would cauterize me from the inside out. But maybe that's not so bad. I'd walk around like the junkies, too gone to do much but fight for more dust. At least I'd burn out this sense of loss that won't leave me alone.

I stick my foot farther out into the rush. It plucks at my shoelace like nipping minnows.

The phone back in the booth rings. A jarring, jangling sound from another era that shakes me back to the moment. I run back to the booth, slam against the phone as my momentum carries me. I fumble with it as I pick up. "Hello?"

"*Quien es este?*" The voice is male, harsh and guttural.

"Berto?" I ask hopefully. "It's Lee."

The sharp edge drops as quickly as a bubble pops. "Lee! *Bueno*! I was hoping it was you, my man."

I'm a little embarrassed at how good it feels to hear his voice, the opposite of the dark pull of the river rushing in front of me. "I thought you might have given me a fake number or something."

"No, no. I just gotta be careful these days. The people that run this shop don't really know about my side hustle in the luck game. I try to keep it that way. Carmen and I are tight, though. She answers the phones. If someone asks for me by name, she gets me the number."

"How's your gut?" I ask.

"All stitched up. Itches like a dog, but that's about it. In a week, it'll be like it never happened. Thanks to you. That was some badass magic you pulled."

"I got lucky," I say.

Berto laughs then cuts it short, sucking in a breath of air with a hiss. "Still a bit sore. But how are you? You all right?"

"Not really," I say. "I traded something away that maybe I shouldn't have."

"The chip," he says gravely.

"You know?"

"I saw it on you in the alley. Didn't understand it at first. Weird dust on that thing. Then a bounty went out with big money for the right kind of dollar Diamond chip. I was worried for you, my man."

"I fucked up," I say. Then I think of Jillian. "Maybe."

"Who'd you give it to?" he asks.

"A guy named Huxley Betancourt."

Berto sucks air through his teeth again but probably not because of lingering gut pain. "He's bad news, my man."

"I know. I'm kind of in a bad way. I need your help. I gotta get that chip back."

The pause on the line seems to stretch forever.

"Give me an hour," he says. "I'll see what I can do."

# CHAPTER EIGHT

The Crazy Asian is an all-night Chinese buffet nestled between a pawn shop and a weed dispensary a few blocks off Fremont. Just past midnight, the Crazy Asian is doing a brisk trade in fifty-cent scoops of food. I'm loitering outside, toeing a discarded scratch ticket—not a winner—and waiting for Berto to show up.

By this time tomorrow, the spinners' card game will be over one way or the other. I think of myself transported to that time and wonder what it looks like for me. Either I'll know what happened to Mom, or if I miss my shot, I'll never get a chance to sit at that table again.

The Swan will probably fold. I'll fail on all fronts.

I'll have failed Alli most of all. What would she think of me now, plunging headfirst into a deadly world of golden dust so that I can make some sense of the shitty luck that severed her from me forever? Would she be proud of me? Tell me to get over myself? I'll never know.

I obsess over that horrible memory because it's the last one I'll ever have of her. It's the last hard truth. But every time I fall into it again, it seems less and less like it's mine and more and more gilded with the slippery golden power of the dust.

One thing's for sure: I'm not the man she married anymore.

Berto taps me on the shoulder from a million miles away.

"*Que pasa, jefe?* You look like you got beat with the Vegas stick," he says.

He wears faded jeans and work boots with the laces trailing on the ground. His reflective vest is flopped over his shoulder. A few tiny drops of red blood on his crisp white T-shirt are the only signs of the knife wound. Anybody not searching would miss them.

He smiles at me, and I can't help but smile back. I size him up.

"What? You were expecting a ghost?" he asks.

"Your shoelaces are untied."

"Yeah, still kind of hard to bend down. The far stitch likes to pop."

I kneel and lace up his boots over his half-hearted protests.

When I stand, he laughs. "You're the craziest luck spinner I ever knew. I really hope you stay alive a while."

"That makes two of us, I guess."

"Gonna be hard, once you hear what I got to tell you." He nods toward the front door of the Crazy Asian. "But first, eat. This is the best shitty Chinese food in town. On me."

"How many scoops do I get? Just trying to plan my attack."

"I'm a generous man, *vato*. Three scoops today. After all, this might be your last meal."

The Crazy Asian buffet winds all along the walls and

covers every sort of Asian cuisine there is. The steam wafting from woks and pots fogs the windows, combining to smell not unpleasantly like a campfire cookout. An old man at the door bows and hands us each a standard elementary-school lunch tray with wax paper on the bottom. I walk along and point at the Szechuan beef and General Tso's chicken, along with some fluffy fried rice. The line cook plops all three right on the tray in perfect half spheres.

We set our trays down at one of the only open tables. I'm eager for whatever news Berto has for me, but first things first: I'm starving. And the food is really good. The sauces taste fresh, and the veggies snap, a minor miracle when it comes to buffet food. When I come up to breathe, Berto is waiting patiently, pushing his own food around.

I take a deep breath. "All right. Out with it. How dead am I?"

"Depends. You sure you want this chip?"

"Very sure."

"Then you're pretty dead. My people asked their people. Found Huxley's buyer."

"And?"

"And it's Jasper Jones."

I set my fork down.

"Look, *ese*," he says, leveling his gaze at me. "I heard about this spinners' card game. It can get ugly. Maybe you take it one step at a time, eh? Try to get a chip next year, when you maybe know what you're doing?"

I snort, even though I'm pretty sure that wasn't a joke. "The Swan ain't gonna be around next year. There's more staff than guests at that place."

"You don't know that," Berto says, even though his eyes tell me he knows it just as well as I do. "Maybe Eddie's got one last trick up his sleeve—"

"My mother is gonna be at that card game, Berto."

Berto sits back and takes a slow sip of cola from a red plastic cup that makes me think of when Mom used to take me to the pizza place down the block as a kid. Greasy fingers on arcade games. Sugar highs and cups full of quarters. Simpler times.

"You're gonna have to be quick," Berto says. "In, up to the tower, and out again in five minutes."

"The tower?"

"That's where Jasper lives. That tower that sticks out from the top of the castle."

I'm picturing the tarot card and the sad resignation on the faces of the poor saps plunging down in flames.

"You having second thoughts, *compadre*?" Berto asks.

"Every second of my life."

Berto chuckles. He snatches a pen from the table next to us and pulls a few napkins from the dispenser. "These days, Jasper is almost always up in the tower, but he makes rounds on the casino floor once every hour. They take five minutes. Maybe ten, tops."

He sketches out a crude overhead map of the casino floor and puts the salt shaker on the side nearest me. "Here's the front of Avalon." He draws a dotted line in and around to the right. "Stay to the right wall of the casino floor." The dotted line keeps going. "Hallway here. Goes right through the cages." As I clear my throat, Berto keeps dotting the line, then he stops and draws a small box. "This is the Shattered Shield, Avalon's main bar. In back is a tall door made of fake stone." He taps the napkin. "Through the door is the staircase to Jasper's tower."

"So around the casino, through the cages, behind the bar, and up the tower. No problem," I say shakily.

"Five minutes."

"What if the chip's not up there? What if it's on him?"

"It's not on him. I watched him make his walk half an hour ago. I'd have seen the dust that chip makes." He checks his watch. "You got twenty minutes until he rounds again."

The enormity of what I'm about to do hits me in the silence that falls between us. I'm not sure what I expected— that I'd have a few nights to mull this all over? That I'd be able to create a nice pros-and-cons list? Not in this town. In this town, it's always now or never.

I rap lightly on the table with my knuckles. "Okay, then."

Berto stands, and I follow.

"I'll take you to the Avalon," he says. "From there, it's up to you. I know this might sound strange coming from an ex-junkie that still fights it every day, but if I was you, I'd load up on luck. You're gonna need it."

BERTO'S old truck paints the air with exhaust as it rolls away. I move quickly down the sidewalk to one of the benches out of the crowd, where I sit and gather myself. In front of me, a thin line of people crosses the illuminated drawbridge toward the Avalon. The animatronic dragon perched above the entrance gate belches fire high into the sky and gets a cheer. I rub my hands together and take a few deep breaths to calm my nerves. I'm doing my best not to puke between my shoes.

The luck isn't hard to find. A solid stream of gold dust flows down the middle of the sidewalk, away from the Avalon and away from the Golden Swan nearby. It's pouring away from everywhere and right to the Diamond in preparation for tomorrow night. Easy enough to tap into

—it's doing it without killing myself that's the bigger problem.

Berto's parting words stick with me. To hear a street-smart guy like him say he fights every day to stay away from this stuff reminds me that I'm playing with some serious fire. And I may have to get a little crispy if I want to bank enough luck to get me through the Avalon and to the chip.

I check my watch—five minutes until Jasper starts his rounds. Berto says he moves counterclockwise, back to front. I just have to do the same, front to back. Theoretically, we'll never cross paths.

I close my eyes.

I fall all too easily into my memory, letting myself breathe in the smell of her hair as she settles one hand over mine. I can remember her lipstick, the taste of it, and her laugh as she settles back in her seat. I remember that she hummed a few bars of our song, "Into the Mystic," by Van Morrison. She always hummed when she was happiest.

Each aspect of the scene paints itself vividly in my mind's eye, like an artist going over a painting again and again until the colors are dripping. The cost of remembering is splitting the scar inside me stitch by stitch, but I don't care. I don't mind the pain. The longing is comforting.

More facets of the moment come to me, the way the tiny stones from her wedding ring bite softly into my palm as she holds my hand across the back seat. The ring itself was too big. She was terrified she'd lose it, so she turned it inward and balled her hand tightly all night long. She never let go until that moment that cut her from me forever.

The terrible snap of metal. The pop of glass. The feel of the stone tearing at my palm as her hand is ripped from mine.

I suck in a ragged breath. I've gone too far. Opening my

eyes, I shoot up from the bench, but the dust follows me. A vein of dust the size of my forearm splits from the torrent running down the street and barrels into me, pouring over the slice I carved out of myself.

The sorrow is pummeled down deep within me, somewhere I can no longer feel. The dust warms me, locking the pain inside and muffling it like a velvet blanket over a birdcage.

Then, abruptly, things change. The velvet blanket is smothering me. I can't catch a breath. Each time I try, the dust pours in. I'm choking, drowning. I try to pull back, but I'm tumbled under again, spinning and spinning, pressed to my knees on the sidewalk under a wave much larger than I thought.

I remember the spin cycle, the dryer Lady Chang threw me in. I need something to bring me out of this, some shock to my system.

I slam my bad shoulder into the corner of the bench and feel it slip just a bit, like a bowl full of burning-hot soup slopping slightly over the edge. The pain sears me, clearing my head enough to bring me back to the present. I try to push the door to that day closed by thinking of other things: the way my mom watched me as I played arcade games, the first sweet sip from that red cup of soda, falling asleep to old episodes of *The Twilight Zone* when I was ten. One time, I woke up for just a moment to find Mom carrying me up to my bed.

The door closes.

When I open my eyes, everything around me is glittering, my wedding ring most of all, as if it's liquid gold spinning round and round my finger, dripping dust like water. I'm up to my eyeballs in luck.

I feel unstoppable and strangely distant, soft and floaty.

I have no hard edges anywhere, no uncertainty. The world around me has lost all its teeth. I can see the way forward with a laughable clarity.

Time to roll.

I cross the drawbridge at a slow, sure pace, weaving in and out of pockets of tourists as I go. At the front door stand two security guards cleverly disguised in medieval livery, shields on their backs and swords at their sides. They take smiling pictures with the guests, but I doubt they'd be happy to see me.

I'm not worried.

As I approach the guards, they both glance my way at the same time. I think how lucky it would be if the dragon's breath got a little too close for comfort, and as I do, a thin stream of dust floats off from my ring, as if carrying my thoughts away.

One guard squints at me. Something snaps in the dragon's head, and the rig around it drops just a touch lower. A quick glance shows its jaws wreathed in dust, my dust.

The guard moves toward me, but as his first step falls, the dragon belches the most enormous fireball I've ever seen right across the bow of the drawbridge, mere feet from the heads of the tourists passing by—high enough to spare us from harm but low enough to scare the hell out of everybody... except me.

The heat is tremendous, and the guards are mobbed by people looking for cover. They lose sight of me. Maybe they never really had sight of me to begin with.

Either way, I pass through the gate and into the Avalon without stopping. Then I press the timer on my watch, and the countdown begins.

The casino floor of the Avalon is huge—three, maybe four times as big as the Golden Swan. The foot traffic here is better than the Swan, for sure, but not enough to fill all this space. The table games in the center are lively, but I see entire rooms of empty slot machines and pockets of the floor where nobody's within chatting distance.

The central attraction is an impressive two-story waterfall thundering into a misty pool. A gleaming sword juts from an outcropping of boulders in the middle. The sword is lit from above by a single, piercing beam of white light while all around it, red and blue lights play off the rippling water and tinge the mist to dramatic effect.

People snap selfies and take group pictures by the water. I wonder how many drunken tourists have tried to christen themselves the next rightful King of All England right here in this pool. The dust likes the sword too. In fact, a thin layer of shimmering gold luck floats atop the roiling mist above the entire pool—more dust right here than the Swan has across our entire casino.

Jasper knows what he's doing.

I keep the wall to my right as I walk. Up close, the pageantry and pomp of the décor fade. The walls are slightly scuffed at shoe level. The shield prints on the glass dividers are peeling here and there, and the drywall is chipped in spots. The carpet is well trodden. I'm not one to judge, mind you, but the Swan is fading a bit more gracefully, like an aging movie star. This place has a run-down-theme-park feel.

A pit boss is coming my way but hasn't spotted me yet. Probably just getting off work, he looks like he's counting tips, but we're on a crash course. As he approaches, I gently wave a thin layer of dust along the folded stack of bills in his hand. He pauses, confused, does some figuring on his fingers, and starts to recount the cash. I slip by on his left, and he never looks up.

I'm not sure if the cocktail waitresses are on the lookout for spinners as well, but I'm not taking any chances. I redirect one toward the craps table as a rowdy group of college boys cheer loudly at just the right time. Another seems unavoidable until I give a bottle of beer on her tray a tiny tug with a strand of luck, tipping it over. She mutters a curse and turns back toward the bar.

I come upon the casino cages thirty seconds in. Four cashiers sit at stations cut out between wide bars, swapping chips for cash and looking bored. To my right is the hallway Berto told me about. Well-lit and looking sterile, it runs behind the cages. A beefy security guard stands right in the middle of it, arms crossed.

This is gonna take more than some parlor tricks to get past. With no better plan, I settle in line with other gamblers looking to cash out. *Forty-five seconds in.*

I'm waiting for something. Not sure what yet—but it's coming. I can feel it.

*One minute gone.*

It occurs to me that for something to happen, I might have to use a fair bit of luck.

I close my eyes and let out a slow breath, loosening my grip on the luck a bit and letting it trickle like sand into some unseen wind, scattering however it will. It blows in the direction of a young guy swaggering up to the cages with a rack of chips in his hands. At least, I think he's young. And a man. I can't tell for sure. He wears a hoodie and dark sunglasses like I've seen the pro poker players wear on TV. He's bopping along to the music piping into his head through earphones, completely boxed in to his own world and totally unaware of the tightening electrical cord of a marble-buffing machine on his left.

I can see it before it happens.

The janitor reaches for that tricky corner spot with his whirling buffer. The cord snaps tight right between the hoodie-man's feet. He can't see it, having sacrificed peripheral vision for the goofy Unabomber look. He takes a swaggering step toward the cages, catches his toe, does a little tightrope balancing act on one foot, then pitches forward.

The full rack flies from his hands, and the chips make a splashy constellation in midair before all of them tumble to the ground in a cacophony that sounds a bit like bowling a strike. He follows close behind, sliding along the floor on a wave of his own winnings until his back thumps the cages.

During a split second of stillness, I catch the wasn't-me look of the janitor as the floor buffer winds itself down. Then everybody moves to help him at once. Some strangers reach to pick him up by the arms, while others grab chips then set them in little piles on the floor, unsure if they should touch them. Others pile them haphazardly in the empty rack. Nobody is stealing anything, but the cage boss steps in nonetheless and firmly tells everyone to back up.

*Now's my chance.* I step calmly out of line and take a right turn down the hallway. Nobody says a thing to me as I pass behind the four cashiers and get the odd sensation of watching a TV show where the camera flips back on the audience. I loose a shimmering stream of dust behind me like I'm tossing spilled salt over my shoulder. The luck floats out in a cloud, fogging the frog-eye cameras in the corners. If anyone is behind the security desk, my guess is they're looking elsewhere for the moment.

I push open the heavy swinging doors to the kitchen. Inside is a flurry of activity: line cooks pulling orders off the ticket queue and whipping up the kind of food you'd find at a Renaissance fair—sizzling turkey legs, deboned birds rotating on spits, meats-on-a-stick, fried foods of every kind. The smell reminds me of a tailgate.

A fat man in a pristine white frock coat that says Ye Olde Chef looks at me questioningly. I grab a trash can at my side, pull out the bag, spin it and knot it then heft it over my shoulder. For good measure, I carry the empty can at my side.

The chef looks back down at the duck he's deboning. Nobody messes with the guy taking out the trash.

Through the kitchen, behind the dumbwaiter for the Shattered Shield pub, is the base of the tower. It sticks out like the rounded wall of a grain silo. The door at the base is tall and thin. No Entry is stenciled across in medieval lettering. A big metal doorknob sits front and center. I'm too afraid to try it. It's probably locked.

However, I can't be *sure* it's locked.

Come to think of it, it's only locked if I try it and it doesn't open. Right now, it's just as open as it is locked.

I set the trash down inconspicuously in the corner and puff a big cloud of dust at the door. I feel my reserves draining, and the first whiff of a hangover, which I'm sure will be both physically and existentially debilitating, is prowling at the edges of my mind, but that's a problem for Tomorrow Lee.

Today Lee has two minutes to get in and out of this tower with the chip.

I reach for the knob, and it turns freely. I push the door open and slip inside, closing it softly behind me. I almost laugh aloud upon seeing a set of keys dangling from the interior lock. Jasper must have had other things on his mind when he set out for his rounds. I've made that airhead move a hundred times in my life, usually coming back from a few after-shift drinks at the bar.

I grab the keys and sprint up the spiral stairs. Electric sconces spaced every ten or so steps illuminate the way up with a soft light. A purple runner carpet bolted to the center of the stairway muffles my feet. Thirty seconds later, I'm at the top of the tower. A tall, thin door is all that stands between me and the luck spinner's quarters now. It's locked but opens easily with a turn of Jasper's forgotten keys.

I push the door wide but stay in the small foyer. I feel like anyone within a thousand feet could hear the hammering of my heart and the whistle of blood flying through my veins. But nobody is within a thousand feet. Jasper's quarters are empty for the next—I check my watch—minute and a half, tops.

One minute to find the chip. Half a minute to get the hell out of here.

I'm not sure what I expected to find at the top of this tower. Maybe a huge four-poster bed with an elaborate silk canopy. Golden goblets of wine. Perhaps an oil portrait of the man himself hanging upon the wall with a dour-looking hound.

Instead, Jasper's rooms are sparse and neat. A dark, circular rug lies in the center. A wooden writing desk left of center smells faintly of polish and is clear of everything but a pen and single blank sheet of paper. Pushed against one curved wall is a twin bed, tightly made, that looks way too small for him. Nothing is on the walls but the windows, two on opposite ends that open upon a breathtaking view of Vegas from on high.

Dust swirls peacefully around the inside of the tower in a gentle counterclockwise motion like the settling of a snow globe—too much dust to follow any one strand or trail that might lead me to the chip. The glittering view, both inside and out, is mesmerizing.

I snap myself out of the stupor with a jerk. *No time for sightseeing.* I check the desk first. The single center drawer slides out easily. I flick through a stack of stationery with a thin double *J* embossed in striking gold embossing. More pens. Some stamps. The chip isn't here.

I close the drawer and drum my fingers on the top of the desk. The window above Jasper's bed is drawing me. To be able to look out on everything, while nobody can look in... What a strange sense of security. And the bed itself is so neat and tidy—everything in its place.

Except for his pillow.

You could bounce a quarter off the bed, but the pillow is offset and dimpled, as if recently squeezed.

I lift it with a single finger. The chip underneath glows with the strange inner light of a diamond, sharp and cold among the soft gold of the dust. Relief falls over me like a physical thing as I pick it up with trembling fingers.

"What are you doing here?"

I freeze at the sound of Jasper's voice—not shocked or angry but low and dangerous, the growl of a large cat.

I turn slowly to find him in the doorway, an iron post of a man. Standing tall and looking immovable, he wears dark slacks and a dark jacket with a high, pointed collar. The fingers of his left hand twirl the air absently at his side. His right hand is buried in his pocket, where I'm sure he's priming that spoon.

Already, the dust is flocking to him. And why not? This is the heart of his territory. If luck can belong to anyone, this luck belongs to him.

"What are *you* doing here?" I reply.

"This is my room."

"But you're not supposed to be back for another solid minute."

His eyes narrow. I should probably shut up. Every time I say something to this man, it seems to make him hate me more, no matter the words.

"I forgot my keys," he says quietly. "And I never forget my keys. Ever."

He takes a step inside. The dust follows him with a bit of a swishing delay, like a golden cape.

"And halfway through my rounds, it occurred to me that the only reason I would ever forget my keys was if someone tampered with the flow of luck in my casino."

Another step.

"And here you are," he says.

"Here I am," I reply grimly.

"I can't help but notice that you aren't putting the chip back," says Jasper.

A gathering of luck as thick as a tow rope snakes around his body and down his free arm. The tiny movements of his fingers are fashioning it into the links of a chain.

I've got enough of the dust in myself to flatten my panic. The logic in my brain cuts through with one certainty: he'll try to hurt me, no matter what I do with the chip.

So I pocket it. It feels good there. I smile. "It's my chip."

Jasper turns his lip in disgust, baring sharp, tea-stained teeth. "You gave it up of your own free will."

"I had no choice. I did what any decent human would have done to save her."

"You were a fool in love," he says, his voice so low and guttural I feel like it's shaking the windows. "A lesson for you: as soon as a luck spinner falls in love, he's dead."

A flick of his finger sends the whirling chain of luck slicing through the air toward me. I guess its path in an instant and plunge my left hand into the dust surrounding me, smearing it like a child's finger painting in the air in front of me. My ring glows brightly, gelling enough of the stuff to form a free-floating wall as thin as a hair.

*Sloppy but effective.* The chain shears in half on my makeshift shield. A blow that would have knocked me senseless only makes me stumble over my own feet instead.

Backward. Toward the window.

The glass panes rumble, chattering as if a helicopter is passing just overhead. Jasper gathers the chain around himself once more while setting the rest of the dust spinning faster around us, pressing it back against the curved walls of the tower. A pressure is pushing me back like a Tilt-A-Whirl gathering speed.

I chance a look outside. It's a hell of a long drop, and I'm not sure there's enough luck in Vegas to save me if I get tossed out.

In the moment I'm distracted, Jasper fires his chain. I barely have time to smear a deflection before it hits, punches through my shield, and buries into my chest. Most of my own luck reserves are snuffed out in an instant, and the exhaustion I've kept at bay, the million tiny points of pain, are suddenly realer than ever.

I stagger back into the window, and the glass groans under my weight. A spiderweb of cracks appears as I push myself off and fall forward to the ground.

Watching me coldly, Jasper flares his fingers, and the spinning dust pushes farther outward. The window chatters again then shatters into glittering shards that are sucked out into the night.

Jasper swings his chain at me again, and this time I don't have the luck to block any of it. I hold my arms out weakly over my face, as if that will help, and brace for the blow to land. When it doesn't, I open my eyes. The chain is stopped inches from my face, pulled thin and amorphous until it, too, is sucked out of the window.

Jasper curses. This was no mercy on his part. In an instant, he's gathered another chain and sets it spinning.

I stand with my back to the open window, so close to oblivion that the wind plucks at my shirt, drying the sweat on my back.

A flick of Jasper's finger shoots his new chain like a javelin. I shift a foot to the left and feel the numbing pain of the dust like breath on my neck, inches from my throat. Jasper tries to whip it sideways into me, but the chain is pulled thin again, sucked out the window and down. It sails into the night, down and away until it plunges into the raging river of dust below. All of it is leaving the Avalon, headed to the Diamond.

Jasper grits his teeth and glares coldly at me and at the river below in equal turn. He takes a huge breath, his chest expanding like a bellows. The spinning dust presses harder at the edges of his tower, blanketing me. I stagger to the ground like I've run a marathon, my limbs impossibly heavy.

I feel another shudder, but this time, the tower itself is shaking. The movement is slight but enough to drop my stomach to my toes. Jasper doesn't seem to notice as his eyes glitter with hate.

"You try to steal from me? From *me*? You're just like them!"

He's talking to me but looking at the river ferrying his luck away, gallon by gallon.

"Jasper, wait! The tower!"

He rises to his full height. The wind reverses course through the window, as if he's sucking it into himself. He takes his right hand from his jacket pocket, and for a moment, I can't see anything there. Maybe the spoon is a lie.

In the raging wind, I blink away tears and look closer. *There —it's so small.* He holds its bowl between his ring and middle fingers. The handle is maybe three inches long, hanging below his palm—all this power in something the size of a golf tee.

"The tarot card!" I yell.

I know he hears me. He just doesn't care.

He lets out a prehistoric roar and pushes the dust out in a wave that shatters the other window. The floor drops an inch or two with a heavy cracking sound like the break in a billiards game.

He heaves, blowing air out his nose like a bull, and in a half moment of jagged quiet, I plead with him, the words tumbling out of me.

"The Tower. This is Zja-Zja's Tower. We're in it together. You'll kill us both."

He looks lost for a moment, almost scared. But then his face falls into a cruel sneer again.

"So be it."

He steeples his hands, the spoon between them, then pulls them apart. The chain grows in the space between, lighting the spoon with a golden fire almost too bright to look at.

"'So be it'? That's it? *So be it*, and we're dead?"

Jasper watches his spinning craft as if mesmerized by the deadly game of cat's cradle.

"There is no running from her cards," he says. "I've tried. But the Eye is always right. In the end."

One of Jasper's pens rolls off the table to the floor, spinning over and over itself, past me and out the open window. The tilt is getting worse.

"What are you doing?" I ask.

The empty document box falls next. The bed groans

then shifts slightly. The tower feels like a slowly keeling boat.

"I'm getting it over with," Jasper says.

"No," I say flatly, words tumbling out. "I have to see my mom again." I'm not sure why I say them, but I know they're true.

Jasper's spin work pauses.

"If I'm gonna die, fine. If it's with you, more's the better. But I don't wanna die without seeing my mom one more time."

The angry brilliance of the dust between his palms fades, and the gusting wind outside dies with it. Whatever I'm doing seems to be working, so I keep talking.

"I have to know, man. I gotta know why she's here. Why she's at the Diamond. Why she never told me about any of this."

A rumble from deep within Jasper. "I have some questions of my own," he says.

"I'll find out whatever I can for you," I offer, desperately. "But I can't give you the chip. I gotta go myself."

Jasper huffs with something very close to laughter. "The chip," he says thoughtfully, pocketing his spoon. The half-formed chain drops from his free hand to the ground in a glittering shower of sand. He reaches into his breast pocket and pulls something forth.

A chip.

In a panic, I reach into my pocket and grab my chip. *Still there.* I pull it out and check it. Still glowing with cold fire, it's identical to the one Jasper holds.

"I have my own chip," Jasper says.

"Are two better than one?"

Jasper shakes his head. "The chip is a key to get in. You only need one key."

"Then why take mine? You paid Huxley a fortune."

"I did it as a favor."

The dust is settling, and I find I can breathe normally again. I scramble to my feet, which Jasper allows.

"A favor? For whom?"

He looks at me carefully, seeming to actually see me for the first time. "For your mother," he says.

His words numb me, and I drop the chip in my hand. It bounces and rolls, heading for the open window. I can't even muster the energy to chase it.

Jasper steps on it and snaps it flat.

"That can't be right," I say. "She gave me the chip in the first place."

Jasper nods. "She did. And then she begged me to take it back from you."

"But why?"

Jasper kneels and plucks my chip from the ground. He studies it, face drawn. "She said she'd made a terrible mistake."

I don't know what to think. I feel sick with exhaustion, drained from the dust. I can barely keep my feet under myself, with the tilt of the tower. I might pass out. "A terrible mistake?"

"She didn't elaborate. Neither will I."

The weight of Jasper's words settles heavily upon me, a suffocating pressure not unlike the smothering of the dust moments before, but deeper, on my heart and my soul.

"She doesn't want to see me," I say. My voice doesn't sound like my own.

"It would appear that way."

Jasper's flat baritone brings me back. I look up at him, at his thinly veiled disgust, and I muster the only thing I have left in the tank: anger.

"And I suppose you would know? Who the hell are you, anyway? Aside from an asshole hermit who shuts himself away in a castle tower when he's not making other people miserable."

"A long time ago, your mother and I were friends."

"She never said a word about you."

If this strikes a soft spot, Jasper doesn't show it. "Things didn't end well." He looks carefully at the chip then at the mess of his tower around us. He frowns slightly. "It didn't fall," he says with a note of disappointment.

"Do you *want* to die?" I ask, shakily.

"I assume you have no intention of obeying your mother's wishes and staying away from the spinners' game," Jasper says, ignoring my question.

"No. I want know more than ever why she wants me out of the picture."

Jasper rolls my chip deftly over his knuckles. "Maybe because she wants you to stay alive, not locked in a room with seven very dangerous people who hate you before they meet you."

When he puts it like that, I can *almost* understand. Maybe she knows I'll be the suckerfish at a table full of sharks. But I don't care. I have to know what she's thinking.

"Giving this stupid thing to me then taking it back. Offering me this world then pushing me away. Siding with the outfit that runs the Diamond. None of this sounds like her. I think something's wrong. I think she's in trouble."

Jasper slowly nods. "Finally, something we agree on."

He flips me the chip, and I catch it in both hands like an egg and clutch it to my chest.

"Get out," he says.

I stumble down the tower stairs, leaning heavily on the walls, knocking a few of the sconces awry as I go. Pushing the heavy tower door open takes the last sip of gas I have. I'm running on fumes and hollowed out, and the self-loathing and raw heartache of a dust hangover is pouring into me.

Everyone in the kitchen stares at me as I limp past. Everyone in the cages turns to watch me go by. The pit boss blocks the hallway once more, his eyes burning with anger, until someone chirps in his earpiece and he begrudgingly steps aside.

I limp on past the pond, through the casino, out the door. Mechanics are working on the dragon I bowed. The knights in livery turn to watch my graceless exit. I cross the bridge like a drunk then set my feet on a path to the Golden Swan and focus on taking one step at a time.

The sidewalk is mercifully quiet this late at night. What few people are walking about stay clear of me. But while Vegas might be winding down, the dust is ramping up. In the quiet of the night, it strikes me as strange that such a rushing river makes no sound, like I'm watching it on mute.

I stay well clear of the luck, having barely survived tapping into it when I was at full strength. If I put one tiptoe in right now, I feel, I'd just explode out of existence, my essence blown to pieces, eventually merging with the glittering stuff.

At least I'd end up at the Diamond that way.

Come to think of it, that might have been a lot easier than what I just did.

My own joke makes me chuckle stupidly. Exhaustion doubles the effects of the punch line, and by the time I reach the Golden Swan, I'm sobbing with laughter. I stumble past the drunken duck on the sign and salute him with the chip. I lean heavily against the double doors, and when they open easily, I fall over, sprawled out on the floor.

How embarrassing, if a customer were to see me. But the Swan doesn't get customers anymore—only a few stubborn regulars. And most of them will be long gone at this hour. The Diamond stole the rest. People go where the action is.

*Maybe I'll just sleep on the cold ground. There are worse places.*

I hear the clicking of leather soles on marble and open my eyes. Shirt buttons barely hold back the ample gut that swims blearily into focus above me. Eddie's head pokes over it, his mouth and mustache set in a severe double frown. His tie swings hypnotically over me.

"Goddamn dust," he says, murmuring just loudly enough for me to hear.

I hold up the chip. "Eddie. I got our ticket to the big show."

Then I think I pass out.

## CHAPTER NINE

I awake to a hammering on the door. My first thought is that I've told Rose, the dogged housekeeper, ten times already that she doesn't need to clean my room. I'm hardly ever in here, and there's really not much to clean.

"No, thank you!" I mumble hoarsely and roll over again.

The second thought I have is that speaking is very painful. And I roll over again... and blink... and breathe.

The night before comes back to me in waves—meeting Berto at the Crazy Asian, marching into the Avalon, facing Jasper, stumbling out of the Avalon. The rest is more than a little fuzzy.

I reach out and feel blindly at the nightstand. I touch the chip, and a jolt of its luck thrums through me, as though I've placed my hand on the hood of a revving sportscar.

That was a mistake. The weird dust of the chip turns my stomach like the smell of tequila the morning after a big night out.

More knocking on the door.

"No, thank you, Rose!" I say.

If I stay very still, maybe the nausea will pass. I've

hidden from hangovers before. However, none ever painted the last seconds of my wife's life on the inside of my eyelids. None ever rattled my soul around in my body like pennies in a beggar's cup.

But I know better by now. Hiding from the double whammy of a dust hangover isn't possible. The flayed heart and creeping dread are a one-two punch. I start to spiral.

Alli's death kicked me off the path I was meant to walk in life, one of light and companionship. If a girl as honest and good as she was can get smeared from existence in the time it takes a car to hit a wall, what is the point of trying to make sense of this stupid floating rock we're on?

There's no *getting over* her. I will be defined by her loss for the rest of my life. And maybe that's not so bad. The last light touch of her hand on my knee, the final whiff of clean sweat in her hair—if I have to be frozen in time, I might as well be frozen on a pretty picture.

Our life together before that last moment was pretty too. And painful. And wonderful. And real. But all the *before* is fading, while the day I lost her, the minute I lost her, is so clear and vivid that the paint is turning to lacquer.

More knocking.

"No, thank you, Rose!"

"Open the door, Lee." The no-bullshit reply comes from Zja-Zja.

I swing my feet to the ground and take a dusty swig of day-old water from the glass on my bedside table. I shuffle to the door in my socks. After popping the bolt, I open the door just enough to stick my head out. Zja-Zja returns my squint with a reprimanding look of her own. If she was able, she'd stand up from her scooter, take off her beaded velvet slipper, and smack me upside the head with it, I believe.

"When I said you and Jasper were tied up in this

together, I didn't mean for you to go over and kick the old bear in his cave," she says.

"He took my chip," I croak then clear my throat. The bright light of the hallway feels like it's shearing through my eyeballs into my brain. "I had to get it back."

"I was looking at the Avalon on my way in to work today. The top tower looks a little funky. Kinda drunk. Some talk about a freak settling of the foundation in the middle of the night."

I nod. "That would be my fault. Or his fault." I scratch at the scruff on my neck. "Both of us, I guess."

Zja-Zja furrows her brow and stares straight up at me... through me.

"You gonna open the door, or are we just talking in the hallway?" she asks after a moment.

"Oh," I say. "Yeah, sure. Come in."

I prop open the door and pull on the scratchy hotel robe as Zja-Zja rolls in. I give myself a quick check in the bathroom mirror and try unsuccessfully to wipe some of the bloodshot from my eyes. My stubble has a lot of gray. The robe is too short. My skinny legs are as pale as moonlight, and I'm showing a lot of thigh.

"Sorry," I say, "I don't really have anything to offer in terms of, like, refreshments."

"I wasn't expecting any." Zja-Zja looks around perfunctorily at all the nothing I own then turns back to me as I lean heavily on a wall. "How are you feeling?" she asks.

"Not great."

For a second, I think she's gonna snap at me, but her gaze softens instead. "Sit down, honey," she says.

I wobble to the bed and sit heavily. Some unsettling stars are popping apart at the edge of my vision.

A purple pouch embroidered with a beaded eye hangs

from the front of Zja-Zja's scooter. She fishes around within it and pulls out two colored sticks, one purple and one pink. At first, I think they're some sort of shamanistic thing, maybe Indian spirit sticks or something. She offers them to me. When I take them, I'm surprised at how cold they are.

"What are these?"

"You were a kid once. You know."

"Freezer pops?"

"Yep."

"Why are you giving me freezer pops?" I ask, but I'm immediately biting the little plastic top off the pink one.

"Jasper kept these on hand. I remember him always asking the kitchen for them after he had one of his long nights."

I start sucking the frozen sugar juice, and I don't think I've ever tasted anything more wonderful in my life.

"My guess is they help a bit with the luck hangover."

I'm too busy slurping with my eyes closed to answer.

"Looks like I guessed right."

A blistering cold headache hits me, and I suck air through my teeth.

"Take it easy there, sugar," Zja-Zja says through a smile.

The headache fades, and with it some of the hollow pain of the hangover. I get back to slurping.

"I see you got what you wanted, then," she says, nodding toward my chip on the dresser.

I finish the entire first freezer pop then take a deep breath and work on opening the second. "I wouldn't say it's what I want." I look sidelong at the chip. "But it's what I need. To get into the spinners' card game at the Diamond. It's where they divvy up the dust."

Zja-Zja takes this in with a heavy nod. "I heard of this game," she says, tut-tutting herself. "Should have put two and two together with the chip being the ante in. We haven't had an invite to that game in years. Jasper just gave it back to you? After you broke into his casino like a damn fool?"

"He already has his own chip. He was just doing a favor for my mother. She's the one who wanted it back."

The words sound no better this morning than they did in the tower last night.

"But she's the one who gave it to you in the first place," says Zja-Zja.

"I know. It doesn't add up. I think she's in trouble with the group she's running with. Max told me about Jack Short. Said he's bad people."

Zja-Zja spits lightly and waves her hands to clear the air of the man's name. "That man and his hotel are eating Las Vegas."

"Yeah," I continue, "that's Max's reaction to the guy too."

"And what's Jasper's take in all this? He's always got an angle."

"He said he knew my mom, and I believe him. Matter of fact, I think it was more than just *knowing*. You saw it, too, when you pulled his three cards. You said he was happy once. In love."

The puzzle pieces click behind Zja-Zja's eyes. "With your mother."

"And when you found him that one night, drunk as sin, wanting you to show him his future? I think he was hoping Mom would be in it again."

"And instead he got the Tower. Same as you." She threads through her jewels and beads until she finds her river stone. She spins it with a quick tap of her long, jeweled nail.

The eye within floats in a blur, but the stone settles with the blank side facing out. She looks down and frowns. "I don't like any of this," she says, finally. "I don't like that you had that chip in the first place. I don't like how you lost it, and I like even less how you got it back. The Eye is closed to these machinations," she proclaims, popping every syllable. "All the luck swirling around these events clouds my sight. But my gut tells me you're being pulled down this path as a prisoner, not letting fate decide your steps. It ain't natural."

"I survived your tower," I say. "I can survive a card game."

"You survived *Jasper's* tower," she says, leaning in. "You listen to me, honey. When my cards paint a picture, it comes true. There's nothing you or I or any force on this earth can do to change that." She leans back, settling herself again in a susurrus of soft tinkling. "No matter how hard I may want different," she adds a bit sadly.

I start in on the purple freezer pop, less like an animal and more as I did as a kid, biting the soft ice into equal segments through the plastic then rolling them each up to the top and letting them melt in my mouth. I'm beginning to feel I might survive this morning, at least.

"Is that what you came to tell me? That I'm still doomed?"

"You know you're doomed. I came to tell you you're late for work. Eddie's been working the bar himself. Said to let you sleep as long as you could."

I wobble up, only slightly steadier on my feet. The bedside clock is facing the wall because the green light bothers me. I turn it back around to find that it's barely morning after all. Noon is near, and Eddie has been covering for me for three hours.

Zja-Zja rolls her way out of my room as I throw off my robe and throw on some pants.

"I was gonna ask you to stay away from that card game too," she says over her shoulder. "But my guess is I'd be wastin' good breath."

∼

I SHAMBLE down to the Swan Song as quickly as I can. Eddie is behind the bar, pouring two steaming cups of tea. He sets one on Nancy's waiting tray. She winks at me and sets off. Eddie pushes the other cup toward me with a brief nod before turning around to spot shine the hanging glassware.

"I'm sorry, Eddie. I—"

"Had a late night. I know. I practically carried you up to your bed," he says gruffly.

So that's how I got to bed. The thought of the big man propping me up and laying me down half dead on my bed... It could just be the hangover, but the thought makes me want to cry.

"Everybody gets one free pass," he says. "But that's your one. Have some tea."

I sit down. I'm not sure I've ever seen the bar from this angle, as a customer would, facing in. The stools are wide and comfortable, and the video poker gives off a calming eighties-video-game nostalgia. The brass foot bar below is the perfect height.

It's a good bar. The tea is good, too, really good, bright and clean and pleasantly grassy. I feel myself take all these things in as if I might not see them again, as if I'm saying goodbye.

"You make a mean cup, Eddie."

The old walrus nods, shining each glass and looking out distantly upon his too-quiet casino. "After Jasper left, I ended up working back here more often than not," he says. "It's not a bad job."

"Best job I ever had," I say.

Eddie flops the bar towel over his shoulder and turns to look at me. "I'm not saying I'd like it back, though. Which is what might happen if you go to that card game Zja-Zja told me about."

I'm not exactly sure how much Eddie knows about the luck that governs this town. I don't want to shock the guy by telling him how I carve holes in myself every time I touch the stuff. But I want to talk to him straight, like he deserves.

"The casino is going under, isn't it," I say, more as a statement than a question.

Eddie smooths his mustache, picks up another glass, and starts spot checking. After a quiet moment, he nods. "I've stared at the books until my eyes hurt," he says flatly. "No matter what we do, we're just not getting the foot traffic."

"It's not your fault."

"Which is strange," he continues, "because I feel like I run a good shop here. I work hard. I have good people. This is a nice place."

"Did you hear me? It has nothing to do with you or how well you run this place. You could offer top-shelf booze and a free steak dinner to everyone who walks in the door. You'd still get this," I say, gesturing out at a casino floor that is so empty I can hear the overhead lights buzzing.

"I don't understand," Eddie says, clearing his throat as his voice cracks.

"I do. They're stealing all your luck."

Eddie looks around as if expecting to find something physically stolen from him. "Who did?" he asks.

"A man named Jack Short."

"The GM at the Diamond? But he doesn't even know me. Wouldn't care to, I suspect. He's a big fish in this pond."

I run my hands across the wood of the bar, smoothed by the passage of time and thousands of sliding tumblers. "Places with history like this attract the dust all on their own. Luck likes timeless places. Your casino should be glittering, and I bet it was, once."

Eddie settles his tie and spies a water spot at the bottom of a tumbler. He holds it up like a spyglass as if he could see through it and back in time, to the glory days of the Swan. I wish I could have been there. I bet this place was a sight. He wipes the past away with a swipe of his rag. I can picture the downfall as clearly as I can picture the heyday.

"Then the Diamond broke ground, and Jack Short came to town," I say, completing the picture. "He took what was probably a friendly card game among the spinners and upped the stakes. Now it's how they divvy up all the dust, and it's 'invite only.' If you don't get a seat, you don't get the dust."

Eddie carefully returns the tumbler and sets both hands on the bar, his jaw working. I know the type of helpless anger he's trying to tamp down. I've been feeling it ever since I stumbled into the Diamond that first time and everything and everyone there, from the concierge to the pristine wallpaper, seemed to tell me I wasn't good enough... and never would be.

"And he has your mother?" Eddie ventures.

That wave of helplessness washes over me. "Yes," I say, staring deep into the last foggy remnants of my green tea. "I have no idea how she fell in with Short or the Diamond. But I aim to find out."

"But she's alive."

Leave it to Eddie to slam me with some perspective. Just finding my mother is alive was a gift I quickly took for granted. How quickly we forget the things we wanted desperately but now have.

"And you're alive," he adds.

I snort with laughter. "With some help from freezer pops and green tea, yeah. It would appear I'm alive."

Maybe it's because Eddie confided in me, showing me a moment of weakness, that I confide in him. "Spinners get their power from pain, Eddie. It's why all of us are so miserable. We rip open the worst memory of our life and bleed it out every time we control the luck. The dust rolls in to fill up what we carve out, and we go to work."

Eddie sets his most recent glass down and looks at me with barely concealed horror. "Jasper never said anything about that."

"Jasper doesn't say a lot about anything."

Eddie looks down, his mustache settling sadly. He grasps another glass without looking as a moment of quiet passes between us.

*Fuck it.* He deserves to know who he hired.

"My memory is the day my wife died. Which also happens to be the day we were married."

Eddie swallows hard but stays quiet. I know this tactic. This is an old bartender's trick to get customers to open up. Bartenders make very good psychiatrists. By volume, we do more therapy than anyone.

"That was my worst day," I say. "Funny thing is almost all the other days I had with her were good, but the more I run my brain over that day, the more I forget all the other good days." I gently push the cup away. "That's the cost. Give up all the memories that make you smile, one by one, and cement the one that rips you apart, and you, too, can take luck into your own hands."

Eddie seems to mull over some words, shifting them around like marbles in his mouth before speaking. "This luck—this dust—has never brought me anything but trouble. And it's destroyed a lot of good people I know. Now, I understand wanting to find your mother," he says, "but don't go into that card game on account of the Swan. This is a good place. But it's not worth what you pay. I'm not sure anything is worth what you pay."

This, coming from the man who has sweated blood for the Golden Swan all his adult life, the man who kept every single employee he hired, even when paying them meant losing money. This, coming from a man who loves this place so much he isn't too proud to clean the toilets.

"Let me be the judge of that," I say, standing. I reach over and grasp him on the shoulder like the old friend he's become in barely a month. "And how about you let me do my job behind the bar. I got a pretty important card game tonight, but I'm still on the clock for the next three hours."

Eddie almost smiles. He flips the bar towel off his shoulder and flops it onto mine. Then he walks around the Swan Song's bar, unrolling his sleeves and buttoning them back to general-manager status. He pauses at the steps and looks my way.

"Good luck," he says.

"I'mma need it," I reply.

As he walks back toward the offices without another word, I take my place behind the bar.

For the next three hours, I work. We're busier than usual, which I think is a residual effect of the river of dust passing by outside. We get a handful of people wandering in, drawn to the energy passing by without knowing why, but a handful is still better than normal. I start pouring top shelf. I feel like I'm tending the deck bar on the *Titanic*.

All thoughts of the dust leave me as I work—the card game, my mother a part of it, the lingering ache from the luck hangover. All that is pushed aside in favor of filling a few frosted glasses with ice-cold beer, popping bottles and catching the caps in the same motion, shaking a few martinis loose, and steeping lots and lots of tea. I see each of the Golden Girls in turn: Barbara, Nancy, and Susan. They joke with me and laugh among themselves in the long downtime. We seem to feel something coming to an end without ever speaking of it.

I order an early dinner that is an exact replica of the first thing Eddie gave me when I walked into this joint a month ago, a medium cheeseburger and crispy fries with crunchy lettuce and a surprisingly fresh slice of tomato. I crush it in ten bites and add it to my tab. Rules are rules.

When Barbara steps behind the bar and starts washing up, at first, I ask her if I can get her anything.

"Shift switch, dummy," she says, rolling her eyes. She shoves me to the side gently, flipping my towel off my shoulder and onto hers. "Unless you wanna work here all night?"

I almost say yes. *Yes, I do want to work here all night, Barbara.* What I *don't* want to do is walk into a card game full of killers and find my mother a part of something awful. I'd much rather steep tea. But by then, she's already joking with the other ladies in Thai and checking the beer stock. So I walk away. I walk away from the bar with a strange sinking feeling, letting my finger trail along the bar top until I run out of wood.

I check my watch—still a couple hours until sunset.

A velvet rope crosses the doorway of the Parlor of the

Eye, and the poster board reads Closed. My guess is that Zja-Zja is in there, lost in her divinations. Even I can feel that the energy is weird today. Maybe she's trying to make sense of it. Or maybe she's just kicking her feet up. Either way, I've bothered her enough. She already said her piece anyway: stay the hell away from the card game.

I know she's right. And I know I can't do that.

Only one person might be able to give me advice about what I'm walking into.

I think I've got enough time to make one more trip to Fremont.

I GET off the bus at the usual stop, where the smoking cowboy gives me a neon nod. The golden hour has arrived on Fremont. Heavy light the same tint as the rushing dust falls upon the street. The temperature is probably in the high eighties, but it feels glorious. The open mall is already crowded. Everyone nearby must feel the pull of this river. It's too big to ignore now, whether one can see it or not.

I steer clear, terrified of what the dust might do to me, of how easily I could jump into the river and wink out, forgetting about the card game, the Swan, my mother. I could just leave it all behind. I wonder just how many struggling luck junkies have done just that since Jack Short started calling all the dust in the city to the Diamond. I imagine seeing all this luck rushing by is something like a heroin addict finding the keys to that room where the cops put all the confiscated drugs.

The energy on the street is electric. Fremont seems enchanted by the flow. Tourists dance to outdoor music, drinks in hand, awash in dust they can't see. They laugh and hoot and twirl, but there's a manic edge to it all. People gyrate as if they've got a touch of the dancing plague. The buskers seem to perform at double time. Street vendors shoot electric tchotchkes into the air with rapid-fire quickness and wave counterfeit bags and sunglasses frantically at all who pass. Revelers roam in packs. Everyone has to speak loudly to be heard.

Max isn't in either of the spots I found him before, not surprisingly. So I keep my head down and keep walking. Eventually, I find him on the other side of the street, across the river. He's nestled in a heavy velvet shadow, sitting cross-legged on top of his pack. To the untrained eye, he'd look like a pile of trash bags, but I can see the glow of dust in his hands.

He looks like a cobbler hard at work on a shoe, hunched over a shimmering orb that glints with all the colors of the rainbow. He puffs away at a cigarette, white plumes of smoke streaming around him. I walk as close as I dare to the river that separates us, trying to get a better look at what he's making. It's something infinitely more delicate than the fury flowing between us.

I don't see how I can cross. The river runs fast and unbroken, like a mountain stream in full snowmelt. I might have to walk a quarter mile to find a spot safe enough to chance it.

"Max!" I yell.

He doesn't look up.

"Max! Over here!"

He holds up a single finger, like Mom used to do when I wanted her attention but she was talking on the phone. His focus remains fixed on the orb of dust in his lap.

I put my hands on my hips and look about awkwardly, like I'm the only person not dancing at a party. Just when

I'm about to yell at him again, Max gestures idly at a swath of dust eddied up to his feet. It freezes into a rigid line that snakes slowly away from him and toward me.

The seam of luck extends itself like a crack in the ice of a pond. It doesn't stop when it reaches the crushing river of dust either. It crosses in a crackling surge like a gunpowder fuse, zipping all the way to my feet.

Max has cut the river in half. Upstream, the dust still surges, but it is piling up against an impossibly strong paper-thin dam. Downstream, the dust runs away like a galloping herd until it's lost around the bend.

I touch the gum-stained and filthy street like a man finding solid ground after floating adrift. I half expect to find little luck fishes flopping around.

"Hurry up," Max snaps without looking, still working with whatever is in his hands.

I scamper across the street, sliding between the revelers, pointedly ignoring the sparkling mound of dust already piled up as high as my neck behind Max's dam. A single dollop slops up and over the invisible barrier and splashes to the ground behind me.

Then I'm over on Max's side.

As soon as reach Max's pack, his dam bursts, felt but not heard, like a change in cabin pressure. I turn in time to see a six-foot wave of molten gold eating up the empty street, plowing through a throng of tourists who let out a delirious yell in unison without knowing why. Lovers squeeze and twirl. Four or five glasses of beer get thrown in the air, all to the pounding breakdown of a perfectly timed guitar solo.

Every light down the street turns green along the storm surge of dust, then yellow, then red with its passing.

"This whole place has gone crazy," I say, letting out a breath. I wipe my sweaty brow with the front of my shirt and ease myself down the still-warm wall until I'm sitting by Max's side.

He looks over at me and startles as if surprised to find me here. His eyes jerk about a bit, then he grunts in agreement. "B-bad night to be out," he stammers. "Like a full moon on crack. Cops already got their hands full."

I look out on the madness. My eye is drawn to a little girl about fifty feet away. She's maybe four or five, standing stock-still and watching the two of us while her parents order food and drink at a street vendor outside the Golden Gate casino.

"What's her deal?" I ask.

Max glances up briefly. "She can see the dust. Or some of it, at least."

This shocks me. "I thought trauma brings on the sight."

"You think kids can't experience trauma?" Max asks simply, his cigarette bobbing along with his words.

"I guess I just never thought of a kid having to come to terms with all this," I say. "It's hard enough for an adult."

"It's easier for kids," Max mumbles. "Kids dance through the dust, more a part of it than they are apart from it. Natural like. Luck magic only starts to kill you when you learn how to twist it."

His grip shifts, and for the first time, I can see what he's tinkering with: a butterfly. He's whittling a butterfly out of pure luck, plucking the dust that floats in the air around him as easily as twirling a finger through pipe smoke. He spins up its left wing with a watchmaker's touch and adds a subtle pattern, a cat's eye as thin as morning mist.

"That's incredible," I say.

Max doesn't reply. He's moved on to the little antennae, long and impossibly delicate, stretching to spirals the size of shirt buttons. Gone are the tremors that trip him up whenever he tries to light his cigarette. The stutter, too, is barely noticeable.

"I got my chip back," I say.

"Good. Game is on any time now."

"How will I know?"

"You'll know."

I settle back and find myself watching the little girl again. She's trading glances between us and her oblivious parents, who are talking loudly and swaying, flush with wine. Her eyes are glistening.

"I think she's trying hard not to cry," I say.

"She's scared," Max says.

"Of us?"

"Of everything." He moves to the other antenna, stringing out the dust so that it floats like a spider's web. "Think if you were little like her, stuck in the middle of all this noise. Loud and hot and strange. Everybody acting a fool, and you don't understand it."

"That sounds like most of my life."

Max whispers to the butterfly, and it floats upward like a napkin caught in a warm summer breeze. "Not yet," he murmurs, ushering it back down. He sets to work on the thorax, a tiny peanut of a shape.

"You think I should go to this card game?" I ask.

"Yes."

"You're the only one. Eddie told me not to. Berto thinks I might die. Zja-Zja seems convinced I will."

"Decent chance of death, yeah," he says casually. "The Eye ain't dumb."

I can't help but laugh. "Then why do it?" I'm not sure whether I'm asking him or myself.

"You know why," he says. "You wanna sit here and let your soul rot off in the Vegas dust? Never knowing?"

"Can I beat them? Jack Short and the other spinners?"

"Probably not," he says.

The butterfly is almost finished. He takes a long look at it then moves to the bottom of each wing, stretching the glowing dust into symmetrical teardrops.

"How did you beat them?" I ask.

Max doesn't answer. He cups the finished butterfly in his hands and lifts it to eye level, smiling fondly. His eyes sparkle with a soft golden glow—not the dust itself but a reflection of the magical creature he's crafted.

He whispers to it again, and its wings stretch out into a long and leisurely flap. My jaw drops.

Max gently blows upon the butterfly, and it takes flight.

We both watch as it flutters up high then dips low, finding its wings and testing its balance. The hot gusts of desert air do nothing to disturb it. The manic revelry of the crowd below doesn't bother it in the slightest.

The little girl sees it immediately. She stops wiping at her eyes and holds out a hand. The butterfly alights gently upon her outstretched finger and slowly beats its wings. For a minute or so, it simply flutters on her finger. From where we sit, it looks like nothing so much as a fairy come to life. Then it seems to step into her hand, sinking slowly until it disappears in a soft puff of glowing dandelion seeds.

I expect tears from the girl, some shock at the loss of the thing, but instead she looks over at Max and smiles shyly, pressing against her mother. Her whole demeanor has changed, and it occurs to me that Max gave this little girl a lot more than a pretty puff of dust.

Her mother glances down at her as if surprised to find her there. She brushes her daughter's hair behind her ears and says something to the man, still in line for a drink. He shrugs and steps out, picks the girl up, and plops her on his shoulders. They walk down the street together, out of the dust.

The girl looks back once and waves.

"Did I beat them?" he asks me. He's looking down at his own scarred hands as if surprised that such a thing as that butterfly came from them. He takes off his sweat-stained trucker's hat, pokes his finger through a hole at the top, and waggles it at himself. "Did I really?"

It occurs to me that all of this, all our strange talks together, might have been nothing more than the ramblings of an insane man.

Maybe Max never played the spinners' game. Maybe he was never a luck spinner.

Maybe the card Zja-Zja gave me was for another person, some buttoned-up street busker a little farther down Fremont with a legitimate business tutoring rookie spinners in the ways of the dust—a guy with a system and a textbook: *Seven Habits of Highly Effective Luck Spinners.*

Maybe this man isn't even named Max.

Maybe I'm still in that hospital, doped up.

Maybe I never made it out of that car.

But then I remember the spinning snow globe of dust I first saw around the man, the way he changed the cards I had in my hand, the way he stopped the river by himself for a few moments.

That butterfly was real. The girl's smile said so.

"The first thing I tried to do when I found out I could control this stuff is use it to steal," I say. "I've seen junkies fight and nearly kill for a hit of dust, just to wipe their brains for a bit. I've seen spinners use it to hurt people and break things, spinners chock full of dust who only use it to get more."

I turn to Max, trying to find his face. "That was the first

time I've ever seen anyone use the dust to make someone happy. So yeah. I'd say you beat them. And I want to know how you did it, so I can beat them too."

Max smiles absently and nods to himself as he produces another phantom cigarette from inside his hat. He pulls his tarnished Zippo from the outer sleeve of his pack, flicks it open, and tries several times to light the flame, but his tremors have returned. I take it from him and snap it alight then hold it out while he pokes the cigarette in and takes a long drag.

He takes his lighter back and holds it fondly, almost delicately, the same way Jasper holds his spoon, the same way I thumb my ring. I keep expecting it to glitter the way our charms do, but no dust rests on this thing. It's still just a lump of metal with a wick and a stained etching that ends in Why Me?

"I b-beat them because I realized there's only one thing more powerful than finding your luck charm."

I wait. And wait.

Finally, I throw up my hands. "And that is?"

"I c-ca…" His stuttering gets the better of him, and he sucks at the cigarette, calming himself. "I can't tell you that," he says. "It don't work that way."

I lay my head back on the warm brick and look up at the fading light in the sky. In all the nights I've been here, I can't remember seeing the stars once. Catching a glimmer here or there is possible, but I'm pretty sure a clear night sky is hard to come by in Vegas even when you don't have a river of gold rushing through. This city does its best to drown out the cosmic lights with a show all its own.

"That's what I figured," I say.

We sit quietly next to each other—Max a little higher,

perched up on his bag; me on the dirty ground. We watch the river flow and buffet the crowd.

When the sun dips out of sight and the last of the light flees Fremont Street, the river stops running. It doesn't dry up or trickle away, it just stops flowing, like a huge bathtub drain somewhere was just plugged up. The dust flattens and spreads away into a million little tiny rivulets that evaporate into the air like a bucket of water thrown over hot pavement.

I get the feeling a lot of tables will be cold in Las Vegas tonight—everywhere except for the Diamond, that is.

Max stops shuffling his cards and looks up. "Jack got all the dust he needs. Time for you to go, boyo."

He digs around in one of his many pockets and pulls out some crumpled bills. "Take a cab," he says. "Arrive in style."

His cackle is contagious. I stand up and take the cash.

"Good luck," he says, and cackles again.

I feel Max watching me as I walk away, right up until I get the cab and close the door. I look back at him from the window and see nothing but a glowing ember in the darkness.

I turn to the weary-looking cabbie. "Take me to the Diamond," I say.

# CHAPTER TEN

The Diamond looks like it sucked up all the daylight in Vegas. The facets of the building seem to cage the light within, bouncing it back upon itself again and again. The rest of Vegas can't keep up. Other casinos look like faded postcards in comparison.

Traffic is thick with people getting in and out of cars and rubbernecking at the strange way the casino blazes tonight. Lining up to get into a casino, where everything is devised to rob you blind, strikes me as particularly absurd.

Then again, this place has all the luck in Vegas right now. You don't need to be a spinner or a junkie to feel it.

I pay the cabbie and step out half a block away, feeling as though I got kicked out of this place just yesterday, dismissed by the concierge with that grating smile and escorted out with a single finger.

I wipe as much of the desert grit from my jeans as I can then run my hands over the scruff on my face and try to give my wiry hair a little life. I pop my nose inside the stretched collar of my T-shirt and give myself a sniff—not great.

I remember thinking I'd hit a new level of tired when I

got off that flight, but I bet I look even worse now than I did then. I've gone round and round in circles to show up at the front door of the place that kicked me out, grasping the same little chip in my pocket.

The more things change, the more they stay the same.

The sidewalk is clogged with tourists taking selfies and prodding at the doormen. Everyone wants to get a shot of the thick crystal lettering resting freely above the front doors. Each letter in the word Diamond seems to glow with its own inner fire.

I hear the rhythmic thump of an incoming helicopter, and everyone pauses to look up. I spot it breaking through the clouds, a darker shadow in an already muddy sky. It passes out of sight, landing somewhere high above. I wonder if I'll be seeing that guest at the table. The thought brings a smirk to my face as I pull up my sagging pants.

A black sedan bullies its way through the traffic and pulls up to a stop on the sidewalk, just feet from the front doors. The chauffeur exits and loops around to open the rear door, and Lady Chang steps out. She's dressed in a red silk dress, accented all about with gold and black thread. She looks beautiful and severe at the same time, like a gleaming knife on a decorative pillow.

The doormen cut a path for her, and she walks straight through, golden heels clicking sharply. She doesn't see me or anyone else. Once she's inside, the crowd folds around again and falls to speculating. I hear everything from "shipping magnate" to "movie star," and a few people even bet she's Far East royalty.

I'm pretty sure I'm the only one who can say I've had the privilege of getting thrown into an industrial dryer by the woman.

The crowds pose a problem approaching the doors. I'm

getting shouldered around and buffeted back. Whatever confidence Chang has in these types of situations is totally foreign to me. I'm not usually the one with the ticket for the big show. I'm usually the guy cleaning the dishes afterward.

I find the doorman I recognize—the "ambassador" that pointed me out with his middle finger.

"Hey!" I yell weakly. "Hey, guy."

No dice—I'm drowned out by the crowd. An influx of new tourists presses at me from behind. I'm getting claustrophobic. This place, with its stupid beveled glass windows and its ridiculous crystalline sign and its blinding lighting—this stupid place that stole all the dust around it like some sort of bloated, preening tick—this goddamn casino holding all of us hostage one way or another—it's really starting to piss me off.

"Hey, asshole!" I scream.

The crowd quiets with a startled hush, and the doorman with the stupid fez—his name is Luc, I see now —looks at me in alarm.

I wave at him. "Let me in," I say.

His eyes narrow as alarm turns to anger... until I show him the chip. I hold it up like a press pass, pinched between finger and thumb.

"I got a golden ticket," I add in a singsong voice.

Everyone on the entire block looks my way during a pregnant pause. I'm hoping that all the blood rushing to my face looks a lot less obvious than it feels.

After a moment, Luc declares, "Make way!"

The crowd parts, barely. I maneuver my way to the front with hundreds of eyes on my back. Luc looks me up and down like a piece of fish on ice. He clearly doesn't remember me. I'm not sure whether I'm offended or relieved.

He presses his hand to his earpiece and asks for someone whose name I don't catch. "Wait here," he tells me.

I'm reminded uncomfortably of a time when I held up a line of angry New Yorkers at a Brooklyn bodega while my credit card kept getting declined. I stand there awkwardly for what feels like half an hour but is probably no more than two minutes.

A second doorman emerges from within. His jaunty fez reads Adam, and I see instantly that he has the look. It's in his eyes, which are a bit wider and more consuming, the skin of his face pulled a bit tighter. He can see the dust. Whether he's a junkie or not is harder to tell, but he can definitely see the dust.

Luc points me out. Adam takes one look at the chip and nods then turns and leaves again, off to do some other bidding. He never even looked at my face. I wonder how many people this casino employs who have some degree of skill with the dust. I bet it's a small platoon. I'm trying not to feel small, but it's getting harder and harder.

Luc looks as if he can't quite believe what he's about to do, but he does eventually open the door and hold it for me.

"Welcome to the Diamond," he says with all the vigor of a funeral director.

"Thanks. Next time, I'll be sure to wear a red dress," I say. The joke passes right by him, and so do I.

A red carpet cuts through the center of the 7,777-karat foyer. Velvet ropes on either side keep the sizeable crowd back. People are checking in, checking out, gawking, and moving to and from the casino, but all of them stop for a moment and turn to watch me. Even the ceaseless front-desk staff pauses to look up. I see the guy with the grating smile who told me robots cleaned the place, and I wave. He doesn't recognize me either.

I'm waiting for an escort that I soon realize isn't coming. I'm truly inside, behind the velvet rope. I'm free to walk of my own volition. Putting my hands in my pockets, I stroll along the red carpet, underneath the hanging chandelier, past the walls of water and the central fountain, into the casino proper. Every twenty or so feet, I pass another ambassador guarding the carpet. They face outward, backs to me, each fez perfectly offset.

Inside the casino, people pay me scant attention. They're far more interested in the table action. Blackjack and pai gow tables are stacked three and four deep for each seat. Craps tables roar like dogfight pits. To these people, I'm just some VIP on my way to the high-stakes tables.

The really-high-stakes tables.

A fair amount of dust floats around the casino floor but nowhere near the amount that the river brought here. About halfway across, I see where the real lion's share went: up the back elevator bay. The single glass tube looks like a magic wand hollowed out and pumped full of gold dust. Trails stream up and down like bottle rockets in the night.

I'm just standing stupidly in front of it again. *Talk about déjà vu.* But this time, no one escorts me away.

Nobody welcomes me either.

I cross my arms and frown in confusion. All I see is a sealed glass door. The elevator itself looks to have departed, likely bearing Lady Chang upward into the haze of dust. If there's a call button, I can't find it. I glance back the way I came, but the carpet is clear, the security looking pointedly elsewhere. This is a one-in-one-out affair, apparently. But I have no idea how to get in, and I don't think they're gonna hold up the bus for my broke ass much longer.

I run my fingers along the glass, feeling for anything that might resemble a button, and just to the left of the door, my pinkie brushes over a hard ridge in the smooth glass.

I feel it out. It's a slot about the size of a quarter... or a chip.

Before I can dwell on how stupid I'd feel if this thing was a weird ashtray and not a call button, I slide my chip in.

The size is a perfect fit. The chip drops down a clear chute out of sight, and I hear a satisfying *clunk* from somewhere below.

Then nothing.

I'm just starting to craft an explanation to tell everyone back at the Swan that I decided to throw the chip I nearly died for down an elevator shaft for no good reason when I hear a sucking sound. I step back, and the elevator zooms down like a glass bead dropped in water, slowing to a smooth stop in front of me. When the doors are flush with each other, the elevator opens.

It's empty. I get in, and the doors close behind me. I search high and low for a button to push, or a panel, or anything, but the elevator starts a slow rise on its own. The casino floor drops below me, and I feel a touch of vertigo.

I turn around and almost fall down. I'm in a glass bubble climbing the outer edge of the Diamond. I can see all of Vegas, which seems small, and I see black desert beyond. Then the desert starts to seem small, and I see little pockets of light—distant towns that must be a hundred miles away.

I don't even notice the elevator slowing or stopping. A soft *ding* on arrival is like the snap of a hypnotist.

When I turn around, the door has already opened to reveal a short, brightly lit walkway with rich red curtains drawn along either side. A big wooden double door is open at the end, and I see movement within, bodies passing by. I hear laughter.

Before I can think too hard about it, I step out and across, and I've arrived.

The poker room is shaped like a hockey puck. Floor-to-ceiling windows provide a three-hundred-and-sixty-degree view of the inky black desert sky. Straight ahead is a sparkling crystal bar with clear bottles of gleaming spirits in every color. Wine is decanting in glassware that curves and loops so delicately it ought to be in an alchemist's lab. An unfamiliar man in a tuxedo is gently stirring a martini in a thick crystal mixing glass.

Behind the bar is a second door that leads out to a helipad—empty, now.

To my left is the spinners' game. Plush crimson wing-back chairs encircle a massive felt-topped card table that looks to have been pulled directly from the heart of an old-growth redwood tree. Spaced evenly in the seats are the spinners.

It's all quite dramatic, but I've stopped registering. I see only my mother.

She's dressed all in black. I've never seen her dressed all in black before. Mom is the queen of color mismatch—pink sweats, purple polka-dotted house slippers, weird printed tees she got from all her days working sales expos for a medical equipment company.

Now she looks like a cross between a monk and a middle-aged assassin, with a high-collared black jacket and a black silk blouse with a darker black cravat around the neck. Black linen pants. She looks like she could buy a car with the dripping diamond necklace she's got on, although the center stone is of an evil shade like the space between stars. She's lost about twenty pounds, which I can see in her face.

She doesn't quite recognize me at first. Her eyes have a strange, watery haze that looks familiar, the same type of half-entranced look Jillian wore when she walked down the aisle.

When they alight on me, though, they clear. They widen. Her mouth goes slack. She doesn't look happy to see me.

In fact, I would call the look on her face horrified, which is another first. Mom's been angry, astounded by some of my decisions, and baffled by a few of the things I've done over the years. I've even seen what I would call misery on her face, when she visited me in my fleeting moments of coherence after the wreck... before she left.

But "horrified" is a first.

I start to speak, but she greets me with such a singular and cutting shake of her head that the words are blown from my lips.

Maybe our relation is secret. Maybe nobody knows we're mother and son. Maybe her alibi relies upon it and she's been caught up in some terrible business, trapped against her will. That would explain why she disappeared and might offer some consolation for the misery I've had to shoulder alone, without her.

Then the man standing behind the bar speaks. "The prodigal son returns." And he's looking at me. "Better late than never, I suppose."

He walks over to my mother and hands her the fresh martini he was stirring as he passes, a simple act that somehow hurts me more than anything that has happened to me in the past three weeks. She takes it numbly. She hasn't blinked since she first saw me.

"Claire told me she had misgivings. She said she'd taken back the chip I gave her to give to you. I guess the luck had other ideas, didn't it?"

Smiling like we have some secret between us, he extends his hand. I find I'm shaking it.

"I'm Jack Short. I spin for the Diamond here in Vegas. Among other things."

I expected a cold, bejeweled oligarch, aloof and distant. I expected a grim mafioso, sneering and petty when he cared to pay attention at all. I expected a... a...

I did not expect this man.

Jack Short is tall, for starters—not as tall as Jasper Jones, who I now notice is sitting across the table, watching everything and everyone with a peculiar stillness, but tall enough. Short is taller than me, anyhow.

He's dressed in a classic black tuxedo, which he wears as easily as I might wear a pair of old blue jeans. His hair is jet-black, and his eyes bright blue. He has a slightly windswept look, and my guess is he's the one who recently arrived by helicopter. His face is clean-shaven, and his teeth are too white. He could be forty or fifty.

"Take a seat, won't you?" he asks, smiling. His southern accent is disarming in an alarming way, like an ace salesman or a hypnotist. I can't see what his luck charm might be. He doesn't wear any jewelry, not even a watch.

"Your mother wanted me to remove the extra seat. But I said, 'Let's just hold off a moment. See if my little river brings in one more fish.'" He talks like he's charming a courtroom. That was an insult, as far as I can tell, but everyone laughs, except for my mother... and Jasper, who watches me quietly, a glass of water in front of him, one hand on the green felt, the other in his jacket.

"What are you drinking, Lee?" asks Jack.

"What's he bring to the table is a better question." This from Lady Chang, seated across from Jasper, sipping green tea from a beautiful ceramic mug.

She gets chuckles and some nods. I recognize the Golden Gate spinner, Lapel Pin with the red beard and the fetish for old sports injuries. He's looking at me like he wants to eat me.

Jack waggles his finger at her playfully. "Now, now, Xie-fu. He brought a chip. He can play the game."

"His casino is bone-dry," says another spinner, a beautiful woman I don't recognize. She wears a shimmering copper gown and smokes from a long ivory cigarette holder that drips with luck. "How much of the luck in your box came from the Swan? A handful at best?"

Jack Short takes a seat and reaches out with long, manicured fingers to gently touch an ebony box at the edge of the table. I hadn't noticed it before, and somehow, I can barely notice it now, even staring straight at it. I feel as though there's a blind spot right where the box is supposed to be in my field of vision. It's so black it's like it punches a hole in my eyes.

I blink and look away, slightly nauseous.

"Not much," he says gently, caressing the box with the tip of his forefinger. "But a little bit. Enough."

Lady Chang exhales slowly from her nose and sips her tea. The fox-fur woman rolls her eyes.

"Who cares? He'll be out soon enough. Let's play," says a huge man seated to Chang's right. He wears a pinstripe suit that looks as though it could safely cover a car in a hailstorm. A golden watch on a golden chain loops from the front pocket, glittering with dust.

"We're doing him a service, really," says the smoker. "The Swan needs to be put out of its misery. That place..."

She gestures grandly with the ivory cigarette holder, looking for a word. "It just keeps *lingering*."

"That's a pretty ring," says the girl to my right. She looks too young to be in a casino, much less a spinner. Her beady black eyes linger on my wedding ring as she plays with her braided hair. Her bangs are pulled back and pinned with a jeweled clip that glitters malevolently. "Maybe the box will eat it. The box can eat anything. That could be your ante. Make the box eat his ring, Jack!"

Her giggle sends shivers down my spine.

Jack seems to consider this. He takes his finger off the box and sits back in his chair. "What do you think, Lee?"

I am meat dropped in a cage of lions. I keep looking back at my mother, trying to read her face, but she's gone horribly blank again.

I turn back to face Jack, thinking for a moment.

"I'll take a scotch on the rocks. If you're making drinks."

The table is quiet. Jack furrows his brow, and I wait for a backhand, either the physical kind or the verbal kind.

"What's your scotch?" he asks evenly.

"Whatever's the most expensive."

Jack laughs lightly and nods as if conceding a point.

"You'll be wanting the fifty-year, then." He glances over his shoulder at a man who is leaning casually against the glass at the back.

He's so still that my eyes passed over him the first time. The man is dressed in his yachting finest and sipping what is most likely expensive tequila.

"Huxley, would you pour Lee a few fingers of scotch?"

Huxley nods and pushes himself up as he saunters over to the bar. "Glad you could make it, Lee," he says as he passes, eyes glittering. He looks like a kid in a candy shop.

"Do you know Huxley?" asks Jack. "He is also in my

employ. Hux will divvy up the dust when everything settles. He also pours scotch if you ask nicely."

"He left me for dead in a twenty-four-hour wedding chapel," I say. "Along with his fiancée."

Jack looks impressed. He turns to Huxley. "You have a fiancée?"

"We've gone our separate ways," Huxley replies soberly.

"Ah, too bad."

Jack turns back to the table, and the conversation seems instantly forgotten. He flattens his hand on the money-colored felt and smiles with boyish glee. The table is full, all eight seats taken. I'd hoped my mother would be playing. I figured if the two of us were at the table, maybe we could help each other. But she's standing a pace behind Jack. She casts me a fleeting glance, her eyes clear and pleading again. I can tell her mind is racing. Mine is, too, but I feel as though we're running separate races. She wants me to get up and go, to run. But I'm not going anywhere without her.

Then the fog returns to her eyes. She stops looking at me and gazes out the window at the view as if seeing it for the first time.

The black stone resting neatly in the hollow dip at the base of her freckled neck glints evilly.

"Let's play, shall we?" Jack asks.

The luck in the room shifts instantly as the other six lean in. I'm last to elbow up. The air is heavy with the weight of moving dust. All the charms in this room seem to thrum. Tendrils of luck lick the table, the drinks, the felt. They run all over the single deck of cards at the edge. I can't tell who is spinning what dust, but everyone seems to be working the scene already.

Everyone except for me. Huxley sets my scotch down

with a flourish, and I take a long, very expensive drink, watching my mother carefully as she steps up to the table and reaches for the deck of cards.

As her hand touches the felt, every thread of dust she comes in contact with goes up in smoke, fast as flash paper. The deck shimmers like a golden bar as all the players probe for a way to turn the cards in their favor, but the moment Mom grabs it, the dust flares brightly and disappears.

The big man flinches as if slapped. The beautiful smoker sucks in a breath and coughs. Even the girl in braids pulls back her twiddling hands as if they were slapped by a ruler.

"Ah, ah, ah," Jack says, admonishing. "No luck on the cards until the hands are dealt."

My mother slides the deck her way, and it cleaves a path through the dust on the table. Wherever she touches, the luck disappears. Now all the spinners are watching her, although she seems too lost within herself to notice.

"My newest associate here, Mrs. Claire Baker, has a very unique talent," Jack says in answer to the gawping. He checks me out of the corner of his eye. "She's what's known as a cooler."

Lady Chang frowns, hissing out a breath. She makes some sign in the air before her, as if to ward off the very word. Jasper leans carefully back in his seat, and I sense that something has clicked in his mind, something that has gone completely over my head.

"A what?" I ask.

"A luck killer," says Jack. "Claire, would you mind breaking the pack and shuffling the cards?"

The fog returns. Mom pulls the plastic from the deck and splits the cards out by suit for all to see.

"I'm very lucky to have her. Coolers are quite rare. A

very valuable talent. She's insurance, you see. For the house. In case things get out of hand."

"And I'm sure she'll treat us exactly the same as she'll treat you," Jasper says drolly. "If things get... out of hand."

"Absolutely," says Jack, and the asshole has the gall to wink at me.

I take another sip and suck the scotch in through my teeth and try to hold on to the soft burn. It helps—a little— pulling my floating head back down to the table.

A cooler. A luck killer.

I recall her face, floating in front of me, haloed in the cadaverous lights of the hospital room. *I have to go, Lee. I did this. All of it.*

My head feels like it's floating up on a string again. I take another slug of scotch to bring it back down and rattle my glass at Huxley for a refill. He flips me off without looking.

"Now, for the benefit of young Lee here, a quick refresher on the rules."

Mom slides the cards in a rainbow and muddles the runs of suits like an old pro. She stacks them neatly again then shuffles them overhand and riffles them together. She stares at them distantly as Jack talks.

"All we're doing here is playing one hand. Five-card stud. No discards, no swaps, nothing like that. You play the hand you're dealt."

Jack tightens his bow tie then flicks it stylishly askew, smiling. "But," he adds, "Claire will deal each card in its own round. Eight cards, one for each of us, set right here in the middle of the table." He taps one finger on the center of the felt.

"Once the first round of cards is in the center, spin

away, my friends. Find the one that suits you. No holds barred."

The beautiful smoker takes a languorous drag and eyes me like she's already stabbed me and I just haven't felt it yet. The big man lets out a low sigh. Jasper shifts in his wingback as if it's got a jutting spring somewhere.

"We do this five times. Until you've got a full hand. Then we show our cards. The dust in my music box will be divvied out proportionally. Half to the winner. Half again to second place. Half again to third—so on and so forth. Everyone gets something. Nobody leaves empty-handed."

"How generous," Jasper says.

"If you were a better spinner," says Lady Chang, "you'd get more dust."

The young goth girl licks her teeth and taps her black nails together.

I take a dainty sip of what's left in my glass, but I'm fighting down a rising panic with every breath.

My mother has the power to stop this. If she's really a luck killer, she could grab any one of us by the ears, even Jack Short, and snuff the dust from the room. Even if she's hamstrung by the necklace, if she's anything like Jillian was under the influence, she'll still be lucid enough in moments to understand what's happening.

Yet she hasn't acted. She's still here, dealing cards.

And Huxley, watching the skies, is strangely quiet. He's waiting. Something is wrong here, beyond the obvious.

"Away we go," says Jack, leaning back as my mother flips eight cards facedown into a pile in the center. The design on their backs sports the silver filigreed logo of the Diamond.

As soon as the last card lands on the felt, the room erupts

in dust. I'm playing poker in the eye of a hurricane. Dust whips from card to card, some strings probing carefully, others groping. Lady Chang spins her bracelet and casts a fisherman's net crafted from dust over the pile. She drags it through the cards and back to her hand, eyes fluttering left to right. Mr. Lapel Pin pulls a thin string like a garotte from his charm and sweeps it across the table like a radar.

Anyone with the sight who happened to be looking at the sparkling crown atop the Diamond tonight would see a storm in a bottle.

Anyone without the sight would simply see a bunch of weirdos at a card game.

The cards themselves don't move, of course. But they do light up in various shades of gold ranging from dirty white all the way to a blazingly pure honey color that looks like it has the power of a stack of Fort Knox bars behind it. I think everyone sees the same colors. I also think the colors are lying.

The beautiful smoker exhales a thin stream of smoke that envelops a honey-colored card, and I watch it change shades before my eyes—honey to red gold, then to a lack-luster yellow gold like a dime-store ring.

An illusion, then, brought on by one of the other players.

"Nice try, Chang," she says. "That one's worthless."

A small smile lifts the corner of Lady Chang's mouth. "Or is it?" she asks. "The first card is only as powerful as the four that follow."

She surprises the table by plucking up her own illusion before anyone can react. The Smoker furrows her smooth brow. Illusions upon illusions. A scramble follows: the goth girl reaches for a card, but the big man snatches it from the table first.

He listens to his pocket watch. "Too slow," he grumbles. I think he's referring to the kid, not the watch, which streams dust in delicate flows with the steady sweep of the second hand—not the kind of luck I'd expect from a man with his heft. The kid winks, flutters her hands to a card on the left, then picks up the card on the right.

Jasper sweeps his long arm over the table, and the cards change hue again. He pauses, grumbling. The Smoker sees something she likes and plucks it up with a smile.

That leaves three cards: one for Jasper, one for Jack, and one for me. All three look lucky enough to me, with nearly identical shades of gold. Then again, I have no idea what I'm doing.

Jasper takes the center card. He doesn't look happy about it, but he doesn't look happy about most things.

Jack hasn't spun an ounce of luck this entire round, only watching and sipping carefully at his silver julep cup full of crushed ice and fragrant rum. He gestures at the two remaining cards with a friendly smile.

"Take your pick. The first round is always a crapshoot anyway."

I look at the two remaining cards. Their colors shift and flicker like a campfire fed on strange wood. A better spinner might be able to make heads or tails of them. Not me. I grab the closest.

I almost look at the card. Everyone else has, Jack included, when he takes the remainder. But something stops me. I think of what Max would do. He was at this table once, watching all these loose cannons play cards and squabble for dust. The thought strikes me as absurd. All I want right now is to be sitting next to him, learning how to spin up a butterfly.

I feel like Max would've played blind. So I slide my

card in front of me and leave it be. Jasper shakes his head. I get a condescending laugh from Lady Chang.

"You know, you can't play the game if you don't see your cards, dumbass," says the big man. "It's about crafting a hand round by round."

"You play your game. I'll play mine," I say.

The Smoker looks disappointed. "You're not gonna last long at all," she says.

"Fine by me," says Mr. Lapel Pin.

Jack Short looks sidelong at me for a moment then shrugs. "Round two," he says, rubbing his hands together. "Deal 'em."

Mom steps up again. The spinners lean away whenever she gets near, as if she was leprous—all except for Jasper. Even though he can't seem to bring himself to meet her dead eyes, he leans in.

Another eight cards are neatly laid in a row. As soon as the second hand is dealt, the dust comes out again, washing over the table from all directions. Luck slaps into luck over the cards like waves slamming into one another in the ocean, spraying golden plumes over all of us, and all the while, the spinners still probe the cards. I can barely follow the game with my eyes, much less spin up the perimeter I see Lady Chang crafting or the gossamer veil the Smoker knits out of thin air to drape over her eyes and the cards alike.

Jack leans in to choose a card, second from the left. The big man shifts in his seat, snaps the case of his pocket watch closed, and pushes a thick band of dust toward Jack Short at the same time. It crosses the table in a blink, singeing my senses as it grazes me. I can't even react quickly enough to take my hands off the table. Jack can't possibly see it, much less stop it.

He snaps his fingers and splits the band in half. The dust cleaves right in front of his hand and pummels into the Smoker, to his right, and Mr. Lapel Pin, to his left.

For a moment, neither moves. The table pauses midbreath. Both spinners look like they're lost, asleep with their eyes open. Then I notice Mr. Lapel Pin is slowly jamming his thumb into the sharp end of his charm until blood wells and starts to drip.

"Oh, David. Not on the felt," says Jack, as if speaking to a puppy.

A full inch of pin is lodged in his thumb. I feel like I'm going to be sick from looking at it, but I can't turn away, even when it starts to poke through the top of his nail. Tears are streaming down his face.

The Smoker's anguished wail startles everyone at the table. She looks at her own hands desperately, and her gossamer veil falls to pieces. She shakes her head to rid herself of whatever demons rode that wave of dust but can't seem to do it. In a desperate moment, she flips her cigarette holder around and stubs out the cherry on her tongue.

She moans in pain but is breathing normally again. David seems to have used the pain to gather himself as well. He pulls his lapel pin free and presses his hand on his cocktail napkin.

"Pardon the blood, Jack. Not bad, Gio. Not bad," he says shakily.

"Wasn't aiming for you," the big man, Gio, rumbles.

David leans forward to choose a card then flicks a needle of dust toward Gio. It flies across the table alongside a few flecks of the spinner's blood, and both the dust and the blood land center left of Gio's chest, right where his heart is.

Gio flinches but says nothing. I'm not even sure the big

man saw it land. But I do know what David can do with a needle of dust, and I want no part of it.

Before David can turn his attention to me, I reach out and snatch the nearest card. It has almost no glow to it and feels pretty worthless, actually. But the sooner I pick a card, the sooner these lunatics will leave me alone, and maybe—just maybe—I won't have to scratch my eyes out to stay sane.

I slide the second card next to my first, facedown. I need to wake up here and start playing defense, building something to keep these people from touching me with their twisted luck. The only thing I got going for me right now is that none of them think I'm worth the energy, but that could change with the flip of a card. I need to gather some luck.

I take a deep breath and start with the light touch of Alli's hand on mine, the strange and wonderful sensation of the ring I just gave her, resting against my own.

I prick open the wound inside me again, and the dust wells slowly up from within.

The sun-warmed car. The smell of leather mixed with her perfume. The soft sound of the church bells pealing in the distance, which will eventually blend into the whine of a siren.

Were there bells? I don't think there were bells, now that I recall. I just put them in there and ran my brain over the addition so much that the bells stuck. And what was it Alli said to me? Something important. Something like *"the first day of the rest of our lives."*

Or maybe she didn't say that. She wasn't as dramatic as that, was she? I just stuck those words in, too—right before that final *pop* that crushes her and jerks her away from me like a marionette plucked from the stage.

I'm trying to make the pain of the loss hurt more, to bring up more dust from the wound. And it's working.

Suddenly, I'm not sure how much of my gilded memory is true and how much I've changed and then frozen for my own ends.

I open my eyes and find Jack Short looking right at me, and it's as if he understands my panic. My left hand is dipped an inch deep in a pool of dust of my own making. It has an intense red color, like blood mixed with gold.

"Don't dig too deep now, Lee," he says, his eyes sparkling.

In a moment of lucidity, my mother leans in toward me. "Run," she whispers.

"Deal the cards, Claire," says Short, and her glazed look returns.

Huxley Betancourt chuckles and checks his watch and looks expectantly at the black sky above Vegas.

Round three—the cards are laid, and the dust returns, stronger now. Each spinner's hand takes on a distinctive color of gold. I can't say whether each is accurate or an illusion meant to throw off the table, and I don't have the dust to spend finding out. I need my little golden pool to turn back an attack like Gio's wave.

Dust piles upon dust in the room. I try to fight the numb floating sensation that comes along with it by focusing on details like the ice melting in Short's glass and the tattered look of the clouds running in front of the moon. Short is hiding something, and Huxley is in on it. I think Jasper feels it too. He hasn't said a word since the game started. If I'm gonna get out of here, I have to stay lucid.

Chang draws a Chinese symbol in the dust on the felt, and the luck right in front of her turns syrupy. She taps a card, considers it, then pulls back. Her touch leaves a dollop of dust on the Diamond filigree like a glittering wax seal.

"I ain't afraid of your eastern bullshit, Chang," says the goth girl. She scratches the seal off with her long black nail and takes the card for herself.

"You should be," Chang says primly. She chooses a new card.

Short glances at the girl's nail and sucks in a breath through his teeth. "Watch yourself there, Sue."

The dust turns sickly yellow under her fingernail and spreads, crawling up her finger like filthy water soaking its way up a rag. Sue lets out a little shuddering breath and tries to flick the dust away, but it sticks.

"What is this?" she asks. "What did you do?"

"Luck is a funny thing," says Chang, looking at her own nails, red like ripe apples. "In China, we say good luck rains down from heaven—*fu dao*. But bad luck is the cousin of death. It creeps up from below."

Sue pushes herself standing from the table, horrified at the yellow ichor now climbing past her elbow.

"Death is nothing to be afraid of," replies Short, watching Sue with academic interest. "Bad luck, on the other hand, is pure fear."

Sue isn't looking at her arm anymore. Her eyes are wide and distant, and she's fiddling with the black gauge in her ear and facing the expanse of dark sky outside.

"The fear that you don't matter," Short continues. "That you're out of sync with this world. The fear that you're an alien and a stranger in this place."

Sue rips the gauge from her ear. A splash of blood slaps onto the glass countertop of the bar to her right. Huxley sets down the cut-crystal tumbler he's been nursing and steps back warily. Sue picks up the tumbler.

"Bad luck speaks the truth," Short continues. "We don't fit in here. This world is a terrible place. We are aliens and strangers. When we hit a string of bad luck, it opens our eyes to an unimaginable truth. That we don't belong."

The pain seems to have brought her back, the same way it snapped the Smoker and David back to the reality of the card game. For a moment, she looks like she's going to return to the table, then she pivots and throws Huxley's tumbler at the window with a shrill cry. She follows it with her body.

The entire table gasps—except for Short.

The window holds. The tumbler shatters harmlessly off the glass and Sue hits with a sickening thud. Her face leaves a dark red trail as she slides to the ground and is still.

Short turns back toward the table as if suddenly bored by the spectacle of attempted suicide. "What we call good luck is nothing but the ability to master the bad luck. To own the fear. It appears Sue has left the game," he adds, then brightens. "How about that, Lee! You're not gonna be in last place, after all."

His genuine chuckle turns my stomach. I pull a little bit of my dust back in, trying to offset the dirty-penny feeling of panic rising in my mouth. In the tense silence of that glass parlor, it's hard not to wonder if Short is right. Maybe all luck is bad luck, and it's just about how you own it.

In my mind, I see that butterfly Max made, along with the face of the girl as she reached out to touch it. His words ring out in my head: *"No such thing as bad luck."* I open my eyes and breathe a little more easily.

The cards are all spoken for, save for one. Even David and the Smoker have drawn their cards, their faces pale and eyes hollow. The dust on the one left is weak by any standards. I slide it toward myself and place it next to my other two, facedown. *No peeking.*

"You ain't even playin'," scoffs Gio. "Just being played."

"Do you want to win?" The question from Short sounds genuine.

"I want to stay alive," I say.

Jasper is slowly building that golden chain he acquainted me with in the tower, pulling link after link from the tiny cup of his spoon as it rests against the palm of his hand. He's watching me.

Short notices Jasper's intense gaze and gives me a small smile. "It appears our quiet giant has other plans for you. Perhaps in round four? Claire, would you please?"

The air is so thick with dust that it makes my eyes water —dust pulled from charms, dust refined and worked, dust floating thick like pollen or probing with little fingers. As my mother sets each card down, the table gather themselves. Jasper adds another link to his slowly building chain. The Smoker lights another thin cigarette with a shaky hand. Her tremor reminds me of Max. I wonder if Max wasn't on the raw end of a few luck punches at this very table.

Gio shuffles his bulk uncomfortably in his chair. His forehead and upper lip are glistening with sweat. He tugs at his collar and works his left hand like it's bothering him.

"How you feeling, Giovanni?" asks David. He pinches a cocktail napkin to stem the blood from his thumb, but that smirk is halfway back already. "You look a little off, big man."

I rub my shoulder at the memory of what that smug asshole did to me at the Golden Gate. *"I got a knack for making bodies remember things,"* he'd said.

My guess is big Giovanni's heart has been on the brink before, and David's luck is making him remember it. Gio knows it too. He shoots a look of such hatred David's way that I accidentally start to like the big fellow.

The final card of the fourth round is placed. My mother, still barely there, steps back into the shadow of Jack Short. No words of warning this time—no sign of recognition.

Gio wastes no time washing dust across the table. He has no intention of dying of a heart attack in this bird's nest. If David goes down, the dust he spun up goes down with him. He pushes another wave toward David then, at the last moment, spreads it wide to target Jasper and Short to either side.

Jasper snaps his golden chain tight and angles it with a flick of his spoon. The golden links bow as the wave smashes against them, but he holds the line. David's thin garotte isn't enough to stop all of it. He gets drenched and seems to deflate until his head is lolling like a man nodding from too much heroin.

Jack Short snaps his finger, and the wave is blown apart like mist in the wind. He points, and the mist shifts like fickle campfire smoke until it's coming my way.

I act on instinct, dipping both hands in my little pool of blood-gold dust and splashing it up and over my face. I pull it through my hair and wipe it under my eyes. I drip it down my neck and run it up my arms to the elbows. I cake myself in the sorrow of my own memory before I can get doused with whatever horror Gio has laced within his dust.

It almost works.

At first, the mist beads off me and drops to the floor, but the wave was big, and the room is thick with its aftermath. Soon, it saturates my clothes and hair in the places I couldn't cover, and with it comes a mounting feeling of loss —no pain, no sadness, just... absence. I feel nothing. And it's horrible.

Before I know it, I'm digging a thumb into the scar at my

shoulder. Even the feeling of prying open stitched-together skin would be preferable to this emptiness. I see why the Smoker burned her own tongue. I see why David shoved his lapel pin through his thumb.

My mother comes toward me, but before she can pass behind Short, he holds her up with an outstretched arm.

"If you help him, I'll redouble the pain," he says simply. "No cheating."

Her eyes are crystal clear again and full of hatred, but she doesn't press.

I want to hold on to this line of thought. It's real, and it matters until it doesn't. And nothing seems to matter at all. I dig harder at my shoulder, looking for a shock to set me straight. I feel the slight slip of my shoulder joint separating and sigh into the pain with a disgusting sort of relief as it fills the nothing... for a moment.

But the moment passes. Short pulls a card. Lady Chang already has hers. The beautiful Smoker sits wearily in a cloud of her own making, but it seems to be protecting her from the mist. She has four cards, too, as does Jasper, who is watching my mother take her place at the table again. Even Giovanni wipes his brow and seems to steel himself. He chooses the card closest him.

David crumples to the ground. Short looks at him distastefully as Huxley pulls him away from the table by the armpits and dumps him unceremoniously by the window, not far from Sue.

I hear a helicopter thumping its way down from the sky, and I know I should be more concerned about that, but caring about it is hard. Three cards are left to choose from, but I've lost what little taste I have for this game. They all look the same to me. All the dust looks the same: miserable.

I slap my hand on one of them and pull it toward

myself. Then I click my shoulder around to set it back in its socket and sigh loudly enough to startle Short, who is turned around and watching the sky.

"Last round," I say, blinking back tears. "Let's get this over with."

"Agreed," says Short. "Claire, would you do the honors?"

My mother moves like a marionette once more. Jasper's eyes flick between me and her, her and me. She sets the remaining two aside then deals eight cards down in a single row, still dealing to the two who have cracked. The second the last card falls, Jasper strikes.

I recognize the flick of movement far too late. He used it on me in the tower, throwing his chain like a weighted whip. I cringe, ready for his luck to hit me like a hammer. But it doesn't.

He's not aiming for me. He's aiming for my mom, and his aim is true. Jasper snaps his chain tight at the last moment, right into my mother's neck. Mom freezes.

Tailings of Jasper's luck drift down over me. He's been linking together a strange brew, nothing like the overwhelming force that marked his earlier attack on me in his tower. This is a shot of ice-cold vodka, a snort of smelling salts.

He means it as an eye-opener, and it works.

My mother speaks to me. "I'm so sorry, Lee," she whispers. Then she touches my shoulder, and the dust that covers me is burned away. Her touch is freezing but not in the way Huxley's cursed charms were cold. This is riverwater cold, mountain runoff cold.

"Look at them," she whispers. "See what I see."

And I do.

I see Lady Chang first. She draws upon a terrifying

memory from when she was a young girl, her father dragging her to a filthy orphanage in the rain. Deafening thunder and blinding lightning split the sky as he ties her hand to a rusty doorknob with a piece of biting leather, the same charmed strip of leather she's turned into a bracelet and wears around her wrist. He slams his fist four times on the front door as she wails. The most powerful moment of her pain is when he tells her she's lucky he didn't drown her, then he runs away into the rain.

Chang takes her final card. I look away and find the beautiful Smoker next.

She's naked, sitting alone on a pile of clothes inside a darkened dance studio. Ballet slippers hang over the stretch bar. She's thinking of how perfectly she executed that fouetté, a whipped throw she'd worked on for years. Her routine was flawless. But it wasn't enough. He'd run his hands over her breasts to check her posture and groped between her legs to check her positioning as he told her how competitive the role was and how she might get an edge if she wanted to.

She let the weight of his old body drag her down. How quickly she'd gone from soaring to sinking.

He left her here, her body stinging and bleeding. He told her he'd call if she got the part. She stayed in the darkness, rummaged around in her clothes until she found a pack of stale cigarettes he'd left behind. She lit one up and took a drag, and after a minute, she stopped shaking, and the smoke around her took on a strange golden sparkle that she'd never seen before.

The Smoker takes her final card. I turn away, but my eyes find Giovanni.

In his mind, Giovanni stuffs himself with food he hates while his father beats his mother to death in a bedroom upstairs. He vomits in the sink in the dead of night, and the memory he gilds—the moment he runs over again and again in his mind until it's everything to him—is how his trembling hands are lit by the sick light of the moon dripping through a skylight as his mother's cries clip off. His father's pocket watch is on the counter, frozen at 11:11.

He wears it now in the watch pocket of his vest. He hasn't wound it since. He has no fight left in him for this game. None of the spinners do. He takes his card.

I whisper for Mom to let me go. I don't want any of this anymore. But she turns me to face Jasper.

I see his memory—well-worn, more lacquered than the others, drawn deeply upon.

It's of my mother, much younger—younger than I am now. She sits on the toilet in the dark in a small, cluttered apartment. She reaches between her legs and pulls her hand forth. In the weak light filtering in from the city streets, he sees a pool of dark red in her palm. She doesn't know he's watching and doesn't know he sees her holding her other hand over her mouth, wracked with silent sobs.

His own mother gave him a silver spoon when he told her he was having a boy. Jasper's frozen moment is when he finds it in the drawer of his nightstand. As the choked sound of my mother's muffled weeping drifts into the bedroom, he tries to snap it in half with his bare hands, his teeth gritting. He can't do it.

It now lies half bent and well-worn in his hand. His thumb scratches at the cup uneasily as he takes his final card.

"That's enough, Claire," says Short, his voice deadly quiet.

For once, I agree with him, but Mom won't let go. She

places both hands on my shoulders, and in a daze, I turn to face her.

"I love you," she says. "Now look at me."

There is no sound in the memory she shows me, only sensation. The rough scratch of the fireman's fluorescent jacket as he holds her back. The pop of little bits of shattered glass beneath her feet like the shells of acorns. The smell of gasoline.

I've been pulled from the car already, rushed to the hospital in an ambulance. Alli is on the sidewalk, a soft shape under a white sheet. The tips of her fingers poke out from underneath. She'd just had her nails done. Soft pink. Mom remembers holding that hand after the ceremony and kissing us both farewell as we stepped into the car.

There are other memories too.

That night with Jasper, when the light of the little seed of life within her fled before her fingertips like smoke on the wind as she caressed her belly. She knew the miscarriage was coming before the bleeding ever happened. She believes her touch chased away the child's soul.

She can't control when this darkness comes upon her. She calls them dark chapters—these times in her life when her power awakens and her touch becomes a curse. The curse can last from an hour to a month before it simmers and burrows down within her again, waiting.

I see another memory—perhaps her first—a frozen snapshot in time: my mother as a young girl weeping in the loft of her father's, my grandfather's, old barn in upstate New York. A litter of puppies lay still in the hay before her, still steaming in the cold autumn air. Her hand had touched each as it was delivered. Their eyes never opened. That was the first time she realized something was wrong.

Leaving me at the hospital broke her heart, but she

couldn't risk snuffing my life out too. She would either find someone who could help her—someone who could explain why she was such a danger to those she loved—or she would die trying.

She found Short.

"Claire, you don't want to go back to how things were, do you?" Short asks softly, his voice bringing me out of the depths of my mother's memories. He lightly caresses the carved surface of his music box with the tip of a thumb.

My mother's touch lingers. I see the man truly for only an instant:

A young boy screams at the wide banks of a rushing river of golden luck. Boiling dust makes the flow that barreled down Fremont look like nothing more than a swollen gutter after a rainfall. His father's hand is firmly on his neck, and Short's heart is filled with a single certainty: if he dies, he deserves it. He is afraid nonetheless, and his fear shames him.

His father's voice comes from behind him. *"Either you take all of it, or you get none of it."* Short's head is shoved down. The memory wavers, a dream on the verge of popping.

In a blink, I'm back at the card table. Short cut me off. He slammed the blinds down, much the same way that Max hid himself in plain sight. He's watching me carefully, perhaps determining how much I saw.

I saw enough to know one thing for certain: Jack Short has no intention of giving up the dust he's collected in that box. He's an all-or-nothing type of man.

Short smiles at me as if he can read my thoughts. It's the smile of a man who is finally able to tell his secret. He slides his final card toward himself.

"Pick a card, Lee. It's time to show our hands," he says.

I pick my last card from the remainder and slide it weakly over to complete my hand. The thumping blades of the helicopter start to rattle the crystal glassware at the bar. My mother's touch is gone, along with all the dust that I had, but a nameless dread lingers. Short started a Rube Goldberg machine long ago that has finally found its way to this moment in this glass bird's nest.

The Smoker quickly turns her cards over. Three queens. A good hand, but all her gloat and confidence are gone. She's spinning the ivory cigarette holder nervously between her fingers and looking toward the elevator beyond.

Huxley watches the helicopter descend and checks his watch. Lady Chang's cards tremble slightly on the felt as she flips each. A flush, all spades. She doesn't seem to care. She's watching Short as if waiting for him to make a move. She's barely suppressing a smile, the same smile she wore as she walked away from that dryer.

The helicopter touches down. It is jet-black and unmarked, and the windows are darkened save for the soft green glow of the instrument panel, which gives it a reptilian look. Jasper stands to get a better look. He turns over his cards almost as an afterthought—a full house, aces full of eights, a very strong hand.

The door to the helicopter opens, but nobody gets out.

"Is that your ride, Jack?" asks Jasper. He steps around and behind his chair, looking at it strangely.

"Yes, it is," Short replies.

"A little early," says Giovanni, turning over his own hand as he heaves himself to standing. Four of a kind, sevens. It's the high hand so far, but Gio doesn't look too happy about it. He rubs at his chest in a way that tells me maybe David's dust did some real damage before he dropped the man.

"Right on time," says Short. "Royal flush for me." He turns over each card in succession. Ten, jack, queen, king, ace—all diamonds, naturally.

"Unbelievable," says Giovanni.

"But true. I'm better than you, Gio. And Jasper. Better even than the formidable Lady Chang. Fact is, I'm better than all of you put together."

My mother has a moment of clarity. She makes a move toward me, her hand reaching out. "Run!" she screams.

A single note chimes from the music box in Short's hands, and a current of electricity seems to run through the room. It makes all of us slump an inch or two, and I feel as if I've somehow run a mile just sitting here. All the dust in the room shifts slightly toward the music box, like smoke seeking an open window.

Short opens the box, and it begins to play. The song is in a minor key, something I imagine I'd hear playing in the quiet corner of an abandoned room. I don't recognize it, but that hardly matters. It leeches everyone and everything of dust with slow, relentless surety.

I lose track of time and place as the tune plinks sadly along. It plays for ten seconds or ten minutes. All I know is that when I come to again, the room is wiped clean of all dust. I watch, hypnotized, as Short sets the lid closed with a single slim finger.

"I suppose now's as good a time as any to announce a slight rule change," he says. His face is apologetic, his tone understanding, as if we were somehow at fault and he was forgiving us. "I'm taking everything," he says. "All the dust."

Lady Chang smiles knowingly, and I realize that she's been in on this double cross from the beginning. Giovanni takes a massive silk kerchief from his breast pocket and mops at his sweating brow.

The beautiful Smoker snaps out of it first. She stands, tucks her cigarette holder down her cleavage, grabs her purse, and heads for the door.

Another somber note plinks from the music box, hollow and longing. I feel it echo across the room and watch as it hits the Smoker. She staggers and falls against the window.

"I'm afraid I can't let you leave, Victoria," says Short.

I'm waiting for Jasper to blow up at Short, to take that chain of his and swing it right into his temple, but instead, he looks furious with himself... and slightly resigned. That, more than anything, sets my heart hammering. If Jasper doesn't think he can fight his way out of this, the rest of us have no hope.

"You already control the flow in this town, Jack," says Jasper. "What good does it do you to pile more luck on top of the mountain you already have?"

Short taps the box. "This luck is leaving Las Vegas, my friend. Lady Chang and I are going east. Far east."

Chang stands and snaps her red leather pocketbook closed with finality.

"You're robbing us," says Gio.

Short thinks for a moment then nods.

"You son of a bitch," says Gio, and in the hand where he held the kerchief is now a small handgun.

I duck on instinct and find myself staring at my cards. An odd feeling passes over me, and the small hairs on my arms do the wave up and down.

"Watch yourself, Giovanni," says Short, his voice friendly in an *aw-shucks* sort of way. He doesn't seem to care one whit that a gun is pointed at his head.

"I'll kill you," says Gio.

Jasper holds his hand up and starts to speak, but Gio pulls the trigger.

Short snaps his fingers at the exact same time the handgun pops. Both sounds seem to bounce off the glass and rebound in upon us.

When I look up, Short is smiling sadly. I wait for a moment, hoping for the movie-scene ending where blood wells up from the center of his immaculate tuxedo shirt. But despite the fact that Gio was three feet away and couldn't possibly have missed, no blood ever shows. Short's smile remains.

"Misfire," he says. "Tough luck."

The snub nose of Gio's pistol is cracked and smoking. His hand is bleeding. He drops the gun, stunned.

"Did you really think you could shoot me, Gio?" Short asks, perplexed. "Really?"

Gio takes his kerchief back out and slowly wraps his bleeding knuckles. He sits down in a daze.

"Huxley, escort Claire to the helicopter, and the both of you buckle in. Time to close up shop."

Huxley adjusts the night stone at the center of my mother's neck with a tap of his finger, and it bubbles like dry ice dunked in water. It's clearly a conduit for some power, something that burns off my mother's luck-killing power but saps her free will at the same time.

"Magnificent, isn't it?" Huxley says. "Same family as the ring I'd planned for Jillian."

Mom looks up at me blankly, and I see within her flat gaze much of the same conflict I saw in Jillian's eyes at that flea-bitten chapel. She walked in the front door of a prison of her own making, but she did it for me.

Even if I ripped the thing off, she wouldn't come with

me—not while she believes her touch can kill me, not while she thinks Alli's death was her fault.

Hux gives me a cocky two-fingered salute and opens the door to the helipad. The thumping of the helicopter assails us. Bottles rattle and glasses chatter. Whipping air stirs the slumped forms of Sue and David and sets them groaning. The wind unsettles my cards on the table. I slap down on them to keep them from scattering but not before the first one gets flipped.

It's the Tower.

"Lady Chang, after you," says Short, bowing and gesturing to her.

Chang walks around the table without so much as a glance at the three of us still sitting. She steps over Sue like a bag of trash, holds her hair in place, and walks toward the chopper with its spinning rotor blades.

I flip the second card. The Tower again. I flip the third. The Tower. Fourth, fifth: Tower, Tower.

Jasper sees each card as it skates around the table in the backdraft. He looks up at me, pale faced.

"What happens to me if I try that elevator?" I ask. The cold dread that started at the nape of my neck is now rippling in my gut.

"You'll find it out of order, I'm afraid," says Short.

"I'll take the stairs, then."

"Under construction." Short lightly bites his lower lip. "Tough luck."

"So we're prisoners here," Jasper says.

"Briefly," Short says, winking. He tucks his music box under one arm and turns toward the door but then sees my hand of Towers—the only cards still on the felt. For the first time all night, I see a moment of true hesitation from him.

He looks up at me with narrowed eyes. "How did you do that?"

"I didn't do anything. That's the hand I was dealt," I say.

"Then that must be a pretty powerful ring you got there," Short says. "Wish I could take it with me, but stolen charms never work quite right. I've tried."

I look at my wedding ring. It once stood for eternity, an unbroken bond, but it now stands as little more than a sad signpost pointing down a path I'll never walk with a woman who is gone. The ring that Alli put on my finger and the ring that wraps it now are not the same thing. It was once a contract between us, one that promised forever, and in a sense, it delivered—just not the way Alli would have wanted. It weighs upon me now, tying me to a moment in time that I know she would want me to move past.

"It's not the ring," I say. "It's the memory that's got a hold of me, the memory that's powerful in all the wrong ways."

"You sound like a fellow I used to play cards with," Short says, thumbing the carved filigree of the music box. "Called himself marvelous, but really, he was just crazy. Ironic, though. Things didn't work out so well for him either."

Short steps over the threshold, out onto the pad. "Don't take it personally, Lee," he says, voice raised over the whir of the blades. "It's all about the luck. And don't worry, I'll take good care of Claire. I am a good shepherd of my prize assets."

He taps the outer glass of the tower. "Unfortunately, this pretty little bird's nest isn't one of my prize assets. My hotel is about to get a haircut, but she'll survive. Can't say the same for you."

He turns away without a word. Jasper, Gio, and I watch helplessly as he walks the length of the helipad. The force of the air tousles his hair and ripples his tuxedo as he deftly steps up and inside. He slides the door shut behind himself as the motor revs into high gear.

The helicopter lifts up and away while we remain, barely standing, not a drop of dust among us. In the absence of the thumping roar, the silence is deafening.

Gio sits down like a man who's found a square of weak shade in the desert. He dabs at his forehead.

Jasper walks carefully around the table. "Where is it?" he mutters. "Where, where, where..."

"Where's what?" asks Gio.

"He had to put it somewhere nobody could sense it," Jasper says. Then he stops. He kneels down and has to bend farther still to look under the table. I follow him.

A black box is affixed to the underside of the table where Short sat, right underneath where that godforsaken music box was. The box has a blinking red diode and a small digital clock face that reads 2:15.

2:14.

2:13.

"I'm guessing that's not a card shuffler," I say.

Jasper grasps it in his huge hands, thinks for a moment, and pulls. Nothing. He sits down and puts a shoe against it, pushing a little. Nothing. He pushes a little harder. Nothing.

"It's drilled into the table," he says, standing. He grasps the table with two hands and lifts—a small creak but nothing more. "And the table is bolted to the floor."

I close my eyes and rub at my face. My skin feels like greasy sandpaper. Vegas has hollowed me out and hijacked my memories. I've got two minutes to live. I want to spend them picturing Alli, but I can't. All I see is the final moment. Every time I try to go back to the lifetime we lived together, my brain skips forward again. I feel I'm being rewritten, losing more of her by the second.

"Maybe all of us could lift it," says Gio. He struggles to standing. Places his bulk against the table.

I stand half-heartedly. "And what? Throw a bomb down onto the Las Vegas strip?"

"Let's try it," Jasper says. "Due diligence."

I know nothing is going to move this table. But we try anyway.

Nothing moves the table. I sit down again and put my head in my hands. Right now, I'm more scared of the fact that I can't remember what Alli looked like on the night I proposed to her than I am of the fact that I'm about to rain down upon Las Vegas Boulevard in a million bloody pieces.

Jasper walks quickly to the elevator and presses the buttons. Nothing. He slams them. Nothing. The stairway door doesn't move when he shoulders hard into it. This place has become a coffin, sealed tight.

Jasper plops down in his chair and looks underneath. "A minute fifteen," he says. "If there was any dust, any dust at all, maybe we could..."

Another precious second ticks by.

"But he took it all," he says. "He took everything." He looks forlornly out the window, and I know he's talking about much more than dust.

I feel him. Maybe the fact that Short took Mom is a good thing. At least she isn't going to die.

*Not today, at least.* The voice in my brain takes on Max's stuttering tone. *"Sure, she's alive. But at what c-c-cost?"*

"There's nothing any of us can do." I'm not sure

whether I'm talking to Gio and Jasper or to Max in my head. I suppose it doesn't matter either way. I take up the set of Towers, all five of them, pictographs burning bright, raining people into the night, and I throw them. "These stupid cards were written in stone. What Zja-Zja sees happens. No escape."

My ring itches me. I'm furious with myself, yelling at nobody and everybody. None of this—not the dust, not the luck, not this weird world I walked into—none of it is worth what I've lost and what I'm losing every time I dig deeper into my heart.

I look around at the spinners left here to die—all broken people, some of us literally. All of us spiritually flayed. And we do it to ourselves, again and again and again—knowing full well that each time we dig deep, we give that memory more and more purchase inside— because for those moments that we control the luck, we're floating and free of that one terrible moment that has come to define us.

We're all luck junkies in the end.

Max is in my mind again, speaking into the darkness on that first night we met, the red cherry of his cigarette bouncing over each word: *"If you can read the dust, you can pick the right card on the table. If you know the d-dust like I do, you can change the cards that are dealt."*

I open my eyes.

And this whole time, I thought he was talking about actual playing cards.

"I don't want any part of this anymore," I say.

"Yeah, no shit," says Gio. "It ain't exactly up to you no more, kid."

I look at my ring one last time and run my finger over its gleaming surface. I may be losing more and more of the moment she put it on my finger, but I still remember enough—enough to say goodbye.

"You're wrong," I reply. "It is up to me."

I grab my ring and work it off. With each sliding inch, it glows more brightly. When I pass it over my knuckle, it sputters to life with a brightness so rich that it makes all the dust I've seen in this city look like dime-store glitter.

Jasper stands and backs away. So does Gio.

The echo of Max in my head: *I beat them because I realized there's only one thing more powerful than finding your luck charm.*

Now I know what it is. The only thing more powerful than finding my luck charm is giving it up.

As I pull the ring from my finger, I hear a subtle pop, like the sound inside your head when you swallow during a pressure change. Somewhere deep inside me, an engine whirs to life, one that had been dormant for far too long. It's a cold start, like a motor rumbling to life out of a deep freeze, cracking thin layers of ice and chasing away hoar-frost until it's a roar inside me, as if every memory of the life Alli and I had together floods back to me at once, as if the pain of her loss was a dam holding them all back from their rightful place.

The true brilliance of the ring—all its power—is sucked into my heart in an instant. I shut my eyes against the blinding gold as I'm blown back into my seat.

This feels nothing like digging into my heart, nothing like mining my memories and trapping the dust there like a caged animal. Nothing like bending the dust to my will.

The dust and I finally understand one another. It's a brief and baffling alignment, like a glimpse at understanding the shifting wind. But it's very powerful. It pays respect to the weight of what I'm giving up.

I open my eyes, and the world is cast in the dripping light of the golden hour. I set my ring in the center of the table. It seems small, dull. It's nothing more than metal now. Everything it was is inside me.

The breath of fate blows gently upon my back.

I stand. Jasper and Gio fall farther back, and I realize with a peaceful sort of understanding that they are afraid. They fear death. They fear dying as the men they are. They fear Jack Short, the dust, Las Vegas. And now, they're afraid of me.

*Here. This might help ease that fear.*

I walk around to Jack Short's empty chair and push it aside. The timer has five seconds left. I can feel it without looking.

Four.

Three.

I cup my right hand and blow into it, like I'm warming it up in winter. Dust flies from my fingers. It falls through the table like flour through a sieve, drenching the bomb beneath.

Two.

One.

One.

One.

Gio holds his kerchief against his lips. Jasper winces, preparing for an oblivion that doesn't come—not quite yet, at least. *Must have been a glitch in the timer. Lucky us.*

I unfurl my hand one finger at a time. "The dust and I have come to an understanding," I say.

I hear my voice as if from outside myself. I see my words as tiny puffs of golden air like a sparrow's song in winter. "The dust is telling me that if we move, we just might live."

Gio tucks his kerchief in his breast pocket and looks at

Jasper. Jasper takes one more look at my eyes, and in that moment, another emotion flits across his face. I've seen hate and anger, fear and pain. But not this. Not until now.

I see hope.

Jasper steps aside and gestures to the hallway and beyond. "Then let's get the hell out of here," he says.

"We take the others," I say.

"Those three?" Gio asks, nodding at the other spinners, prone on the ground.

Only the Smoker is moving, and barely at that. David and Sue are out cold but not dead.

"They're dead weight," he says.

"I won't leave them," I reply. "It's as good as murder."

"They'd leave you," Jasper says quietly.

"I know that. But I'm not like them. Gio, you take the Smoker—"

"I'm having a heart attack, kid," says Gio.

"Which is why you get the one that might be able to stand. Quickly."

Gio takes one last look at me, up and down, then shuffles over to her. He needles her hard in the rib with the tip of one polished shoe. "Up and at 'em, sweetheart. Today might be your lucky day."

Jasper moves over to David, the only one of the three I know I couldn't carry. He kneels down and picks up the bulky man as easily as a sack of flour. The goth girl is thin and small, with a gymnast's build. But dead weight is still dead weight. I get down on one knee and flop her to a seated position, where she settles in the crook of my shoulder. I count to three, breathe, then stand with her in my arms. The precarious balance might work if we keep moving.

"The elevator," I say.

"It's locked," says Gio.

He's sweating again, but the Smoker is on his shoulder, propped under his arm, half standing on her own. She looks at me with dazed eyes that are widening in fear, which makes sense. I think I'm literally smoking gold.

"The elevator," I say again.

The three of us walk around the windblown demise of the card room. I'm the first down the hall.

We stop at the elevator. Gio props the Smoker against the wall and leans against her to keep her upright, blowing like a bull. He slams the buttons to prove his point. They stay dark.

I look out the window and around the corner at the exterior elevator shaft. It's right there, clinging like a drop of water to the glass of the Diamond right outside the window, maybe five feet up. It may be dark—locked up tight—but to my eyes, it glows with a pulse, an inner beat that speaks to me.

"Please tell me we're not breaking the glass," says Gio.

"We're not breaking the glass," I say. "Stand close, both of you. Right in front of the door."

I find the fire alarm and grasp it with one hand. "I want everyone to take three deep breaths. As soon as these doors open, step out. No matter what."

We take three deep breaths, as deeply as one can breathe with the timer of a bomb stuck at one. I pull the fire alarm. The glass pops, and for one terrible second, I think the thing isn't even connected. Then I hear the claxon of a siren climbing its way up the building.

The elevator doors open. Jasper and I step in, and Gio falls in behind with the Smoker. All of us hit the floor hard. The elevator drops before we can even right ourselves. Air is screaming all around us. If I'm guessing right, and I know I am, this bird's nest is connected directly to the fire command. Every elevator bay along the top half of this elevator shaft will be open by now, with some serious fans pulling air up and out through the roof.

As we drop away from the bird's nest, a smattering of dust slowly seeps back into the elevator. Jasper and Gio gather it to themselves as quickly as they can. For Gio, it's a patch-up job, something to keep him from keeling over. Jasper tries to fashion his chain again, but it's an ephemeral thing, wispy and weak. Jack Short sucked a lot of dust into that devil's box of his. It's safe to say there's no luck in Las Vegas tonight.

No luck outside of me, that is.

The elevator slows as another sound builds underneath the roaring evac fans: the sound of panic.

"Get ready," I say.

The elevator settles. Gio pats at the beads of sweat on his brow. Jasper softly clears his throat. The Smoker moans.

The doors open to a cacophony. Fire alarms are blaring, gamblers and tourists running and shouting. The casino floor is as bright as a supermarket with emergency lighting—nothing sexy or glamorous about it now.

People are grabbing their chips from the gaming tables and punching out tickets on the slots. Every machine seems to be blaring at once. The casino cages are lowered and locked to our left, distraught cashiers securing their posts, ignoring the crowd trying to cash out.

Jasper props David over his shoulder and reaches into a pocket. He pulls out his spoon and thumbs it, looking anywhere and everywhere for some dust. Gio staggers to a corner and drops the Smoker unceremoniously against a wall, which he slides down shortly after, sucking wind.

I set the goth down as lightly as I can next to the Smoker. She slumps over gracelessly.

"What are you doing?" Jasper asks. "We have to get out of here."

"Better inside than out," I say. The words form golden puffs from my mouth.

The pulse of this place is frantic and afraid, but it taps out a steady song, one I feel has already been written. I know when the beat is about to drop.

Jasper has an inner beat too. His spoon glows brilliantly, a magnifying glass in the sun, but the dust won't come. He understands what's coming and frowns for a brief moment before setting David down as well.

"I told you," says Jasper. "Her cards don't lie."

"The tower must fall," I say. "But that doesn't mean we have to fall with it."

The beat drops. A single clap of thunder from thirty floors above punches at my sternum and sends everyone crouching on instinct. The walls and floor shudder violently, and the lights flicker, flicker, and fail. We're plunged into a red-tinged darkness. The casino erupts in screams.

A stampede is coming next. I know this. A crush of humanity will be rushing toward the doors. The panic in the room is a palpable thing, a taste like pennies in the air. It's already starting, but any scream of warning on my part would be drowned out in the chaos.

The first wave pushes through the front doors, only to meet a rain of fire. I can see it even from where we stand, glass falling on glass, a tinkling sound that is strangely beautiful. Then the first big debris, a metal girder, crashes to the ground. Another slams into the tapered glass exterior of the Diamond and splinters the thick glass. A flaming chair bounces down and out into the crowded streets—one in eight chance it was mine.

People that wanted out now suddenly want back in. They press back, squeezing those stuck in the middle.

I sense the fire above and the falling debris with the same timing as the elevator and the walls. I feel the timing of everything, all of it like synchronized gears spinning and clicking and whirring within the guts of a magnificent watch.

I fling rich dust like gouts of golden blood from my fingers, out and over the foyer, where the beat is hammering hardest. The central fountain is already offset from the shuddering of the explosion. It wants to fall. All I have to do is give it a little nudge, popping hoses and snapping jets. The spray clears the people—an area in the foyer about the size of a kiddie pool—just as a single beam of steel slices through the glass ceiling above and slams vertically into the floor. The beam stands upright for a span of heartbeats then tips, tips, and falls onto the fountain, crushing it like tinfoil. It spews water that hisses on contact with the hot iron.

Nobody is hurt. Lucky, lucky, lucky.

The tick of the great watch continues, louder now at the front of the hotel where, to my sun-drenched sight, the huge glass panes of the street-facing windows are vibrating like golden guitar strings fit to snap.

I hear the roar of sirens coming in fast—too fast.

No leaning fountain here—nothing at all is available to clear the area—just people way too close to a patch of ground that is about to be pulverized.

A young woman is holding the hand of an old man sitting stunned on the ground feet from the thrumming window. She looks up briefly and glances back toward the guts of the casino to take in the full scope of the mess she's in. With a flip of her copper hair, I see her face clearly for a second—sharp cut, aquiline, but with that button nose. I know that nose.

"Jillian."

I say her name softly. Nobody, not even Jasper next to me, hears my voice. But the dust hears. Her name floats from my mouth in a puff of gold that hangs in the air in front of me like smoke on a still night. I'm surprised at how cool it feels when I skim the outer edge with my fingertip. The smoke gathers itself at my touch, slowly spinning and curling until it vaguely resembles a bird. It stretches its wings and comes into focus with a tiny heart of dust that beats furiously. The bird revs and revs until it takes off like a bullet through the casino and slams bodily into Jillian's back.

I wince. But she doesn't.

Jillian stands taller, seeming to see the glass in front of her as I do—thrumming with warning, moments from disaster. She takes a moment and glances back into the depths where I stand, and I know she's looking for me, but the moment is broken when the incoming siren reaches a fever pitch.

Jillian dashes to the wall and punches a lever behind the blackjack table that spits a half inch of something that looks like corrugated metal from the wall—blinds, perhaps, to keep the dipping sun from baking the casino floor or maybe a divider for poker tournaments. Either way, she pulls it after herself, pushing people to the back of it, shrouding the windows just as something hits the ground outside with the sound of freight-train cars slamming together.

As soon as she closes off the window, tires screech and brakes squeal. The blinds are buckshot with debris. In an instant, I'm taken back to that final moment with Alli, and I'm certain that horror will repeat itself, but I force my eyes to stay open, to bear witness this time. Jillian turns her back toward the gate, shielding the older man as a car punches into the blinds, bulging and rending the metal until the slats snap one after another like rubber bands.

The car squeals to a stop maybe a foot from her shoulder blade. It's a cop car whose siren dies as she slowly turns around, her eyes wide and drinking in the red and blue light. She could kiss the grille if she wanted.

I want to collapse with relief, but I still have work to do.

The car missed the crowd, but they are thrown back anyway in a struggle to get away from the windows. I scan the floor. Nothing is thrumming with killing tension any longer. The worst of the bird's nest has hit the ground.

But the stampede is becoming a riot. The worst danger to these people is themselves. If only I could speak to everyone here as I did to Jillian. I'd tell them that their own fear is their biggest enemy.

The words mist gold around my head, a little personal cloud of luck that dissipates five feet from me.

Max's voice sounds in my head: *"If you want to tell them, just tell them."*

Speaking the language of luck to a thousand people will take every last ounce of dust I have within me. And without the ring, it's likely to be the last time I ever spin luck again.

*Fine. So be it. It's a loser's game anyway.*

I take a breath that taps into the base of my lungs. After pulling all the dust from my blood, I craft a single thought within my mind: *save yourself by saving others.*

I picture what it might look like if the panic was blown from this room and gold dust fell down like cool rain. And I exhale.

I know immediately that I've tapped too deep. Gold pours from my mouth. I hit something, some vein inside, and luck is spilling out faster than I can control it. This must be what it feels like to give blood until you die. A cold weakening creeps up my legs, to my groin, gut, now my chest. It slows my heart and chills my lungs.

The last thing I see is a pool of gold high above me. My pool of gold, a thunderhead stretching the length of the casino floor, breaks open and rains upon the crowd below.

## CHAPTER ELEVEN

F lashes of consciousness. I'm being carried. My eyes flutter open, and I see Jasper, his face grim. Holding me in his arms, he pushes his way through a door. My limbs are leaden. Flickering lights above feel like they're drilling a hole through my head.

I close my eyes.

Surfacing again. Heavy knocking, hard and fast. Jasper waits. Curses. Knocks again. The sound is horrendous. Like his fists are pounding against the inside of my head. I try to tell him to stop, but the words come out as moans. He looks down at me, alarmed.

Something is unlatched. A door swings open.

"What took you so long?" asks Jasper, furious. "He's dying, for God's sake."

"Then you'll watch your tone, if it's the last thing he ever hears," snaps Zja-Zja. I'd recognize that voice anywhere. "Now bring him in. Quickly."

Jasper shoulders through the door. My head bumps softly against the doorframe, and stars pop in my brain.

. . .

I AWAKE AGAIN to complete silence. I'm on my back. The sky is a heavy velvet above me, the stars are soft glints in the distance. I recognize that sky—not really a sky at all, but the heavy studded tapestry draping the ceiling of the Parlor of the Eye.

My arms still feel encased in lead, but my fingers are my own. I curl them and unfurl them slowly then rest. I smell incense, soft and sweet. Zja-Zja hums beside me, a wordless tune that strikes me as impossibly familiar, something my mother sang to me when I was very young.

*I see the moon, and the moon sees me.*
*The moon sees someone that I'd like to see.*
*Over the mountains and over the trees,*
*Shine on the one I love.*

Turning my head toward her takes almost more effort than I have within me. Out of the corner of my eye, I see her sitting at her velvet table. Her kerchief is spread. The river stone sits atop, and the knife anchors the bottom. She spreads the cards with her hands, slowly, like kneading bread.

"Sleep, Lee," she says without looking up from her work. "You're safe for now."

When I next open my eyes, the room is still—no incense, no humming, no shuffling of cards. Outside are the muted sounds of activity, the daily comings and goings of the Golden Swan, but more so—strange for a casino on its deathbed. I find I can sit up. With my feet planted on the ground, I take stock.

My body is intact. I'm clothed. My face, my hair... They feel there. I stretch my neck about and massage my bum shoulder until my raw fingertips can't stand the touch any longer.

A note on Zja-Zja's reading table says, "Ice pops in the freezer."

That's enough to get me up and moving again.

# CHAPTER TWELVE

I have to stop myself from running my hands along the worn wood of the Swan Song. My fingers still sting a bit, but more than that, it just looks weird. Twice now, Barbara and Nancy have had to clear their throats to spur me back to the mixological aspects of my job.

I didn't think I'd ever tend this bar again. I thought that damned card game would be my own swan song. But here I am.

Four days after the explosion at the Diamond, I'm back working a full shift. I'm drinking so much green tea I have to pee every hour, and I think I may have a cavity or three from all the freezer pops I'm sucking down, but the dust hangover is a shadow of what it was. I think I'd be dead if I channeled that much dust through a charm, the heartache way. But my last spin was different. I was drained like a marathoner, not like a junkie. The recovery has been painful, for sure, but not like the morning after a bender gone wrong.

Barbara comes back again, tray empty. "Two Bloody Marys, one whisky cola, two green teas, and an orange juice." She huffs out a breath and smiles at me. "Busy morning."

The casino isn't packed, not like the Diamond was or even like the Metro, but it is busy. People are here gambling, laughing, drinking. Eddie stands at the edge of the foyer, watching the bustle like a kid on Christmas morning, still not sure this is real.

I pull our scratch Bloody Mary mix from the bar fridge and two mugs from the freezer. I wet the rims of the mugs and dip them in the celery salt, flip them, and fill them with ice. The cold vapor from the glasses mingles with the gold dust covering the bar. I pour up the drinks and slide them through the luck to where Barbara's tray waits.

The luck drought lasted about two days, I'm told. I slept through it in the Parlor of the Eye, but Eddie said it was a grim scene all across Vegas. No luck at all—not good or bad. Nobody won much, but nobody lost either. The kiss of death for a Vegas casino—no action at all. Eddie said he was beside himself. The attorneys were preparing liquidation papers. He had inspectors and appraisers walking through the casino all week long, and they were going to see a husk of a business with even less cash flow than the honest numbers he gave them.

He went to Zja-Zja in desperation and asked if she could do anything. She said to wait.

As soon as I stepped up behind the bar, I saw the dust, noticeable but faint and very still—so still I almost didn't recognize it for what it was. Ever since I landed here, the dust I've seen whirled and moved, bucked and spun, or rushed this way and that. But not anymore.

When the dust came back to the Golden Swan, it came seeping through the floor like low-lying fog in a quiet bog. The Swan Song is the center of it all, this bar specifically. I realize now that the Swan Song is to this casino what the Elvis statue is to the Golden Gate: a source. It's a well tapped into whatever bedrock of luck flows through this city.

I find myself running my hand along the polished wood again. What Barbara doesn't know, or Eddie or Zja-Zja or anybody, is that the dust seems to have forgotten me. Without the ring, my left hand doesn't stir anything—no hint of movement at all. I might as well be a tourist myself.

Just to make sure, I think of Alli—her smile and her warmth, the feeling of her beside me in those final seconds. The sadness comes, but it's different now, realer. Before, it smothered me. Now, it washes over me, more like a wave, intense and slamming but also passing.

I open my eyes and try to call the dust to myself. Nothing. I have no rift inside any longer, nothing for the dust to rush in and patch up. When I placed my ring in the center of that table, something shifted within me.

I can see the stuff, but I can't work with it anymore. The Diamond truly was my last hurrah. My memories are my own. I should be thankful. I'll never wake up flayed and broken again on account of a memory. So why do I feel like I've lost something precious?

I straighten up and sip some tea from my cup beside the register. What's done is done. Time to move on... or try to move on... or at least look like I'm trying to move on.

I check on a couple playing video poker at the bar and pour fresh beers for them, and when I turn back around, Jasper is walking through the front doors with a short, very tan man dressed in white linen. I swallow hard, fluttering my naked ring finger, my mind racing. I'm supposed to keep him out of this place. Keep all spinners out—that's my job. But I can't do that anymore if I can't spin dust myself.

Eddie walks up to the tan man and holds out his hand. They shake. The man gestures back at Jasper, who is waiting patiently behind. Eddie nods to Jasper and shakes his hand as well.

I breathe again.

Sooner or later, the truth is gonna come out, that I went from bartender to spinner back to bartender again, that I have about as much chance of protecting this bar from bad luck as I do of pulling that sword from the stone at the Avalon.

I take another sip of tea. *One thing at a time.* Right now, Jasper is walking up to my bar.

He sits down and looks thoughtfully at the cracked glass, patched now with clear epoxy. You'd never notice it unless you knew it was there.

"I hope this is a friendly visit," I say.

Jasper nods. "I'm escorting Avi Green," he says. "Avi is my employer. He owns the Avalon. He's speaking with Eddie about a joint venture to bring more people toward our end of the Strip."

His eyes take in the bar he once tended. I know he's seeing the dust, how it sits like still mist on a lake. That first visit, when he broke the mirror, the dust on this bar seemed to make him angry—jealous, even. Now he looks nostalgic, as if he's flipping through a photo album in his mind.

"What can I get you?" I ask.

His eyes run up and down over me. I wonder if he can see that the engine inside me that could command dust has burned out. If he can, he doesn't mention it.

"Tea, please. The Hangzhou green, if you still have it."

"I think we have one or two packets left." I pull down the tea box and start sifting, glad for something to do. I clear my throat. "I'm pretty hazy on the end of that night, but I do remember you carrying me out of the Diamond. Bringing me to Zja-Zja. Thank you."

I can feel him watching me as I gather the tea service. "We'd all be blown to pieces if it wasn't for you. And who knows how many might have died in that panic you quelled."

The tea steeps, and a silence falls between us. I take down a perfectly clean martini glass from the hanging rack and polish it anyway. Then I set it back.

"So now you've seen her," Jasper says quietly. He presses the tea bag carefully against the side of his cup. "She's enthralled to that lunatic, Jack Short. Do you feel any better?"

"Enthralled is better than dead."

"Barely," says Jasper.

He presses the tea bag harder, and a thin black line spools in the cup. He stares into it with a clenched jaw, and I understand that my loss is also his loss. Just when I think he's about to shatter another cup at my bar, he backs off, sets the spoon down, and exhales.

"Barely," I agree.

Jasper stares at the spoon and taps briefly at the pocket where he keeps one of his own. "What did you see when she touched you?" he asks, his voice a low rumble.

I grab another perfectly clean martini glass. "Moments."

"What kind of moments?"

"Bad ones."

Jasper nods then takes a sip of tea and sets the cup carefully back in its indentation within the saucer.

"You know I'm not your father, right?" he says.

I snort. I can't help it. Jasper looks at me and narrows his gaze.

"For a second, maybe I thought... but no. I'm not tall enough, for one."

"Not nearly tall enough," Jasper says.

"Plus, I got kind of a Zen thing going on, where I'm trying to come to peace with myself, you know? And you're..." I gesture for the word with a fluttering of my singed fingers.

"I'm what?"

I clear my throat. "Well, you're sort of an asshole."

Jasper looks at me flatly, and for a second, I think I've gone too far. Maybe he's gonna start knitting that chain together right here and now. Then a half smile lifts the corner of his mouth.

"That's fair."

I let out a breath and rerack the martini glass. Then I turn back to Jasper, face-to-face. "I know you wanted to be a father. With her."

Jasper breaks eye contact, looking down. "I wanted nothing to do with it. Until she became pregnant. Then I wanted nothing more."

I let those words settle on the bar and wait until they're covered with seeping dust. "Me without a dad. You without a kid. In some weird alternate time line, maybe things line up."

Jasper shakes his head sadly. "There's only this time line," he says. "Only now."

Eddie and Avi walk back into view near the foyer. Both men are smiling and nodding, a good sign, I suppose. Jasper stands and reaches for his wallet, but I wave him off.

Jasper places both hands on the bar and looks squarely at me. "Short wanted us dead, and we're not dead. He'll come back at us," he says. "You know this isn't over."

"No, it's not."

"And you know we will get her back," he says.

"Or die trying."

Jasper watches me in that careful way of his. Whatever moment of vulnerability he allowed over the steam of his cup of tea is now gone. The man standing before me is once again the maker and breaker of chains.

"Good," he says.

He turns away without another word. I watch him go for a span of seconds before Nancy slaps an order on the bar by the busing station.

"Hop to it, Lee," she says. "We got a crowd tonight."

"Right," I say. "On it."

My shift passes in a blur of steady work. I time warp the way I used to in Brooklyn on industry night when the orders never stopped coming. It's a good feeling. Soon enough, I'm on autopilot, reaching for bottles and finding them there, washing glasses and pouring drinks and filling tickets and chatting up the bar in a singular dance.

About half an hour before my shift is up, I get another customer I recognize—not one I expected to ever see again.

"This seat taken?" Jillian asks.

My autopilot comes to a crashing halt, and I forget all about the margarita I'm mixing.

"All yours," I say before I realize it has to be cleared. I've never had a backup at the bar seats before. "Sorry, hold up." I pluck up empty beer bottles and clear away some crumpled cocktail napkins. I give the space one good wipe with the bar rag... then another.

Jillian sits down and hangs her purse behind her. She looks up at me plainly and honestly, waiting.

"What can I get you? The tea is great."

"I'm more of a martini girl."

"We've got cosmopolitans, lemon drops, the whole nine."

"I'll do a vodka martini. Dry as a bone."

"Freezing vodka. You got it."

I ice a martini glass while I pluck the booze from the top shelf. I can feel her watching me as I measure out the vodka and just the barest hint of vermouth. She's waiting for me to talk first.

"I gotta be honest. I did not expect to see you again. After—"

"After what I said on the bus. Yeah. I..." She looks down at her hands. "I think I was a little harsh."

"I get it," I say, sliding the drink in front of her. "You caught me at a very strange time in my life. I'm sort of flailing around out here. Barely staying afloat. I think I may have... grabbed on to you. A little bit."

"You were trying to help me. You did help me. Saved me, really, from *him*." Her lip curls slightly. She takes a deep sip of her martini, and her lips leave a soft pink print on the rim. "But it's a hard thing to take. Waking up like that after all these years. Seeing him for who he is. I feel foolish. Like I should have known."

"Huxley deals in objects that entrap people. Very powerful objects. Anyone would have fallen under his spell."

Jillian slowly spins the glass, watching the legs of vodka drip down. "He wasn't always like that. I know it's hard to believe, but he was a good man once."

"People change," I say. "And working with corrupted dust like he does can't be good for your soul, long-term."

I don't believe Huxley was ever a good man, but I keep that to myself. Maybe he wasn't always the flat-out evil person he is today, but I cannot believe the man who escorted my enthralled mother away from me with a grin on his face was ever truly good. Dust changes people, true, but I don't think it can rewrite a person entirely. The seed has to be there first.

She places her lips exactly where the imprint is and sips again. "I thought I would just up and leave that night. Like I said. But I got back to the Diamond, and I took about an hour-long shower and ordered room-service ice cream, and then I fell asleep. When I woke up, I ordered more room service and watched crappy TV, and then another day passed. And another. And then I finally called my mom back. And my dad. And my brother. And each day, I talked with one other person who left me a voice mail. And soon enough, a week had gone by. And I realized I was waiting for something."

"You probably felt all the dust. The Diamond was sucking up all the luck in Vegas for weeks. And you're sensitive to the stuff to begin with."

"Maybe. Or maybe I was waiting for you."

Heat rises from my face, and I come within an inch of dropping the vodka bottle while trying to reshelve it. *Real smooth.*

"You were there the night of the explosion, weren't you?" she asks.

"I was."

"I felt you. Things were about to pop in there. All around me, people were panicking. I felt the fear in the room like a real thing. Like quicksand. And then I swear I heard you calling my name. I *felt* your voice."

I nod again.

"And then everyone felt your voice," she says, looking deeply into my eyes, her drink seemingly forgotten. "It was like walking across a blaring highway and into a secret garden. All the panic, all the fear was just... gone."

"All gone," I say, smiling. I try to grasp the dust pooling on my bar, and my hand falls right through it. "All gone."

"How did you do that?"

"I gave it all up," I say. "Let it all go."

"Your ring?" she asks quietly, looking at the space on my finger.

The absence is like an imprint on a dusty shelf where a favorite book sat.

"The ring, yeah, and also the memory that let me work the luck like I did. When I gave it all up, the luck and I lined up like lucky sevens for one last time."

"It was beautiful," she says softly.

"I wish I could have seen it," I say. "But it drained me. Almost killed me. And now, the luck seems to have forgotten about me. I probably shouldn't tell you that since my job depends on it, but I'm about fed up with secrets these days."

Jillian sits back and cocks her head at me. She looks at the bar and at my hand, then her eyes trace their way up to mine. "I don't know anything about this luck you work with. But I do know you're a pretty hard person to forget, Lee." She places a twenty on the bar and plucks a cocktail napkin off the stack. After taking a pen from my side of the bar, she writes a phone number under the drunken duck. "They closed the Diamond for repairs. Gave everyone a week free at their sister hotel, out south in the canyon, the Sapphire resort. It's a luxury-spa type of place. No casino. I think I'm gonna stay out there for a while. If you ever want a break from all this, give me a call."

I pick up the napkin, fold it carefully, and put it right in my pocket.

"See you around," she says.

I watch her go, wishing I had a great one-liner. When she's gone, it comes to me. *"Looks like some of that good luck stuck around after all."* Or maybe *"You'll always have a seat at my bar."* Oh, I like that one. *That would have been cool. Dammit.*

Oh well. If I play my cards right, maybe I'll get another shot.

Another customer slides in where she stepped out. In fact, every seat is filled. I can't remember ever seeing every seat filled at the Swan Song. I walk the line, filling orders and chatting up the guests. Strange guests—odd people, young and old. Most of them are new except for ol' Agnes, of course, who watches the bar from her perch at the Lucky Goat slot machine, sipping her orange juice. She catches me looking her way and gives me a wink.

I catch a couple at one of the high tops whispering and nodding at me. They seem a little starstruck when I take their order. The young woman fingers an alphabet-charm bracelet around her wrist. I pause and back up.

Her face falls slightly, and she moves to stand. "I'm sorry. I'll leave. I just heard…"

"Heard what?"

"That the Golden Swan was open for everyone. They say you can make the luck rain from the sky. That you're not afraid of anything."

I almost laugh out loud. I feel like I'm afraid of every-thing these days. But an open-door policy might not be such a bad idea. If I can't police spinners, maybe they'll police each other. At the very least, we'll keep the seats filled. I've got enough friendly eyes around here to keep folks straight. And like I said, I'm pretty fed up with secrets these days.

"I can leave," she says again, getting up.

"No, no. You heard right. Welcome to the Golden Swan. Let me know if I can get you anything. And watch your ass."

Her eyes widen for a moment until I smile. Then she laughs, and her partner does, too, a bit more forced.

I walk back behind my bar, a full slate of orders in hand. Things are about to get weird in here, but I find myself smiling. I'm good with weird.

So if you're ever in Sin City and you want to see the real Vegas, the Golden Swan is open to one and all. Come on in and belly up to the bar.

We've got hot tea and ice-cold beer, and I hear we're one of the luckiest spots in town.

## ABOUT THE AUTHOR

B. B. Griffith writes best-selling fantasy and thriller books. He lives in Denver, CO, where he is often seen sitting on his porch staring off into the distance or wandering to and from local watering holes with his family.

See more at his digital HQ: https://bbgriffith.com

If you like his books, you can sign up for his mailing list here: http://eepurl.com/SObZj. It is an entirely spam-free experience.

## ALSO BY B. B. GRIFFITH

Made in United States
Troutdale, OR
10/11/2023

13610659R00190